A SMALL TOWN, FRIENDS-TO-LOVERS ROMANCE

FOR YOU
I'D MEND

BOOK 2 OF THE PEACE FALLS SERIES

HANNAH JORDAN

About This Book

Peace Falls Series **Reading Order:** *For You I'd Mend* is a stand-alone novel; however, Poppy and Theo are featured throughout Book 1 of the *Peace Falls Series*, *For You I'd Break*. *For You I'd Mend* occurs chronologically after *For You I'd Break* and so contains spoilers for the first book.

Content Warning: This book contains potentially upsetting subject matter, including multiple references to self-harm, addiction, drug use, anxiety, post-traumatic stress disorder, incarceration, and accidental death. It also contains multiple blush-inducing sex scenes, so if you're looking for a sweet, small-town romance, best put this one down.

Published by Hannah Jordan Books 2024

Cover Design: Kaytalin McCarry, Duskbound Books

ebook ISBN: 979-8-9905868-2-6

Paperback ISBN: 979-8-9905868-3-3

https://hannahjordanauthor.com

For anyone fighting for their mental health. Never stop.
And for Matt, as an apology for letting go.

CHAPTER ONE

Poppy

MY SHOCK FACTOR SOARED when I bought a hearse. People stared whenever I rolled down the road in Tallulah, especially after I added the fire decals. A not-so-subtle warning that I'm hell on wheels.

It's easier to be shocking than likable, at least in my experience. So, instead of smiling at strangers and learning the "art" of small talk, I stomped through life with my combats boots, making as much noise as possible despite my small feet. I dressed in all black, my accessories heavy, loud, and plentiful.

Why? Because I want to make people feel. Shock, annoyance, curiosity, the emotion doesn't matter as long as it's strong. After all, emotions are the only thing separating us from the AI robots. I don't always go for shock. Most of my sculptures are about losing my dad as a kid, the heartbreaking duality of grief and love. I put my softer feelings into my art and saved the rest for the world at large.

Unfortunately, I've struggled for inspiration lately, and all those soft feelings have knotted into a big ball of annoyance. My small studio, aka the shed in our backyard, was usually my sanctuary. Not so much anymore.

The electric heater grated my nerves, the incessant hum an unrelenting reminder that only it was working.

I sure as hell wasn't. The clay on my worktable looked the same as when I scooped it from the bucket a half hour ago. Normally, I saw a piece in my mind before I touched the clay. It felt like the sculpture was already inside, waiting for me to carve it out. For the past few weeks, the lump of clay has just been a lump.

I played with the zipper on my fleece-lined hoodie. Despite its persistence, the heater hadn't quite squelched the chill. At least the zipper cut the monotonous hum. Up, down. Up, down. Until the sound added to my irritation.

I grabbed my clay knife and stabbed the lump. The handle sticking from the blob was the closest thing to art I'd created in weeks. I could call it *Death to Inspiration*. I gave the old lazy Susan I stole from Mom a solid spin and watched the knife whirl around. Nope, still not art.

Fuck it. No sense wasting time I didn't have. I wiped the knife clean on a cloth and dumped the clay back into an airtight bucket, so it'd be ready to torture me another day. I switched off the heater and relished the silence a moment before I tromped across the brittle grass to the house, my breath forming angry little clouds with every step. The kitchen light cast a warm glow across the gray afternoon and my dark mood. Rowan darted past the window on her way to and from the pantry, preparing for her second baking sprint of the day. Fifteen minutes with an icing bag and my sister was just what I needed to feel better.

By the time I opened the back door, Rowan had already taken her place in the small corner between the stove and the sink. "Back already," she called as she measured from one of the extracts lined up on the counter like a battalion awaiting her commands. She might as well have been using a pipet for how exact she measured.

"Cookies won't ice themselves." I unlaced my combat boots and put them on the waterproof mat Mom insisted everyone use. My Oscar the Grouch socks sneered up at me while I wiggled out of my hoodie. The kitchen felt like a sauna after the studio and smelled like brown sugar and bacon from whatever Rowan had in the oven. Mom's old appliances barely got a rest these days. I ran cold, so I knew I'd be comfortable in a few minutes, but Rowan stood closer to the stove and looked in serious need of an iced beverage.

I washed my hands at the sink before I headed to the prep table to decorate the snowflake cookies Rowan baked earlier. Mom gifted us the large stainless-steel table for Christmas and let us put it in the space where the kitchen table used to be. I laid out decorating bags, piping tips, food coloring, edible glitter, pearl dust, and enough royal icing to drown my bad mood. When I had everything ready, I tucked my short hair behind my ears and got to work.

My love of all things shocking started with my hair. In the ten years since middle school, I'd worn it every color except my natural red. To be fair, that first dye job was less about shocking people and more an attempt to limit comparisons to my perfect older sister.

Rowan got straight A's, never spent time in the principal's office, and never, ever complained. So instead of repeating everything Rowan did, only three years after she did it and not as well, I made it obvious we were nothing alike. Despite my best efforts, my face could still unlock her phone.

The similarity stopped at the physical. I'm goth to her girlie. Blunt to her charming. Sarcastic to her sweet. I should have hated my sister on principle, but the bitch was too nice, too supportive, too *Rowan* to be anything but loveable. Which meant I was unlovable.

I guess my family loved me, but that's hardwired in their DNA. A few friends tolerated me in small doses, but real love, the kind that changed a person for the better, wasn't something I inspired. Just ask all my ex-boyfriends. I hold the dubious honor of being dumped by each and every person I've dated.

I eased into a rhythm while I worked. The muscles in my neck, then shoulders, relaxed as I squeezed all my frustration into the piping bag. I tried out different icing colors and designs before settling on one I liked.

"Have you made your New Year's resolutions yet?" Rowan asked.

"I don't believe in them," I said, putting the finishing touches on the snowflake I wanted to copy for the rest.

Rowan wiped her arm across her forehead and joined me at the table. "Resolutions can be helpful."

"You want to change? Do it. Why wait until the weather's crappy and the sun sets before dinner?" I held out the cookie and admired how the pearl dust made it shimmer like a real snowflake. I preferred the dust's subtle sparkle to the edible glitter I'd tried on another cookie.

"Wow, that looks incredible," Rowan said, leaning over my shoulder.

My chest warmed at her compliment, but I shrugged and put the cookie on a wire rack to dry. "So, what are your resolutions?" I asked as Rowan cracked open the window over the sink.

The cold breeze made goosebumps rise on my arms, but I didn't say anything. I could always put my hoodie back on. Rowan was down to a pair of shorts and a tank top and still flushed.

"To find a place for Red Blossoms Bakery since we can't keep operating out of Mom's kitchen. And to marry Cal, of course."

My sister got that dopey, lovestruck look she'd been sporting for half a year, and I mimed gagging. Truth was, I couldn't wait for the wedding.

Talk about inspiring a love that changes a person. Rowan had turned our fuckboy neighbor Cal into a doting fiancé in less than four months and grew her own backbone in the process. Metaphorically speaking. Her real back was still shot from an accident that happened last summer, which was how she got tangled with Dr. Caleb Cardoso in the first place.

Caring and unquestionably hot, Cal was a perfect match for my sweet sister. Which unfortunately meant Cal's best friends had become regular fixtures in my life. Aiden O'Malley was an ass of epic proportions. I'd rather let my hair grow out my natural color than date him. But I'd had a full-blown crush on Theo Makris long before Rowan and Cal got together.

Nope. I wasn't thinking about Theo. I was icing cookies. Lots and lots of cute, identical snowflakes. I laid out a dozen and iced the same portion white before switching to a bag of silver to add details, keeping them all the same. As usual, the simple repetition relaxed me enough for my mind to wander.

There was nothing cookie cutter about Theo. Tall, chiseled, and covered in tattoos and piercings, he looked exactly like every other bad boy I'd ever dated, but unlike my exes, the badness stopped at his spiky exterior. He's thoughtful, kind, and unbelievably talented. In other words, a damn unicorn of a man.

We'd grown close when I took his art class last winter, months before Rowan moved back to town after her first marriage ended in spectacular fashion. I'd hinted to Theo I'd be down for more. I'd outright flirted. I'd done everything except straddle him, but I've been frozen in the friend zone for over a year.

The holidays were brutal. Cal only has his parents, and Theo only has Cal's family, so of course, Mom insisted we all celebrate together. I suffered through Thanksgiving turkey dinner, Christmas pancake brunch, and New Year's Eve apps where I received a one-arm bro hug from Theo at midnight. A lady has limits. Even me. So I'd set a secret New Year's resolution: Stop lusting after Theo Makris.

Step one: Try not to think about him. (Clearly, that was going to take some work.)

Step two: Spend less time with him. I figured I could limit my Theo intake to a couple times a week, in the context where he belonged: teaching art classes.

"Do you think our price point is too low for those cookies?" Rowan asked, without turning from the dough she was kneading. "They seem time intensive."

They were only time intensive with all the details I'd added, and right now the repetitive work was exactly what I wanted. "I doubt anyone would pay more than we're already charging for sugar cookies, no matter how pretty they are."

"They would for custom orders," she said, turning to face me. She got that look in her eyes that meant she'd be researching the hell out of custom cookies later. I knew without researching they'd fit within her twenty-page business plan because who wouldn't pay more for something uniquely theirs?

"Are there cookies?" my brother Chris asked, bounding into the kitchen and grabbing one of my perfectly iced snowflakes. My kid brother could demolish a dozen baked goods in ten minutes flat.

"Were you listening at the door like a creeper?" I slapped his hand when he reached for a second cookie on the rack and pointed to my pile of castoffs.

Chris shrugged. With his dark hair and massive height, he looked so much like our dad, I sometimes wondered if he'd gotten any genes from our mother. "I was in the dining room trying to calm down Mom."

Rowan shot a worried glance at the dining room door. "Maybe I should make her some tea."

"Better yet, pour some rum in a teacup," I said. "There's a bottle under the sink."

Rowan scrunched her forehead. "What's it doing under the sink?"

"You'd have to ask Mom," I said, laying out another row of plain cookies. "The rest of the liquor is there too, but rum looks the most like tea."

Chris laughed and grabbed the snowflake with edible glitter. "I wondered where she stashed it."

Rowan put her hands on her hips in a perfect imitation of our mother. "Christopher Stevens, did Mom catch you drinking?"

My sixteen-year-old brother wasn't a saint, but he wasn't stupid. He'd never take alcohol from Mom. He'd been old enough to remember the punishment I got seven years ago when I snuck into the liquor cabinet my junior year of high school. It'd taken two toothbrushes, but the kitchen and bathrooms had never been so clean.

"If I wanted to drink, I'd just ask Aiden to buy me beer."

Rowan fisted her hands at her sides.

I glared at Chris. "He said if, Rowan." He got the message and nodded. "Mom hosted Bible study last week."

"Ah," Rowan said, and her shoulders visibly relaxed.

Chris pressed his lips together and did his best not to laugh. "Bible study" was what Mom and her friends called their weekly gatherings where they'd read a Psalm and spend the rest of the evening drinking wine, discussing romance novels, and watching reality TV before stumbling home. If my sister didn't spend all her nights down the street at Cal's house, she'd know the booze was under the sink because Mom was hiding it from herself as part of her Whole 30 challenge. It was still best to change the subject.

"If I must make a New Year's resolution, I guess I could curse less, especially in public and in front of Mom," I said. "Try to be more ladylike. I also second finding a space for the bakery."

Chris looked around the cramped kitchen and nodded. Three ten-inch rounds cooled by the sink. The island held dozens of cupcakes waiting to be filled, then frosted. Rowan only had her small corner of counter space to make the rest of the desserts we needed before tomorrow's deliveries.

Not to mention, the health inspector had looked a little flustered during our initial inspection last fall. We cleaned the kitchen to exacting standards, but it was still a private home.

"Well, I might as well resolve to kick ass on the SATs," Chris said. He sauntered to the cabinet under the sink, pushed aside the Drano, and grabbed a bottle of Captain Morgan.

Rowan took the bottle from him and poured a couple shots into a teacup then pushed through the swinging door to the dining room.

I slapped Chris's hand with a flat-edge frosting knife when he reached for one of my identical iced cookies after he'd taken down all the castoffs. "Stop that."

"Please, Pop," he said, giving me those annoying puppy dog brown eyes.

I shoved an uniced cookie at him as Rowan returned with the teacup. She threw it back and swallowed.

"Dr. Evers should have given her a Xanax," Rowan said, adding the cup to the pile of dirty dishes in the sink. "I can't stand seeing her so upset."

Mom had maintained a fear of all things medical since Dad died. I couldn't blame her. I'm terrified of needles after watching all those IVs shoved in Dad's arms, but Mom's fear was next level. She broke into a cold sweat any time she entered a doctor's office, which was why Dr. Evers started making house calls for her. When Rowan was in the hospital last year after getting hit by a Segway—true story—she waited to tell us until after she'd been released. That's how much my sister hated seeing our mom upset.

Chris gave Rowan's shoulders a squeeze. "Just stay back here, Ann. I got Mom."

Rowan's eyes looked a little misty as she watched him push through the door.

"That rum must be hitting you fast," I said.

She shook her head. "He isn't a little boy anymore."

"Hasn't been for a while."

"I'm so glad I'm here for his last years of high school."

"Me too," I said, feeling my own throat tighten. Damn it. There was no reason for me to get choked up. A year ago, Rowan lived with her shitty soon-to-be-ex-husband in DC and worked at a boring finance company while I suffered through shifts as a barista at my friend Lauren's café and bookshop, Karma. Now my sister was back in Peace Falls, and we'd launched our dream business together. Sure, she'd practically moved in with Cal, and Chris was now a high school football star who had little time for his sisters, but I liked having time alone. Really.

I cleared my throat and my mind and fell into a rhythm with the piping.

"When does your class start?" Rowan asked, trying to sound casual and failing miserably. She knew I liked Theo, and being the perfect sister, she'd done everything in her power to encourage him to make a move. I felt a little sorry for Aiden. In the past few months, Rowan had planned countless romantic outings for Cal, herself, Theo, and me, leaving him out.

"Thursday."

"Are you looking forward to it?" she asked cautiously. "The class."

"Of course. It's art," I said and glared at her.

Rowan took the hint and started washing dishes.

When I finished the cookies, I got to work on a three-layer cake for Cal. I needed the crumb coat to set overnight before I covered it in fondant. Rowan had whipped up a chai buttercream that smelled so good my mouth watered.

"What time do you need the fondant tomorrow?" Rowan asked as she dumped sugar into her massive mixer to start the rest of the frosting I needed for the cupcakes. Most men would be in the doghouse for gifting their fiancée a kitchen appliance for their first Christmas, but Rowan had squealed when she unwrapped the box. I completely understood. Having the right tools meant everything. Though all the new art supplies my family gifted me had done nothing to kick me out of my slump.

"Noon should do. I want to finish early so I can spend some time in the studio." Probably staring at the same lump of clay.

"Sounds good. What are you thinking for the top?"

"A model of Skye, obviously, with a banner in her mouth saying something cheesy like 'Congrats Dad.'" Cal's ten-year-old Weimaraner had more personality than three dogs, making her the best topper for my future-brother-in-law's celebratory cake. All my other ideas involved resistance bands, since he's a physical therapist, or bank loans, since he'd needed them to buy the practice from his retiring boss. Neither seemed festive.

Rowan scrunched her nose. "I've never heard him refer to himself as her dad."

"Oh come on, Rowan, that man treats his dog better than most parents treat their kids."

"He does, doesn't he?" she said, looking extra dopy. "He's going to make a wonderful father someday, but I'm not sure you should call him Dad on the cake."

"How about something like 'Now you can bring me to work cause you own the joint.'"

Rowan laughed. "That's perfect. I know you'll make it look amazing. You always do."

I ignored the compliment and got to work with the buttercream. I saw the cake clearly in my mind. Skye was a high-energy dog who tended to get in a bit of trouble. I'd make an exam table out of Rice Krispies Treats and modeling chocolate and write the message on edible paper that looked like the thin tissue stuff medical offices use to keep things sort of clean between patients. Cal would love it. I'd add some details in florescent pink as a nod to Cal's receptionist, Cammie, who loved obnoxiously bright colors. Not to mention, giving my future brother-in-law a cake covered in pink flowers and butterflies would make my week. Maybe I'd throw in a unicorn or two.

"I've been thinking," Rowan said. "We should cross train. I can teach you a few simple recipes, and you can teach me some basic piping. Nothing as complicated as those cookies or the custom cakes, but enough I could limp along for a few days if necessary."

I frowned. I hated baking. Toss in a little too much of something and everything went to shit. Leave something in the oven a couple minutes too long and, at best, you throw away all the work you just did. At worst, you need the fire extinguisher. Don't ask.

It's not that I was afraid of mistakes. I made them all the time when sculpting or decorating cakes and cookies. Worst case, I had to reform the clay or modeling chocolate or toss a cookie, and sometimes "errors" led to something wonderful. Something fresh and unexpected. I adored those moments of forced creativity. They felt like a gift every time. I'm sure things like that happened in baking, but I'd yet to experience it.

"I suppose you're right. You're going on your honeymoon soon, and I could accidentally mow over a squirrel in the yard and contract the bubonic plague."

Rowan's mouth fell open. "Your mind is a scary place. Is that even possible?"

"Google it."

Rowan held up her hands. "I believe you. We'll start with fondant tomorrow. It's super easy."

"Sure it is."

"So, since you won't talk about Theo, want to share what you're working on in the studio?"

"No."

Rowan smiled and turned on the mixer. It wasn't odd for me to keep my work to myself until I'd finished. It *was* odd for me not to be working on anything. I usually had a few pieces in progress simultaneously. But what with getting Red Blossoms Bakery started and actually having a social life now that my sister was back in town, I'd finished all the pieces I'd started without beginning new ones. Hopefully, the class would inspire more than fantasies about a certain tattooed teacher.

The doorbell rang as I finished crumb coating the cake.

"That'll be Dr. Evers," Rowan said, stealing a few cookies from the wire racks.

"Not those." I squeezed the bag too hard and frosting shot across the worktable. "Son of a biscuit."

Laughter carried from the front of the house. Dr. Evers had no doubt come prepared with jokes to loosen up Mom.

"Stingy much?" Rowan said, grabbing another cookie to put in a bakery box. Rowan had wanted red. I'd insisted on matte black. "How many doctors do you know make house calls?"

"I'm not denying the man deserves baked goods. But they're vanilla. Dr. Evers is a chocoholic." Plus, those cookies took a shit-ton of time to ice.

Rowan narrowed her eyes like she could read my mind. "And you know this because?"

"He always ordered mocha lattes at Karma with a brownie to go."

Thankfully, someone other than me now filled the good doctor's drink orders. As customers went, Dr. Evers was a peach, but I never wanted to serve him or anyone else another latte. It'd been four months since I took off my gag-worthy teal barista apron. I fought the urge to hug my sister every day I didn't have to stand behind a counter and pretend to be pleasant.

Rowan looked into the box and frowned. "Shoot. I haven't made the brownies yet."

"Put six chocolate cupcakes in a medium box," I said, filling the icing bag with the last of the chai buttercream while my sister selected the cupcakes. Rowan set the box on the table, and I quickly piped a swirl on each with a 1M Open Star Tip. Next, I grabbed a Hershey bar and shaved chocolate onto the frosting.

Rowan sighed. "Those look great, but I should have filled the middle with fudge or Nutella.

"Next time." I closed the box and sealed it with a sticker covered in pretty red flowers and *Red Blossoms Bakery* in delicate script. Rowan had insisted. "I'll take these to him."

She blew out a breath and grabbed another dirty bowl. "Thanks."

I went to the dining room, but Dr. Evers and Mom had settled in the living room with Chris.

"Ah," Dr. Evers said, eyeing the box. "Just the person I wanted to see."

I held out the box, assuming it had elicited his enthusiasm rather than me. "Chocolate cupcakes with chai buttercream frosting."

A huge smile stretched across Dr. Evers's face. "Thank you. I can't wait to eat one."

I hate to admit it, but I kind of missed seeing people's reactions to being handed a treat. I needed to sneak Skye a bone. It'd have the same effect without the chit chat.

Dr. Evers placed the box on the coffee table and called my name as I started for the kitchen. "I looked at your file before I came over. You're behind on your tetanus booster, Poppy."

"If I cut myself with something old and rusty, you'll be the first person I call," I said, stepping toward the hall. Chris blocked the doorway with his stupid big football muscles. I shoved his chest. "Move."

"Should I hold her down?" Chris asked.

I lowered my shoulder and ran into him. He let out a huff like I'd knocked the breath from his lungs, but wrapped his arms around me and picked me up. "It'll be over before you know it, Pop."

"Maybe you should put her on the sofa," Mom said, wringing her hands. Her red hair had faded a bit since I last dyed it with henna, but otherwise, Rowan was her carbon copy.

"Mom," I pleaded like a little kid. Rowan appeared like an angel of mercy. "They're trying to give me a shot," I yelled.

"Oh," she said, twisting her hands just like Mom. "Is it something she needs?"

"No," I said as Dr. Evers, Mom, and Chris said yes.

"You know how often she works with reclaimed metal," Mom added. "She's liable to cut herself at some point."

"Better put her on the couch then," Rowan said. "Last time she passed out."

I take it back. I hated Rowan. I hated Dr. Evers, Chris, and Mom. I hated everyone. Well, maybe not Theo. He hadn't done anything yet to piss me off. Frustrated me sexually, yes. But pissed me off, no.

Chris tossed me on the couch and sat on my legs while Mom and Rowan each held down an arm.

"Just close your eyes, Poppy," Dr. Evers said in a soothing voice.

I should have listened. Instead, I watched Dr. Evers pull the instrument of death from his scrub pocket.

To their credit, Mom and Rowan were crying when I came to, and Chris looked like he wanted to puke. Dr. Evers had the decency to avoid eye contact with everyone.

"Fucking needles," I said, burying my face in a couch cushion before the first tear escaped.

CHAPTER TWO

Theo

THE ART CLOSET LOOKED exactly like I'd left it in November, which surprised me. Several people had the key, and I'd put everything away knowing the community center had scheduled single-day classes in December for kids to make presents for their families. Figuring they'd need to dip into the supply closet for a few things, I'd put the older brushes and water-soluble paint toward the front and tucked the oils and newer brushes in the back. I would have liked to help the kids make ornaments and picture frames, but I didn't want any of them missing out because of me.

I only taught adults. Older ones mostly. If someone didn't like my tattoos or piercings or past, they could leave. In my experience, kids didn't care what I looked like. But their parents often did. And I wasn't going to be the reason some first grader didn't get to play with paint.

As I started pulling out supplies, the classroom door opened, and Poppy Stevens strutted in. I did my best to push down the surge of need that always rose whenever she neared.

"You're early," I said, placing a stack of plastic palettes on the nearest table.

"Thought I could help you," she said, walking toward me. Her compact body had curves in all the right places, and she wasn't shy about showing them. Her black skirt hugged her thighs and the V on her shirt dipped halfway to her belly button. I caught a flash of red beneath the black lace and realized I could see most of her bra. Poppy always looked sexy, but that was a lot of cleavage for an art lesson. Not that I was complaining. No doubt Mr. Twillings, the retired high school principal who always took my classes, would tell her to button up like he still had a dress code to enforce.

"Not much to set up tonight," I said, turning back to the closet. "We're beginning with color mixing."

I started collecting some acrylics but stopped when Poppy's arms wrapped around my waist. "That's not the kind of help I'm offering."

I sucked in a breath as she ran her hand down my stomach to the button of my jeans.

"Poppy," I said, placing my hand over hers. "We're just friends."

"Do all your friends make you hard?" she asked, running her other hand over my erection. Because of course my dick had turned to stone the second she touched me.

"Please," I said. Was I asking her to stop or keep going? Fuck, did I want her to keep going?

I turned to face her, still unsure if I was going to step away or pull her close. She dropped to her knees before I could decide and unzipped my pants. Then she looked up at me and wet her beautiful lips.

"Kardoula mou," I said. She smiled like she understood what I called her but had never dared translate. My heart. I watched as she took me in her hand and licked my crown before sucking every throbbing inch of me into her delicate mouth. I should tell her to stop, but her mouth felt amazing. All hot and wet and impossibly deep. She reached one hand under her skirt and began touching herself. Fuck, that was hot. My balls tightened. She moaned and the vibration set off my orgasm.

I came and came until I woke panting.

"Damn it," I said, using the sheet to wipe the mess from my stomach. I glanced at my phone and groaned. 5:00 am. I'd gone to bed at one and hadn't planned to be up for another four hours.

A normal man would jerk it before bed, so he didn't wake up covered in cum before dawn. Or at least fall back asleep. I felt too guilty to do either.

An unread text from Mana only added to my mountain of guilt. But unlike my relentless attraction to Poppy, that guilt I could ease.

I knew what the text would say before I opened it.

Mana

Pos eisai?

How are you?

kalo

Pos eisai?

Mana

Kalo

Patera?

She replied that my father was also good before telling me to be well.

Na se kala, I texted before tossing my phone on the nightstand. The frequency of the conversation changed, but the contents seldom varied beyond pleasantries that served as proof of life. At least my mother checked in. I hadn't received a call or text from Patera since my parents moved back to Greece nine years ago.

I worried I'd forget the language with how little I used it and started listening to Greek podcasts last year. When I was younger, I'd hated when Mana made me speak to her in her native tongue, especially in public.

It was hard enough being the kid with spanakopita instead of PB&J in their lunch box without everyone staring every time I talked to my mom at peewee football. Add to that the fact I could switch hands while I took notes without changing my handwriting, and I stood out, even then. Now, I can't walk down Main Street without everyone gawking, either because of the way I look or the mistakes I've made.

I swung my feet to the worn carpet and rubbed my eyes before reaching for the gym shorts by the bed. Maybe I'd have fewer wet dreams if I wore them at night, but I'd rather deal with another load of laundry and guilt than give up the luxury of sleeping naked.

I slipped on the shorts and a pair of sneakers for my morning workout routine, which hadn't changed much since I started it in prison. But first, I stripped the sheets and trucked downstairs, so I could finish the laundry before the shop opened. When I got back to my apartment, I tossed the comforter over the mattress, since leaving my bed unmade made me anxious, and started my workout.

My best friends, Cal and Aiden, had given me an annual membership to their gym for Christmas, but burpees before breakfast happened whether I worked out later with them or not. The Xs I'd tattooed on the backs of my hands glared up at me when I started my pushups. Sex, or the lack of it, was the only part of being straightedge that felt like a deprivation. I'd never done drugs and giving up alcohol was easy since the last time I drank was the worst day of my life. I tried to limit my sugar intake as well, but giving into a cookie craving now and then doesn't have the same repercussions.

Plenty of people have tattoos like mine and still enjoy sex in committed relationships, but since I'd never drag someone into the shit show that is my life, I gave it up a few years after serving my time. When I realized all my one-night stands and friends with benefits acted as an escape from the reality of my life, I tattooed the Xs on my hands and committed fully to the lifestyle. Well, my mind was committed; my body still needed convincing.

By the time I'd finished working out, a few lights were on in the other buildings on Main Street. Marked didn't open until noon, but most of the shops and restaurants opened earlier. Not too many people were eager to get a tattoo before lunch, and quite a few arrived at Marked a couple drinks into the evening. My boss, Max, insisted we close at eight for walk-ins to prevent most drunken mistakes, but he allowed me to work later with established clients, the ones who expected extraordinary and knew they'd get it with me.

I could work for Max a hundred years and never repay him. He started visiting me, a complete stranger, in prison after hearing about my case in the news. Not many people would donate their time like that, and even fewer would give a twenty-year-old paroled felon a job and a place to live. As apartments went, it wasn't much. But it was more than I needed, and I can't beat the commute. After a year crammed in a tiny cell with a car booster with questionable hygiene, it felt downright palatial when I moved in eight years ago.

I glanced at the clock and groaned. I had a lot of time to kill before my first appointment. The apartment was immaculate, as always. I didn't feel like painting, and it was too cold to go for a hike, so I shot off a text to Aiden and Cal to see if they wanted to grab coffee before work. Usually, Aiden would already be on a job site, but his business slowed in winter. He texted right back.

Aiden

Karma in 30?

Works for me. Cal?

Aiden

Don't bother. He's banging Rowan

I waited a minute, but when Cal didn't reply, I jumped in the shower and got dressed before checking again.

Cal

> You're such a dick, A. I was walking Skye but I don't have time for coffee

Aiden

> Because you haven't banged Rowan yet or you're late because you already have?

Cal

> Because I have a patient at 8

Aiden

> So grab a coffee on your way in and one for that hot piece in your office. Or I could bring her a drink after I meet Theo

Cal

> I'll be there in seven minutes. I'm not waiting for y'all to order, so move your asses

Aiden

> Wow. Tell Rowan if she ever needs more than a two-pump chump, she can call me

I shoved my phone and wallet in my pocket and walked the three blocks to Karma, going slow to avoid the ice that lingered on the sidewalk from the snow melt the day before. When I reached the café, Aiden climbed from his truck and greeted me with a fist bump.

"Did you speed getting here?" I asked since he lived a good fifteen minutes from Main Street, out in the farmland that surrounded Peace Falls.

"Nah, I was already here when Cal finally answered."

Cal pulled to a stop behind Aiden and flung open the door of his SUV, his wet hair swirling in every direction.

"Couldn't even last five minutes," Aiden said.

Cal pointed at Aiden. "Fuck you."

Aiden laughed as Cal joined us on the sidewalk and gave me a one-armed hug.

"Morning, brother," I said.

Cal narrowed his eyes and pressed his lips in a line. "How much sleep did you get last night?"

"Enough," I said, walking toward the café.

"Doubt it," Aiden said, opening the door to Karma.

The inside was warm and filled with people enjoying their morning coffee, some talking in pairs and groups, others clicking away on laptops. Aiden tossed his jacket on an empty chair to claim the last free table and headed toward the counter. The owner, Lauren, glared at him. Then she noticed Cal and me and broke into a welcoming smile.

"Morning, Theo, Cal. What can I get you?" she asked, completely ignoring Aiden.

I stepped up beside Aiden. "Shot of espresso, please." I didn't drink coffee often, but when I did, I always ordered espresso since it came closest to the coffee Mana used to brew in her briki. An intricately decorated snowflake cookie in the display case caught my eye.

"Want to add a cookie?" Lauren asked, sliding open the case.

"No thanks. I avoid sugar."

Lauren waved her hand and reached into the case with a piece of wax paper before sliding the cookie into a paper bag. "On the house," she said, handing it to me. "You can admire Poppy's handiwork, then give it to Max."

I accepted the bag with a nod. Aiden and Cal both had doofy grins on their faces. I questioned why I'd asked to meet them.

"I'll take a coffee with a little cream and a Cinnamon Toast Latte for Cam. Both large and to go," Cal said, glancing at his phone.

"Sure thing. Anything else?" Lauren asked.

"I'd like a triple-shot coconut milk cappuccino with extra foam and a pump and a half of vanilla syrup," Aiden said. "Extra hot. For here."

Lauren ignored the stack of colorful mugs and poured the dregs from a pot of decaf into a paper cup. She slid it across the counter to Aiden who took a long sip and hummed in appreciation. "Thanks, beautiful," he said, shoving a fifty in the tip jar.

Lauren took it out, rang up all our orders and handed me the change. "I'll have your drinks ready in a minute."

"Thanks, Lauren," I said, dropping the change in the tip jar.

"You're welcome, Theo. Go ahead and take a seat. I'll bring your drinks."

Aiden grinned as he wove through the crowded café to the table he'd claimed.

"What did you do to Lauren?" Cal asked as we settled around the table. "You're literally the only person on her bad side."

Aiden shrugged, took a sip of coffee, and winced. "So, Theo what has you up and chipper this early?"

"Bad dream," I said.

They both nodded.

"When does your class start?" Cal asked.

"Tomorrow." I hated how easily they accepted the half-truth and moved on. My mental health, or lack thereof, was too established to warrant an extended conversation they knew I didn't want to have.

"Here you go," Lauren said, dropping four drinks on the table. We thanked her, and Cal slid the coffee with cream across the table to Aiden before taking a sip of the hot chocolate he hadn't ordered.

"When are you going to be a man and start drinking coffee?" Aiden asked.

"When you stop pushing Lauren's buttons," Cal said. "You know I'm marrying her best friend. She's going to be part of your life now. You need to make peace."

"I'm working on it," Aiden said, quietly.

If I didn't know better, I'd say he sounded hurt. "Ordering complicated drinks you have no intention of consuming probably isn't helping," I said.

Aiden nodded. "But helping the Stevens sisters find a space for their bakery should earn me points. We're meeting with my realtor later today."

"You are?" Cal said. "First I'm hearing about it."

"Your goth pixie called last night and asked me to set it up," Aiden said to me.

"She's not mine."

"She's either your goth pixie or my Hell cat. Take your pick."

"She's Cal's future sister-in-law," I said.

"She was your friend before I got with Rowan," Cal said. He looked out the window and frowned. "The sidewalks are icy. What time are you meeting them?"

"I got it, Cal," Aiden said. "I promise Rowan won't fall."

Cal blew out a breath. "We got her MRI results yesterday. She needs spinal surgery."

Well, that sucked, but it wasn't a surprise given how much pain she was in. Even so, Cal was probably devastated. He'd kept working with Rowan long after her official physical therapy ended, hoping she'd improve. "You did everything you could," I said, gripping his shoulder. "And you'll be there after to help her recover."

"You're the best PT in the state," Aiden added.

Cal rubbed his forehead. "She wants to push the surgery until after the wedding. So, no slipping on ice. I mean it, Aiden."

"Do you know how many women I've kept safe on the ice over the years? One or another of my sisters is always pregnant."

Cal nodded and glanced at his phone. "I've got to go. See you at Church." He grabbed the latte for his receptionist, Cammie, and hurried out the door.

I'd never tire of hearing the abbreviation for Church Street Brews. Most locals also frequented one of the many churches down the street from the bar, but the double meaning of "going to church" never got old.

I watched Cal juggle the to-go cups as he opened the door to his SUV before turning my attention back to Aiden. "Cammie will be at Church. Try to behave yourself."

Aiden nodded and took another sip of his coffee. "Cal knows I'm just messing with him. I'd never make a pass at Cammie. She's like his little sister. He avoided my sisters during his man-whore phase, even though Fiona wasn't married yet. I'll extend him the same courtesy. I would like Cammie to feel more comfortable around me though. She looks terrified whenever I'm around."

"Don't take it personal. That girl has been through it. She used to be that way around me too."

"How'd you get her to stop?"

"Had a panic attack in front of her. Emasculated me enough she doesn't view me as a threat."

Aiden shook his head. "You're still a huge-ass motherfucker."

I shrugged. "What game are we watching this week?" Aiden loved sports, so he accepted the subject change with enthusiasm. Several minutes later, I caught sight of a tall brunette crossing Main Street and heading toward Karma.

"So is the sister rule why you never dated any of Logan's?" I asked as Everly Hendricks pushed into the café. The espresso burned my stomach, but I smiled at her. Aiden jumped from his chair when he saw her and wrapped her in a tight hug. I stayed seated but waved when they stepped apart.

"How's my favorite Hendricks sister?" Aiden asked, holding her at arm's length.

"Better not let Maddie hear that," she said, giving his hands a squeeze before dropping them.

"Want to join us?" he asked.

"Sorry, I can't. I'm on my way to the office."

Aiden shook his head. "Who would have thought little Everly Hendricks would become a kick-ass lawyer? Logan would be so proud."

Everly smiled, but it didn't reach her eyes. Aiden cleared his throat, and a look passed between them. She dipped her chin ever so slightly.

"You two should stop by sometime," she said. "Check out my new office."

"We will," he said, answering for me.

"I better get going. It was great seeing you both."

She walked to the counter, and I exhaled the breath I hadn't realized I'd been holding. Aiden and I finished our coffees while Everly ordered and then waved goodbye when she left.

"The sister rule doesn't apply to Poppy, you know," Aiden said, rolling his empty to-go cup in his hands. "Even when she's Cal's sister-in-law. You knew her first."

"Does it apply to Everly?"

Aiden's eyes widened. "You want to date Everly?"

"Why would she want to date the man who killed her brother? I meant you. I'm not a mind reader, but I'm positive you two had a silent conversation just now."

"Yeah," he said, leaning back in his chair, "about that. Everly wants to petition the court to have your conviction reduced, then work to have it expunged."

"Absolutely not."

"Just think about it, Theo. She doesn't want you to carry a felon label your whole life. Neither do I. If you'd been a couple years older, or if we lived somewhere other than Virginia, the small amount of alcohol in your system wouldn't have been considered a factor at all. Everly talked it over with her family, and they agree. They all want to testify on your behalf."

"No. And don't bring it up again. Not with Cal or anyone else. I deserve that label."

"You deserve a lot of things," Aiden said quietly.

"I've got to go." I left the cookie on the table and stormed out of Karma, almost busting my ass on the ice.

CHAPTER THREE

Poppy

I TWIRLED IN MY swivel chair until I felt queasy, hoping it would give me a new perspective. When I felt two rotations shy of puking, I gripped the side of the table and waited for the studio to stop spinning. The clay sat in the familiar lump, drying. Two hours of staring at it and not a flicker of an idea.

"Knock, knock," Lauren said as she busted through my studio door.

"You're supposed to wait for me to invite you in."

"You'd have ignored me."

"Because you're interrupting my process."

Lauren poked her finger in the mound of clay. "Is this the same one from Monday night?"

"It is."

"Uh oh. What's wrong?"

"When did you decide I couldn't be left alone with my thoughts?"

"You mean sulking." Lauren flicked the long braid she always wore over her shoulder and smirked.

"Do you want something or are you just here to annoy me?"

"Rowan said you two looked at spaces for the bakery today. See anything good?"

"She was there. Why didn't you ask her?"

"I did. Now I'm asking you, so I can figure out how it really went."

"What the hell does that mean?"

"Rowan worries too much. You don't worry enough. I'll blend the two accounts together and get a good idea of what you saw. I'm not leaving until you tell me." She lifted the edge of a drop cloth that covered a failed piece from last year. "Is that a tree?"

"Stop snooping," I said, grabbing the drop cloth from her grubby hands. It was a tree. A sculpture that hadn't quite worked out, but I liked too much to toss. "There were a few places, none of them perfect. Aiden has some ideas about how to make one of them work. He's drawing up a rough design with measurements he took today."

"That's weirdly nice of him," Lauren said, taking a seat on the lumpy futon I kept in the studio to crash on whenever I worked late and was too tired to walk across the yard to the house. She toed off her UGGs and tucked her feet under her butt. "He's usually such an asshole."

"What did Aiden ever do to you?"

"Did he or did he not kidnap you last summer?"

I waved my hand. "That was nothing. He was being a good friend."

"By kidnapping you?"

Technically, he'd handcuffed us together and took me to a field so I could be with Theo on the anniversary of the accident. Aiden's methods were a little rough, but I'd wanted to be there, despite Theo not inviting me. "Aiden can be an ass, but he's decent. He offered to do whatever work we needed to fit out the bakery as a wedding gift to Rowan and Cal."

"Huh." Lauren flopped back on the futon and stretched out like she intended to stay awhile. I wouldn't have minded if she fell asleep and took a nap while I stared at the blob. I had no idea how the woman hadn't worked herself to death with the hours she kept at Karma.

She closed her eyes but just when I thought she'd nodded off, she let out a huff. "I still don't like him."

"Yeah, I've noticed." I was curious about the tension between Lauren and Aiden, but I figured if she wanted to talk about it, she would. I was just relieved she had the ability to dislike someone. I worried Lauren's whole earth mother vibe made her too forgiving sometimes.

"So," Lauren said, opening her eyes and sitting up straight like she was about to run a board meeting. "How's the wedding planning going, really? Rowan keeps saying everything is fine."

I punched my fist into the clay and started stretching it into a pancake. "Rowan's stressed. She's afraid her divorce from dickhead won't be finalized in time. I told her April was cutting it close, but she didn't want to miss any business during the summer wedding season."

Lauren narrowed her eyes. "Is Brad fighting the divorce?"

I hissed at her. "We do not speak his name."

"Sorry," she said, holding up her hands. "Is *dickhead* fighting the divorce?"

I shook my head, fighting the urge to smile because hearing Saint Lauren call someone dickhead made my day. "It just takes a while, and for whatever reason Rowan and Cal can't stand the idea of waiting to plan the wedding until after it's done."

"Because they're in love," Lauren said, matter-of-factly.

"You don't need to wear uncomfortable, overpriced clothes and eat an elaborate cake in front of everyone you know to prove you love someone."

Lauren laughed. "I wouldn't say that too loud if you want to keep growing your custom cake business."

My phone buzzed on the worktable.

Theo

> Mr. Twillings talked your neighbor Mrs. Adams into registering. Half the class is from Sullivan Street now

> Great. Everyone will be knocking on my studio door asking for help

> Sorry. I didn't think of that, but you really should be teaching the class

> Hell no. If I was the teacher, I couldn't tell Twill to bite me when he got on my nerves. And he will get on my nerves

> You probably could. It's a volunteer position

> No, thanks. I'll just help you with whatever you need

Three dots appeared, then disappeared.

"Texting Theo?" Lauren asked, smiling at me.

"How'd you know?"

"Because he's the only one who makes you grin like that. You are so not just friends."

"I wish," I said, abandoning the clay to flop onto the futon beside her. My phone buzzed in my hand and we both looked at it.

> See you tomorrow

"I don't get that one," Lauren said, frowning. "Normally, I'd say you weren't sending him the right signals or something, but it's pretty obvious you like him."

My stomach dropped. "Is it?"

"In a good way," Lauren said, giving my arm a squeeze. "I mean, you never snap at him like you do everyone else."

I shrugged. "Never had a reason to."

"Oh," Lauren said clapping her hands together. "That's it?"

"What's it?"

"I've never seen you back down from anything, Poppy. Why haven't you just yelled at him to kiss you already or done it yourself?"

"Because," I said, looking at my silent phone. "What if I repulse him, but he's too nice to tell me until I push the issue? You can't come back from an embarrassment like that. Our friendship would end, and he's the only person in this speck of a town who gets as excited about art as I do."

"Trust me, you do not repulse him. You're hot."

"I am not."

"I've heard talk at Karma. There's plenty of guys in Peace Falls who think you're gorgeous."

"Too bad the one I want doesn't want me."

"Maybe he's gay."

"He's definitely not gay."

Lauren raised an eyebrow at me.

"I've seen his art," I said with a shrug.

"And you can tell the man's sexual orientation from his art?"

"That and the fact he screwed half a dozen girls in his early twenties who won't stop talking about it."

Lauren cringed. "That had to be fun to hear."

My face warmed. I knew way more about Theo's penis than I should. Guess women don't forget a dick with hardware. I may or may not have asked follow-up questions. I'm pretty sure I could sculpt an accurate representation, if I wanted.

"Bet he's packing," Lauren said, fanning herself.

31

"Can we change the subject," I said, feeling my body temperature rise as well.

"God, I miss sex."

"So have some. There's bound to be someone willing at Church. I'll be your wing woman Friday."

Lauren sighed. "Pretty sure I've been out with every single man in Peace Falls."

"What about Aiden?" I asked.

Lauren patted my knee. "On that note, I'm off. What's the address of the place you think might work?"

"47 Main."

"Nice! That's smack between Karma and Cal's office. Are the other two on Main as well?" she asked, shoving her feet back in her boots.

I shook my head. "One's in Jericho and the other is by the high school."

"The Main Street one sounds like a no-brainer."

"It needs a lot of work, and Rowan got twitchy with the rent numbers."

"Yeah, that figures. Which do you like?"

"I don't care as long as it's not my mom's kitchen. All I need is a worktable and peace and quiet."

Lauren frowned. "So maybe not Main Street then."

I sighed. "No, Main Street makes the most sense from a marketing perspective. I already told Rowan we're *not* selling baked goods to randoms off the street. That part is business-to-business only. I only want people in the bakery if they're placing an order for a custom cake or a huge event."

"Well, I approve seeing as I can't mark up your baked goods at Karma if you're selling the same ones down the street." Lauren opened her arms.

I made a show of begrudgingly accepting her hug before she left, but I might have let her squeeze me longer than usual. Sculpting was my emotional outlet. Without it, I found myself leaning into any affection I could grab. Theo's continual rejection wasn't helping either.

I settled back in my chair, grabbed the clay, and started working it through my fingers, clearing my mind of everything. I closed my eyes, because nothing else had worked, and let my hands move where they wanted.

"Crap on a cracker," I said when I opened them a half hour later and found a thick one-eyed monster staring up at me. I squished the clay back into a ball, which was likely as close as I'd ever come to touching Theo's penis.

CHAPTER FOUR

Theo

THE BIKER STARED AT his chest in the mirror but didn't say anything. I waited a full minute before I asked, "What do you think?"

A tear slipped down his weathered cheek. "It looks just like him." He pressed his hands to his eyes and took a few stuttering breaths. "I can't thank you enough," he said once he had himself under control. "Now he can ride with me until the day I die."

"You're welcome," I said. After I covered the new ink with a bandage, he reached into his wallet and shoved a hundred toward me. I shook my head. I never took tips for memorial tattoos. "Donate my tip to an animal shelter."

For a second, he looked like he was going to cry again, then he pointed at me and said, "You're good people, man. I'm telling everyone in my club to come to you."

"I appreciate it. And again, I'm sorry for your loss."

He nodded and sucked in a deep breath before heading out.

"Did you just give that guy a cat tattoo?" Max asked as the door shut behind the biker.

"Not just any cat. Mr. Snuggles. He liked to ride inside the guy's leather jacket."

Max shook his head. "Thank the Lord you took him. I don't think I could have done that piece with a straight face."

"Bullshit. You'd have cried. They had a beautiful relationship."

"Yeah, probably," Max said, running a hand through his thick gray hair. "I've been a softie since my girls were born."

"It suits you," I said, clapping him on the shoulder. "I better clean my station if I'm going to make class on time."

"I'll take care of it. There's something we need to talk about. Have a seat," he said, pointing to one of the chairs in the waiting area. He took the one across from me and started rubbing his beard. Then he put his hands on his knees and dropped his head. "This is hard."

My heart started pounding. My boss was one of the calmest people I knew. Seeing him freaked out sent a surge of adrenaline through my veins. "Spit it out, Max, before you give me a panic attack."

He looked me dead in the eyes and said, "I'm evicting you."

I sat back in the chair, too stunned to speak. "Are you firing me?" I finally asked.

"Of course not. Damn it, I knew I should have brought Linda. I practiced the whole conversation with her this morning, but I'm already screwing up."

The fact Max had rehearsed what to say with his wife meant I was as good as homeless. Linda was the only chance I had of convincing Max to change his mind.

Max took a couple breaths and all the tension seemed to leave his body, which pissed me off. I wished it was that simple to calm down when my mind turned against me.

"I'm proud of you, Theo."

"Kicking me out of my home is an odd way of showing it," I snapped.

Max held up his hands. "I get that you're angry but let me explain before you rip into me."

I crossed my arms over my chest and nodded.

"Like I was saying, I'm so proud of the man you've become. Not only are you the best artist to ever work at Marked, myself included, you're one of the best people I've ever had the privilege to know."

My throat tightened, and I looked up at the ceiling a moment. Max was without question the best person I knew, so hearing him say that about me felt surreal.

"You got dealt a crap hand," Max continued.

I locked eyes with him and shook my head. "I deserved it."

Max blew out a breath. "Yeah, that's your problem. You still think you got a debt to pay. It's why you've lived in that crappy apartment long after you could afford something decent."

"I do have a debt. I'll be paying it the rest of my life."

Max's eyes grew sad. "I get it. I did some things when I used that I'll never forgive myself for. But you have to move forward, son."

Every time Max called me that, my chest hurt. I appreciated him for stepping into that role in my life, but it always made me think of Patera and the family I lost.

"It's different for me. You never killed anyone."

"Only by the grace of God," he said, kissing the cross he wore around his neck.

Few people knew Marked was an abbreviation of the company's registered name, Indelibly Marked, a nod to Max's conversion to Christianity. He practiced a different flavor of religion than the Greek Orthodox I was raised. That church thought tattoos desecrated the temple of the living God. If my father hadn't already disowned me for bringing shame on the family, he'd be horrified by the ink I'd gotten since he saw me last.

"Look, Max, the truth is, I like the apartment. I'm not living there to punish myself."

"Bull. The shower head is so low you have to bend in half to wet your hair. There's no room for you to paint anything larger than the piece I have over my mantel. It's hot in the summer and cold in the winter."

"But it's home. Cut the shit and tell me the real reason you want me out."

Max pulled on his neck. "Someone else needs it. There's a kid named Aaron. He's an addict in recovery; did time at Wallens Ridge for dealing. I met him during my prison ministry, and we've kept in touch. I think he has real potential to build a better life, but he's got no family, no one to help him. He's almost out of time at the halfway house, and I'm worried he'll fall back into old habits once he leaves. Plus, we could really use another pair of hands around here to set up, clean, and wrangle customers."

My shoulders sagged. "I can't argue with that. When would he need to move in?"

Max shifted in his seat. "February 1st."

"What the fuck, Max? That's not even a month."

"It's not ideal, but he just got notice he needs to be out by the end of the month. I want to help this guy. He's twenty-four, same age I was when I got clean. You know how hard it is to adjust after doing time. Toss in addiction, and the cards are stacked against him. But we can help level things for him."

I rubbed my forehead. How could I say no? If Max hadn't helped me, who knows where I'd be now. Cal's parents would have kept a roof over my head, but Max gave me a job and then trained me for a career I love. I had an obligation to pay it forward, even if it meant moving in the dead of winter with two weeks' notice. "Fine."

"First thing tomorrow, I'll help you look for a new place. If we can't find something right away, you're welcome to my guest room."

He didn't say what we were both thinking. That he trusted me in the same house as his wife and young daughters but not a newly released felon in recovery.

"Now, you'd better get going or you'll be late."

I glanced at the clock on the wall and jumped up. I'd be lucky to get to the community center on time, which meant everyone would already be there. At least I wouldn't be alone with Poppy. After her text yesterday, I couldn't get that dream out of my head. Well, until now. Max had given me enough to worry about to push aside those thoughts of Poppy. Almost.

"We good?" Max asked.

I nodded.

Max stood and opened his arms. "Bring it in, son."

Despite the bomb he'd just dropped on me, I returned his bear hug. He cleared his throat and stepped back. "I hope you have a kid someday, so you can understand how hard that was for me."

I pushed down the rising panic and forced myself to smile. "One step at a time, old man. I need a place to live first."

Chapter Five

Poppy

I maneuvered into a parking spot at the community center and glanced at the dash clock. Damn it. Even driving like a granny, I'd arrived fifteen minutes early. I needed to cut my alone time with Theo if I wanted any chance of getting over him. A wiser woman wouldn't take his class, but unless the high school let me audit a course, the community center was all I had. It's not that I couldn't learn on my own. If I'm being honest, Theo hadn't taught me anything I didn't already know, but art was the one topic that made me remotely social. It was nice to watch other people learn and to share what I knew. As a bonus, Theo's classes usually inspired my work, whether from his assignments or just staring at him while he taught. I was doing what any sensible woman would in my situation. Still, I needed to kill some time in the hearse because my attraction to Theo ramped up whenever we were alone.

I drummed my fingers on the steering wheel a few minutes before I started talking to Tallulah like she was a person instead of a hearse. "I know this skirt is a little short, but it already has paint on it. And I wore the fishnets with the sheer underlayer so my legs are mostly covered. Maybe leggings would have been better. But come on, I'm wearing a turtleneck sweater.

No one looks hot in a turtleneck sweater, even if it's a little cropped. Theo won't think I dressed up for him. Besides, what he thinks doesn't matter. And last but not least, I'm wearing my cramp panties. I've got this."

I tapped the steering wheel affectionately. The underwear was a brilliant idea, if I do say so myself. The granny panties were oversized, faded, and torn a little at the elastic. I usually only brought them out on the worst days of my cycle. I felt like a troll whenever I wore them. They practically guaranteed I wouldn't flirt accidentally. And yes, flirting by accident is a thing. It's practically a reflex near Theo.

I still had ten minutes to go until class started, but it'd be odd for me not to help set up. Pep talk complete, I climbed out of Tallulah and made my way to the art room. The lights were still off, which was strange. I groped around for the switch and flicked them on, pausing to look around before I stepped into the room. Theo wasn't the type to wait in the dark to jump scare someone, but I'd learn to take precautions growing up with Chris.

Instead of my usual place by the front, I dumped my bag on one of the back tables and kicked out a stool with my boot. The door opened as I took a seat, and Theo's Fan Club shuffled in. They glanced around the room for him and let out a collective sigh of disappointment.

"What are you doing all the way back there?" Gladys Akon asked me as she shoved her walker to the Fan Club's usual table at the front.

"Wanted a change of scenery."

Millie Tomson laughed. "Honey, there's no way the scenery is better back there. None of us have had a backside worth looking at in decades."

"Speak for yourself," Gladys said, fluffing her hair, which resembled a puff of cotton candy swirled to perfection. She pulled a mirror from her purse and started applying bright pink lipstick with a shaky hand.

"Sit wherever you want, dear," my neighbor Mrs. Adams said, taking a seat at the table with them. "I bet she's using us to shield his hotness," she added in a whisper loud enough for me to hear, but not loud enough for Esther.

"His hotdog?" Esther Mensch said. "Oh no. Theo is a fine young man. He won't be flashing his hot dog."

"His hotness," Millie screamed as Mr. Fitzwilliam strolled through the door.

"Why thank you, Millie. You're looking stunning yourself."

"Sit down, you old coot," Millie said. "I wasn't talking about you."

Mr. Fitzwilliam waved to me before taking his usual seat in the middle. My old principal and neighbor, Mr. Twillings, arrived next and grabbed a stool beside Mr. Fitzwilliam after nodding to me.

I glanced at the wall clock and twisted back and forth on my stool. In the year I'd taken Theo's classes, he'd never been late. Not once.

The door opened at exactly 7:00 pm, but it was Wilson. He looked at our usual table in the front, next to the Fan Club, then scanned the room until he found me in the back. Everyone started talking at once when they realized Theo was officially late.

"Hey Poppy," Wilson said kissing my cheek. "Where's Theo?"

"No idea." I woke my phone to check for any missed texts or calls. Nothing.

"I'm sure he just got held up," Wilson said, groaning onto the stool beside mine. "How's the sculpting going?"

I shrugged.

And because Wilson was such a rare gem, who never tried to get me to talk unless I wanted to, he quickly changed the subject. "I bought one of your snowflake cookies at Karma yesterday. It was almost too pretty to eat, so I took a picture and enjoyed every crumb with my tea last night."

Wilson smiled at me and for some reason I wanted to burst into tears. He was the closest thing to a grandpa I'd ever had, and I wasn't the only one who loved the man like family. The town's beloved pharmacist was citizen of the year my entire childhood. Now he alternated the honor with Lauren, who seemed on a mission to save every damaged animal and person within a ten-mile radius of Peace Falls.

After my dad died, Wilson checked in on us often and helped out as much as Mom allowed. I was only nine at the time, so it wasn't until years later that I learned his wife had died in childbirth decades before I was born, and his newborn daughter only lived a few days after. He never remarried, which broke my heart even now since he clearly enjoyed being around people. Wilson patted my hand, but didn't say anything, proving once again what a treasure he was. We waited in companionable silence until the door flew open.

The moment Theo stepped into the room, I knew something terrible had happened. Apparently, so did everyone else. All chatter ceased. Theo's eyes darted around until they found mine. I rose from my stool and walked to him while everyone stared. So much for keeping my distance. He might as well have snagged a hook in my fishnets and reeled me in.

When I reached him, he gripped my hand and led me into the hall. His fingers felt clammy in mine, and his chest rose and fell in short bursts. As soon as the door closed behind us, he pulled me into a tight hug. His full lips and short beard brushed my neck as he nestled his face against me. My core clinched like it always did on the few occasions he'd touched me, but even as my body reacted to the nearness of his, I knew this was a plea for comfort. He cuddled Skye when he felt panicked. I made a mental note to consider later how I felt about being interchangeable with Cal's dog.

"Breathe with me," I said, rubbing my hands up and down his back. His heart hammered against my ear as he exhaled in frantic bursts, which despite the circumstance, felt so good on my neck my breathing became rapid. I kept rubbing his back and forced my breaths to slow. After a few moments, his breathing steadied as well.

He'd never held me this long. At best, I could count on a brief hug, a teasing sample of his strong arms and stomach-fluttering pheromones. He surrounded me now like the sepal of an unopened flower. Even though I was comforting him, I'd never felt so protected. I wanted to stay locked in his embrace forever, but I knew it'd only last until he felt calm.

"I'm good now," he said. He dropped his arms, cleared his throat, and straightened to his full height, an entire foot above my measly five foot, two inches, taking my arms with him. I pulled them back and tilted up my head.

"What's going on?" I asked.

"I need to start class."

"They can wait."

"We should have started five minutes ago," he said, turning toward the door.

I wiggled between him and the doorknob and opened it first. "All right, listen up. All y'all know each other, so we're cutting the usual ice breaker. Instead, I want you to sketch something you think you draw well, then something you struggle to draw. I don't care if it's a pair of stick figures. Sketch pads and charcoal pencils are in the closet. Any questions?"

"Are you teaching the class now?" Principal Twillings asked.

"Heck no. Just draw your sketches. We'll be back in ten minutes."

A series of ohs and ahs erupted from the class. You'd think they were a bunch of middle schoolers the way they carried on.

"Ought to take more than ten minutes," Mr. Fitzwilliam said.

"Not if he knows what he's doing," Mrs. Adams countered. "My Frankie can make me—"

I slammed the door shut. I'd heard enough from the Adams's house the few times I'd dared to keep my bedroom windows open at night. "Want to talk here or outside?"

45

Theo slid down the wall and sat on the linoleum floor with his long legs stretched out in front of him. He still looked pale, but his hands no longer shook. I considered how best to sit without flashing my cramp panties and finally dropped to one knee, then flopped on my ass beside him. My combat boots looked like the kiddie version of his and only reached his knees once I pressed my back against the wall. I waited a good twenty seconds for him to start talking before I said, "Spill it."

"Max evicted me," he said quietly, his deep voice still powerful enough to rumble into my side where we touched. "I have to find a new place before February."

"Why on earth would he do that?" I asked, twisting to look at him.

He turned his head and those warm brown eyes were so sad, my breath stalled in my chest before a surge of hot rage erased the chill of the sticky linoleum against my legs. Max was officially on my shit list.

"It's time," he said. "He's been wanting me to find a better place for a while, and someone else needs the apartment more than I do."

"That'd make sense if you had another rental lined up or more time to find one. Where does he expect you to live?"

"If I can't find something right away, he offered his guest room until I did."

Well, that changed things. I'd been five seconds from jumping off the floor, oversized underwear be damned, and speeding to Max's house to give him a piece of my mind. Clearly, Max didn't want Theo to be homeless any more than I did. But unlike me, he was secure enough in their relationship to push Theo in the direction he wanted him to go. "What about all your furniture and stuff?"

"The apartment came furnished. Everything I own should fit in a couple boxes and a suitcase."

That sounded a heck of a lot more manageable than when I moved Rowan and all her crap from DC in the back of Tallulah. And if he had a temporary place to live, moving out of that shithole over the tattoo shop wasn't necessarily a bad thing.

"Are you worried you can't afford something else?" I asked and winced. "Never mind, that's really nosy. Forget I asked."

He chuckled and grabbed my hand. My stomach flipped, both at the sound of his laughter and his touch. He'd initiated more contact in the last five minutes than the entire year I'd known him. His hand swallowed mine, and he did this little caress with his thumb that made my toes curl. Thank the stars we were sitting on the gross floor, or my knees might have started shaking.

"Money isn't the problem as much as my record."

"Oh." It's not that I didn't know Theo had been to prison. He had the badass tatted-and-pierced look of someone who shouldn't be messed with, but it was just part of his wall. He was sweet as caramel to everyone who treated him with a sniff of kindness and ignored the people who didn't. "Anyone who knows you won't care. Besides, isn't that discrimination?"

"Being a felon isn't a protected class. A lot of guys I know had a terrible time finding housing after they got out."

"Always or just when they were released? You've been a model citizen for eight years," I said squeezing his hand. "You even volunteer your time to teach a bunch of old farts how to paint."

He tensed and I instantly regretted mentioning class. "We better get inside," he said.

He stood and pulled me to my feet, tugging harder than necessary to lift my puny frame. I slammed into him and his eyes darkened as he dropped his hands to my waist to steady me before putting an absurd amount of space between us. "Thanks for talking me down, Poppy. You're a great friend."

"Anytime, pal," I said, doing my best to crush the snark from my tone. "Come on. Let's see how many penis drawings they did."

"Six minutes, thirty-four seconds," Mr. Fitzwilliam shouted as Theo and I rejoined the class. "Twillings?"

"Their clothes appear undisturbed, but there's gum on Ms. Stevens's skirt."

"What?" I said, spinning around like Skye chasing her tail.

"Nope, just a piece of pink construction paper," Mrs. Adams said. "It flew off when she twirled. She could have picked that up in here."

Everyone looked around and grunted in agreement.

"All right then," Mr. Fitzwilliam said, eyeing a paper in his hands. "Wilson and Alison called it. You can collect your winnings after class."

"For the record," Wilson said as I climbed onto the stool beside him. "I was hoping I'd lose. I've been rooting for you kids since I brought you to class last year."

"Same Wilson," I confided quietly. There was no shame between us. The man snuck me condoms when I started dating my first boyfriend in high school. Not that I needed them then, but I sure wish I had a use for a box now. If it was up to me, Theo and I would have been naked and sweaty on the art tables after the first class. OK, maybe not that soon. But at least by Groundhog Day. I'd been walking around in a turned-on stupor for the last twelve months with only my vibrator for relief.

"OK." Theo clapped his hands, snapping everyone's attention to him. "Let's start with you, Mrs. Adams, since you're new to the class."

"Call me Alison, hon."

"All right, Ms. Alison, would you like to come up front and show us your sketches?"

I loved how Theo refused to drop the Ms. every time a member of the Fan Club asked him to use their first names. I took some comfort in the fact he didn't call me Ms. Poppy. He might not want to date me, but at least he didn't lump me in with the retirees.

Mrs. Adams picked up two sheets of paper and clutched them to her chest as she stood before then class. "I like to doodle flowers when I talk on the phone with my daughter, so I guess I'm best at those," she said and nervously held up the first sheet. She'd filled the page with decent renderings of all the blooms in her flowerbeds but without any dimension or shading. "I'm terrible at drawing people," she said flashing the second sheet with a stick figure sporting a potato head and a crooked smile. It was cute in a minimalist way. I felt the corners of my lips tug up, but quickly forced them down. I didn't want Mrs. Adams, who had never asked *me* to call her Alison in the twenty-three years I'd lived next door, to think I was laughing at her.

"That's wonderful," Mr. Fitzwilliam shouted and clapped. Mrs. Adams blushed and hurried back to her stool.

"Better be quick," Wilson said, shoving an open sketch pad in front of me. I stared at the blank page and shook my head. Wilson tapped his finger on the paper. "Do you want Alison thinking you're too good for your own assignment?"

I groaned. I'd never hear the end of it from Mrs. Adams if I didn't sketch something. I could do this. I'd been drawing since I could hold a pencil. Besides, maybe the block was only with clay.

I grabbed the charcoal Wilson rolled to me and got to work. My hand made quick slashes on the pages while everyone presented their sketches. I didn't think; I just drew. Based on the giggles, Mr. Fitzwilliam and Millie both presented penises.

"Great work, everyone," Theo said after Wilson showed his drawings.

"Don't forget Poppy," Wilson said and winked at me.

I rose from my stool and ignored the smirk he gave me as we passed each other. I totally could have gotten away without doing the assignment. Theo smiled as I neared and my stomach did that weird flip thing again.

"Well, here's a drawing of Rowan," I said holding up the first sheet. "I look at her all the time, so I think I captured her face and expression pretty well."

"Beautiful," Mr. Fitzwilliam shouted. I couldn't help but like the guy, even if I'd had to dig through the trash a couple times at Karma to rescue his dentures. Twill and Theo's Fan Club smiled and nodded.

"You need to frame that for your mother," Mrs. Adams said. "She just got Rowan home and now she's moving again."

"Down the street, Alison," Twill snapped. "Rose will see her every day."

"Ignore him, Poppy," Millie said. "Put it in a frame and give it to her. She'll cry like a baby."

I wasn't sure I wanted to make Mom sob, but I nodded. "And this one," I said, glancing down at the second piece of paper, suddenly nervous. "Well, I guess it's my dad."

I held up the portrait of a man with a blurred face. I'd drawn the eyes, nose, and mouth, but then smudged the charcoal with my finger.

Mrs. Adams pressed her hand to her heart and someone sniffed.

I shrugged. "We have pictures, of course, but I can never get his face quite right."

"They're both excellent, Poppy," Theo said after a long pause. "Better than anything I could do."

"So why are you teaching the class?" Twill shouted.

"Because he's a hell of a lot nicer than me," I snapped and glared at him. Theo's Fan Club all swiveled in their stools and did the same.

Theo smiled at me and I shot off for my seat before I humped the teacher like a demented rabbit, giving Twill an extra-long glare on the way.

CHAPTER SIX

Theo

"Finally," Aiden shouted when I entered Church Street Brews. He sat alone at a corner booth by the door with a small "reserved" sign on the table. The Friday-night crowd had already filled the rest of the bar. "I've been getting death glares since I got here. Think fast," he said and tossed me his truck keys.

"Thanks, man," I said, putting them in my leather jacket before I peeled it off and hung it on one of the hooks on the side of the booth. The thought of him or Cal, or really anyone, potentially drinking and driving tied my stomach in knots. Aiden knew I had a better chance of enjoying the evening if I had his keys.

I slid onto the bench beside him and gave him a fist bump. "Where is everyone? I thought I was late."

"Poppy's finishing the cake, and Lauren is helping her bring it. Rowan, Cammie, and Cal are coming from the office. Rowan's back was giving her trouble, so Cal wanted to work on her or something. Your usual?" Aiden asked, quickly changing the subject. We'd grown pretty attached to Rowan and seeing her in pain bothered us both.

I nodded.

"What should I get Hell Cat? I figure the rest of the ladies are good with mango margaritas, but I don't want a repeat of last summer."

"No, we do not," I said. The last time Poppy drank fruity drinks she had too many and got sick. I paced her studio all night while she slept it off on a futon just to make sure she didn't have alcohol poisoning. Cal and Aiden both gave me shit for it, saying I would have rolled them on their sides and slept on the floor or gone home. "Whiskey on the rocks for Poppy."

"Yeah, that stuff tastes so bad she won't drink too fast." Aiden raised his hand and our usual server at Church—who happened to be Max's sister—hurried to the table. "Hey Brandi. We'll take a pitcher of whatever IPA is freshest, a whiskey on the rocks, a Liquid Death, and a pitcher of frozen mango margaritas. And a mixed app platter," he added, smirking at me. "Just in case the lightweights need something more than cake to soak up the booze."

Cal, Rowan, and Cammie joined us a few minutes after Brandi left.

"Sorry we're late," Cal said as he slid into the booth beside Aiden in the corner.

"Not like we could start the party without the man of the hour," Aiden said, giving Rowan a wink as she sat beside me.

"Hey, Theo," she said, smiling. She lowered her voice and added, "I thought Cammie would be more comfortable sitting beside me or Cal."

Cammie gave me a little wave as she slid in next to Cal. I considered it progress. When she wasn't working at Cal's office or Karma, Cammie acted jumpy around men. Since Cal had basically adopted us both as his honorary siblings, she'd been around me enough to relax a little, but Rowan's thoughtfulness made my chest warm. I couldn't have picked a better partner for my best friend.

"Here's your drinks," Brandi said, carrying a large tray to the table. "Apps should be out soon."

Aiden pushed a twenty across the table like he always did whenever she brought him anything. "How's Max?" he asked.

"Good. We finally got the insurance approval to start occupational therapy," she said, folding the bill into her apron. "Theo, before you go, my Max drew Big Max a picture today. Would you mind taking it to him? I'm scheduled until Monday, and the kidlet is impatient for his uncle to get it."

"I'd be happy to," I said. Hearing Max's name made me think about my impending homelessness. I wanted to be mad at him, but I couldn't argue with his reason for evicting me.

"Congratulation, Cal!" Lauren shouted, poking her head around a group of college-aged guys clustered by the door.

"Open your eyes and move," Poppy snapped.

They parted and Poppy hurried to the booth carrying a huge black cake box.

Lauren slid in beside Rowan after greeting everyone. Poppy squeezed into the last remaining seat beside Cammie. She was so far away; I couldn't even say hello without shouting.

"The suspense is killing me," Cammie said, gripping her hands together.

"Calm your tits, woman," Poppy said. I watched her delicate fingers untie the string that held the box closed. She loosened each edge of the box before folding down the sides to reveal a bright pink three-tiered cake with a detailed model of Skye pulling the protective paper off an exam table. The sides of the cake were covered in colorful flowers and butterflies, each dusted with something glittery. It was incredible and, apart from Skye, looked nothing like the type of cake I'd imagined for Cal. He laughed and Cammie clapped her hands.

"Um," Rowan said, taking in the cake. "That's an interesting color palette and—is that a unicorn?"

Cal laughed harder.

"I've been telling him he needs to get used to girlie shi—stuff if he's going to live with you," Poppy shouted. "You'll have floral throw pillows all over his space before the ink dries on the marriage license. I also figured Cammie would like the colors."

"I do," she said with a huge grin. "I feel like I should have gotten you something, Cal. Especially after the raise you gave me."

"You're worth every penny," he said.

"If you're going to quit Karma, please give me a head's up," Lauren said looking slightly panicked. "I don't know what I'd do without you in the evenings and weekends."

"I love working at the cafe," Cammie said. "And I love working with you, Cal. To the best PT in the state!"

We all cheered and toasted. After we ate the appetizers and cake, which was some chocolate concoction I couldn't resist tasting, and had a couple rounds, the girls retreated to the bathroom. When they returned, they reshuffled to different parts of the table, and Poppy somehow ended up beside Aiden. Every muscle in my back tensed when he pulled her into a side hug and kept his arm around her.

"How's my Hell Cat?" he asked.

"Primed to scratch you."

Aiden laughed. Poppy smiled at him. I shifted and my boot accidentally connected with Aiden's leg.

"Watch where you park those boats, man," Aiden said, letting go of Poppy so he could rub his shin.

"You OK, Theo?" Poppy asked, those endless green eyes finally capturing mine.

She hadn't said it very loud, but Aiden and Cal stared at me like two overprotective mama bears.

"Is there a reason he shouldn't be?" Aiden asked loud enough for Lauren, Rowan, and Cammie to pause their conversation and look down the table at me.

Poppy narrowed her eyes. "You didn't tell them?"

"Tell us what?" Cal asked.

"It's nothing," I said. "We're celebrating you tonight."

"That's right," Cal said, crossing his arms over his chest. "And I'd like to know why you've looked like you wanted to throw up all evening. I thought maybe you weren't feeling well."

"Yeah, I was wondering if he caught the stomach bug going around," Aiden said. "I've already had it, so I figured it wouldn't hurt to sit near him."

"And no one thought to tell me he looked contagious?" Lauren said beside me. "Is that why you're over there, Poppy?"

"He's not contagious. He just got evicted." Poppy put her hands over her mouth and shot me an apologetic look.

"What?" Cal and Aiden shouted together.

Now Poppy looked like she wanted to throw up.

"It's OK," I said. I wished I could take Poppy's hand to let her know I wasn't upset at her, but I'd already touched her too much this week for my own good. "Max needs the apartment for someone else."

"When do you have to move?" Cal asked.

"By the end of the month," I said.

"The hell you do," Aiden shouted. "Evictions have rules. He can't just toss you out."

"He wants to help a guy," I said. "Who am I to say no to that? I owe Max everything."

"You could stay in my guest room," Cal said.

Aiden shook his head. "You don't want to stay there. Imagine all the sex noises you'll hear."

"Gross, Aiden," Poppy said, shoving his shoulder. "That's my sister you're talking about."

"You know I'm right, Hell Cat."

"As much as I hate to agree with him, he probably is," Lauren added.

Aiden smiled at her and she flipped him the bird, which made Rowan, Poppy, and Cammie all gasp.

"That's the most un-Lauren thing I've ever seen," Rowan said.

"Back to Theo," Cal said, redirecting everyone's attention to me. "Have you started looking at apartments?"

I nodded. "No vacancies anywhere in town. At least not for me. I have appointments at a couple places in Jericho tomorrow, but I have less of a shot there than here."

"Bad credit?" Cammie asked. "Been there."

"Felon," I said and took a sip of my carbonated water.

Cammie's mouth dropped open, and she looked around the table.

"You didn't know?" I asked.

She shook her head.

"Don't," Poppy snapped. "You're a cool chick, and I know you're like family to Cal, but if you treat Theo any different, I will drag you out this bar by your hair."

It shouldn't have been sexy, but I fought the urge to pull her over Aiden and into my arms. Over the years, Cal had gotten into several fights because someone said something to me he didn't like. It pissed me off every time, but for some reason, watching pint-sized Poppy charge to my defense made me want her even more.

"Geeze, Poppy, take it down," Cammie said. "My daddy's serving a life sentence, and I love that man to bits." She leaned across Lauren's lap to grab my hand. "I was just shocked I hadn't heard about it since everyone in this town loves to gossip. I know better than most, the label doesn't make the man."

Judging by the surprised looks around the booth, Cammie had kept that little tidbit about her family to herself. She could have said any number of things to settle Poppy's wrath and end the awkwardness, but she'd shared a hidden piece of her story to put me at ease. I squeezed her hand before I released it, and she leaned back to her seat.

"It's pretty shocking you hadn't heard about me," I said. Not shocking, absurd. Cammie moved to Peace Falls a year and a half ago and had spent countless hours with Cal and Lauren. I couldn't believe neither of them had mentioned my past. Hell, a few years ago, I couldn't walk down the sidewalk without hearing people whispering about it.

"Well, now I feel like a bitch," Poppy said.

"Only if you mean a female guard dog," Cammie said and blew her a kiss.

Poppy nodded, but she seemed to curl into herself.

"Come on, Hell Cat," Aiden said nudging her shoulder. "Let's see if you can still kick my ass at darts when you're not completely wasted."

"Oh, this I have to see," Lauren said. She and Cammie scooted out of the booth as Rowan and Cal stood aside to let Aiden and Poppy out.

"Why didn't you tell us?" Cal asked, taking the seat Aiden had left beside me with Rowan glued to his side.

"It's nothing for y'all to worry about. You're planning a wedding and have your own businesses to run. You don't need to deal with my shit on top of all that."

Cal shook his head and gripped his hands together.

"Don't be pissed. I'll figure something out."

"I'm not pissed," he said. "I'm hurt."

I glanced at Rowan, expecting her to be as surprised as I was, but she was nodding in agreement. "I'm the one getting evicted. How is that hurting you?"

"Because I'm supposed to be your best friend," Cal said. "You should have told me."

"I just found out last night."

"You had time enough to research the entire Peace Falls rental market, but you couldn't shoot me a text? I get that what you and Poppy have is special, and I'm glad you at least told her—"

"Don't," I said, forcing the word through gritted teeth. "We're just friends." Even if it felt like more to me, I'd never cross that line with Poppy. No matter how much I liked her, I had to keep my distance. "Max talked to me right before class last night, and Poppy helped calm me down like Skye does."

Rowan narrowed her eyes. "How convenient. If you'll excuse me, I think I'll go watch my sister, who unlike Skye has opposable thumbs and can play darts."

My stomach sank as she scooted out of the booth. "That didn't come out right, did it?"

Cal smirked. "Not the smartest thing you've ever said. But you and I both know how much you love my dog. Rowan doesn't realize that any comparison to Skye should be taken as a compliment. Which by the way, proves my point. Poppy is more than a friend."

"She can't be."

Cal sighed and rubbed his forehead. "You should have told Aiden and me about the eviction. Between the two of us, we're bound to know someone who can help. Aiden has a realtor on speed dial. Ever think of buying something?"

"I doubt I could get a loan."

"Maybe not in two weeks, but that doesn't mean never. Like I said, you're more than welcomed to my guest room."

"Thanks but looks like I've landed on your fiancée's bad side."

Cal waved his hand. "She's fiercely protective of Poppy and Chris, but she forgives easily."

"Thank goodness for that," I said. "Even so, you and Rowan have enough going on without adding a houseguest."

"The offer stands."

I nodded. I could feel my emotions building: panic that I was about to lose my home, guilt that I'd upset my friends, and sadness, always the bone-crushing sadness that I'd ruined so many lives, including my own. I craved physical pain to still my racing thoughts and blunt the anguish. A single slice of a razor blade. Maybe two. But I'd promised Cal and Aiden last summer I was done cutting, and I meant to keep that promise, even if it upped the number of panic attacks I had. And I'd do everything in my power to keep them from seeing me fall apart. "I think I'll head out. I don't want everyone focused on me."

"You sure?"

"Yeah, brother, I'm sure. Call me when you're ready to leave, and I'll drive you home."

"Won't be necessary. Aiden can crash with me, and Cammie and Lauren already had plans to stay at her place. We can all walk. We'll be too drunk to feel the cold."

We both climbed out of the booth, and he gave me a crushing hug. "I'll tell everyone you got the runs and had to leave."

"Fuck you," I said, pounding his back.

"Here," he said, handing me his keys. "Did Aiden already give you his?"

I nodded and put Cal's keys in my jacket pocket. "Thanks, brother. Tell Aiden I'll pick him up tomorrow whenever he's ready and drop off your keys."

"Will do. I'll make some other excuse for you ditching us, but you've got to admit, the runs works pretty well."

"Good night," I said and smiled at him despite how tense I felt.

I watched Cal weave through the bar to the back where a small crowd had gathered to watch Poppy and Aiden go head-to-head at darts. I wanted to join them and wrap my arms around Poppy between throws. Maybe drive her to my place after I dropped everyone safely home and spend the rest of the night worshipping every precious inch of her body. Instead, I slid into my jacket, feeling the comforting weight of Aiden's and Cal's keys, and listened to my dad's voice remind me that I didn't deserve to be that happy.

CHAPTER SEVEN

Poppy

INSTEAD OF GIVING THEO the option to see me or not, I stood outside Marked, working up the courage to open the door. I typically visited him after the shop closed. On the few occasions I'd stopped by while Max and Theo were working, the buzz of the tattoo gun had made my head spin. I let out a shaky breath, gripped the door handle, and yanked it open so hard the bell overhead had a hissy fit.

Max walked from the back room and smiled at me. "Morning, Poppy. Thought you were my one o'clock."

"Definitely not," I said, relieved the shop was quiet apart from the classic rock blasting through the speakers. "Is Theo here?"

"Upstairs. He's not scheduled until two."

"Oh." I shifted back and forth, my combat boots squeaking against the waxed floor. "Sorry to bother you." I turned to go, but Max stopped me.

"He's up. I heard him moving around before I started the music. Come on to the back and knock on his door."

"He isn't expecting me." And I was taking him not working as a sign I shouldn't ambush him, even to apologize for letting slip that he'd been evicted. He'd bolted from Church right after I blabbed and hadn't read any of my texts since. "I'll just talk to him later."

"Please," Max said, with a hint of desperation in his voice. "I've wanted to check on him since I got here."

I narrowed my eyes at him. "So, you're aware of the shit storm you started?"

Max nodded.

"Did you know he had a panic attack on Thursday?"

Max banged his fist on the counter before gripping his forehead. "Damn it."

The guy looked genuinely torn up, and I felt like a bitch. Yet again, I'd opened my big mouth and said something Theo probably wanted to keep to himself, or at least from Max. "Forget I said anything," I mumbled. "Just forget I stopped by."

"Oh no," Max said, locking eyes with me. "Either you're knocking on his door or I am. And if I do, I'm giving him hell for not telling me he had another panic attack."

"Like he'd have told you. You're the reason he had it."

"I know," Max said, dropping his head.

He looked exhausted, defeated. I wondered if he'd been second guessing himself ever since he evicted Theo. I know I'd be if I were him. Let's be honest, if I were him, I'd have let Theo stay until the walls fell down in his crappy apartment. But I knew Max only wanted the best for Theo. "Fine. I'll knock on his door. But if he doesn't answer, I'm out of here. Either way, you're not mentioning the panic attack to him. Deal?"

"This way," Max said, motioning me toward the back like I hadn't been to Theo's place dozens of times before.

He walked me to the door that opened to the staircase leading to Theo's apartment but turned and went to the front room before I had a chance to knock. I rapped just loud enough I could look Max in the eyes and say I tried. A couple moments later, the door swung open.

My stomach bottomed out like I was downhill on the world's tallest roller coaster.

Theo stood at the door in nothing but a pair of dark, paint-splattered jeans. Almost his entire torso was covered in colorful ink, his body a work of art, both from the tattoos he'd added and the carved muscles beneath them. My eyes traveled down his sculpted chest and abs to his bare feet. I didn't have a foot fetish, but damn. I could stare at Theo's all day.

He cleared his throat, and my eyes snapped up.

"Sorry." For telling everyone you were being evicted. For showing up unannounced. For ogling your feet like a perve when you clearly don't find me attractive.

"Um, just a sec."

Then he shut the freaking door in my face, confirming my status as a pathetic simp. I considered leaving, but Theo quickly returned wearing a t-shirt, his feet still enticingly bare.

"I thought you were Max," he said, shoving his hands in the pockets of his jeans. "Sorry I answered the door like that."

"You're fine. I mean, it's fine. You're fine too." I needed to leave.

"I'm using oils."

He might as well have spoken in Greek. Was he dousing the apartment in essential oils for the new guy? Cooking breakfast? It didn't smell like pancakes or sandal wood or however else people use oil in their homes.

"Want to see it?"

"Sure." I had no clue what it was, but I lifted my chin high and walked past him up the stairs all the same.

Even with his bed shoved against the wall, Theo's studio apartment was cramped. Cramped but tidy. All his books and art supplies were stacked neatly in the built-in bookcase. The old plaid couch and laminate coffee table had seen better days, but there wasn't a speck of dust or dirty sock in sight. The two-burner stove sparkled. The chipped Formica counter was cleared of everything except a palette loaded with paint. Oil paint. Because, duh, he's a painter, wearing paint-splattered jeans. A canvas sat on the easel in the corner, the back facing the room.

Instead of walking three steps around to see it, I froze. Theo stopped beside me and waited.

"Do you often paint without a shirt on?" Because that was the most awkward question I could possibly ask.

He shrugged. "Sometimes. I was working out before, so I just changed from my shorts."

And now I was imagining him naked and sweaty. "I'm not sure I could sculpt topless, even if the shed didn't have windows." Because if I had to see Theo half naked, I might as well attempt to make him as hot and bothered as me.

He nodded and pressed his lips in a hard line. Yep. Not even a flirty comeback. Every time Theo ignored an opportunity I lobbed at him to leave the friend zone, he chipped away at my self-esteem. It'd become harder to pretend like it didn't bother me.

It was time to switch topics to something we could comfortably discuss, like art. Unfortunately, my brain and mouth failed to communicate. "Yeah, I don't think sculpting topless would work for me, especially not with plaster and chisels."

"Yeah," he said, gripping the back of his neck. The movement made the muscles on his arms flex. "That could be dangerous."

I needed to stop embarrassing myself, or Theo wouldn't even want to be my friend. "I'm rambling. Sorry. That's what I came here to say. I'm sorry I told everyone about the eviction. It wasn't my place and—"

"Hey," he said, placing his warm hand on my elbow. The least-sexiest part of anyone's body, yet my stomach fluttered. "Don't apologize."

"But you left. And you weren't reading my texts." Could I sound more desperate?

He pulled his hand from my elbow and rubbed the scruff on his face. "I didn't want to talk to Aiden or Cal, so I turned off my phone."

"Oh," I said, lacing my fingers together to keep from wrapping my arms around my waist. I needed a damn hug, and Theo obviously wasn't offering. "Well, I'm sorry anyway."

"I'm sorry I made you worry," he said, reaching for me. He pulled his hand back and motioned to the canvas. "Want to see what I'm working on?"

"Sure."

He dragged a stool from the counter where we'd eaten several meals together and pulled it around to the canvas. He grabbed the palette and settled onto the stool he'd presumably been sitting on. Unlike me, Theo didn't mind talking while he painted. He probably conversed with everyone he inked, so I guess it made sense. He placed the palette on his lap, grabbed two brushes from a jar on the windowsill, and started using both.

I hopped onto the stool beside him and took in his work in progress: A woman with beautiful curly black hair, her profile graceful as she stared off the canvas. Theo worked on the background on either side of her, painting first with one hand and then the other.

"I've never seen you work like that before," I said in awe. Any awkwardness I felt dissolved as I watched his alternating brushstrokes.

"I don't usually," he said, using his left hand to add a swirl of rich indigo behind the woman's head.

It took me a moment, but when I saw what he was doing, I gasped. "You're mirroring each stroke in different colors."

He nodded. "Most, but not all."

"If you wanted to show how your hands are equally abled, why not make it identical?"

I'd never ask another artist a question like that mid-work, but I knew Theo had already given the process a lot of thought. He'd probably painted the entire thing in his mind before he picked up a brush, or in this case, brushes. What I wanted to ask, but didn't, was who was the woman? It sure as hell wasn't me. Her eyes were a rich brown, gentle and soft. The expression in them reminded me of something.

"It's to show that no two things are the same. Even if they appear to be. Even things you'd think would be. Like coffee."

A laugh escaped before I could stop it. Theo paused mid brushstroke and flashed me a tentative smile. I squirmed on the stool and almost tipped over when I shifted my weight too much.

Theo reached for me but stopped when he remembered the oily brushes in his hands. "You OK?"

"Yep. So, coffee?" I couldn't be more awkward if I tried.

He turned back to the canvas and started painting again. "Greek coffee is different from American. Thicker, stronger."

He was talking about a beverage, but my body temperature shot up a few degrees. I nodded, a ridiculous response since he wasn't looking at me.

"So many things you'd think would be similar, like refrigerators, aren't. Not only what's inside them, but the shape, the size."

"So, the woman is living in two worlds, basically."

"Mana," he said, pausing his brushstrokes to stare at the woman on the canvas.

"What's that?"

"It's what I call my mother." He set the brushes on the palette, and I instinctively reached for his hand. He didn't take it right away, and my cheeks flamed with embarrassment before he locked his fingers with mine and started speaking again.

"I think she adapted to life here better than my father because she wasn't willing to let one culture replace the other. Patera only spoke Greek at home because he wanted everyone to know he was fluent in English. Mana always spoke Greek with me, no matter where we were. She could make a Thanksgiving meal as easily as roasted lamb for Tsikopempti, Smoke Thursday." He turned from the canvas and grinned at me. "It's like Fat Tuesday but with meat instead of pancakes."

"Sounds delicious," I breathed. A day pigging out on smoked meat did sound tasty, but it was his rare, full grin that had taken my breath away.

He gave my hand a squeeze and dropped it like he'd had enough and couldn't stomach touching me another moment. "Anyway," he said picking up the brushes again. "I figured painting it with both hands came the closest to what it felt like to be in both cultures simultaneously. I guess it could have been a self-portrait, but I wanted to see her face again."

Well, go ahead and stab me in the feels. Theo had never talked about his family before, but everyone in Peace Falls knew they'd abandoned him after the trial. Rowan would have known how to sweetly talk with him about his mother and how he felt. I just sat and watched him paint, knowing whatever came out of my mouth would likely be the wrong thing.

"Thank you," he said quietly after a while, his eyes glued to the canvas.

"For what?"

His hands stilled, but he didn't turn to look at me. "For always being there for me. For being you."

"Yeah, sure," I said. "I can't be anyone else. Believe me, I've tried."

When he turned his head, his dark eyes flashed with anger. "Why would you ever want to?"

I shrugged, my face heating. I wasn't about to list my flaws out loud. What if he agreed with all the reasons I'd considered for why he didn't want me? "I'm an acquired taste," I said instead.

"People like you are rare, *kardoula mou*," he said, laying down his brushes again and swiveling his entire body to face me.

So were plague-riddled squirrels. Being rare wasn't necessarily a compliment. "One of these days, I'm going to spell that close enough for Google to translate."

"It's how I'd say Poppy in Greek." He reached over and cupped my cheek, then pulled his hand back like I'd burned him. "I better get cleaned up for my first client."

I nodded because my throat was too tight to speak. I ached for him to touch me again, but each time he pulled away hurt just a bit more.

CHAPTER EIGHT

Theo

WHEN I ARRIVED AT Cal's house, I gave myself a good minute in the truck to calm down. The roads were icy as fuck, and I'd white knuckled it the entire drive across town.

The front door swung open and Cal stuck his head out. "Are you coming in or not?"

Skye shoved between his legs and barked with enthusiasm. Cal caught her collar as she tried to dash onto the porch. I climbed out and Skye wagged her tail so fast it blurred.

"Hurry up before she breaks free or bruises me," Cal said, but he laughed.

"Go back in. It's icy as shit out here. I'm taking my time."

The smile fell from Cal's face. "How bad is it?"

"Black ice everywhere. I slid three times." Just as I spoke, Aiden's truck skidded to a stop an inch from my bumper.

"I hate winter," he said, climbing out. His feet slid out from under him, but he caught himself on the open door. "Hope you left the sheets I used last night on the guest bed, Cal. No way in hell am I driving again until this melts. You should take the couch, Theo."

I nodded. If I couldn't walk home, I'd rather sleep on a sofa than drive in this shit. "Need a hand?" I asked Aiden.

"So you can use me to break your fall when your big ass goes down? No, thanks."

By the time we shuffled up the sidewalk, Cal had pulled Skye back inside and was shaking Morton's table salt on the porch steps.

"What are you doing?" Aiden asked as Cal tossed a handful of salt at his feet.

"This is all I've got. I've been salting the steps every morning for Rowan. I meant to grab another bag of ice melt yesterday and forgot."

Aiden sighed and turned back around. "Buckets of brains and not an ounce of common sense. Why were you salting before? It hasn't been icy like this in days."

"I didn't want to risk it. Where are you going?" Cal asked.

"To get the ice melt I keep in my truck, so your fiancée doesn't bust that fine ass of hers on the steps later," Aiden shouted without turning around.

I gripped the railing and pulled myself up the stairs. "Rowan's coming over?"

"She's inside, but she thinks she's walking home after the game starts."

"I don't think. I am," Rowan said, joining us on the porch as I finally made it up the stairs. "I have a batch of brownies and popovers to bake. Hey, Theo."

"Rowan, I wanted to—"

She held up her hand to stop me. "I owe you an apology. You've been a great friend to Poppy this past year, and I realized you didn't mean anything offensive when you compared her with Skye. I feel terrible you left early last night."

"If anyone put their foot in their mouth, it was me."

"Can we just hug and forget it happened?"

I held open my arms, and she wrapped hers around my waist, squeezing tight. I only returned half the pressure when I bent down and embraced her, but knowing how much she hated being treated like something fragile, I lifted her slightly. She giggled like she always did when I erased the height difference between us. She used the same lavender shampoo as her sister and the smell felt like a punch to the stomach.

Poppy's hair had been slightly damp when she stopped by this afternoon. Her sweet scent had equally calmed and frustrated me the entire time. Not to mention her ponderings on topless sculpting and the way she'd looked at me when I opened the door half dressed. I'd had to shove my hands in my pockets to stop myself from touching her.

"You give the best hugs," Rowan said, squeezing me again after I placed her gently on the porch.

"The best, really?" Cal said, wrapping his arm around her shoulders the moment she stepped away from me.

She shrugged. "You can't be best at everything, Caleb."

"He's certainly lacking on the emergency prep," Aiden said as he shook ice melt onto the sidewalk.

"Would you mind salting Rowan's sidewalk and steps after you do mine?" Cal asked.

"Chris has several bags of ice melt," Aiden said, working his way up the staircase. "I know because I made sure he did in November. I texted him earlier to put it down. I assumed you were old enough to know how to prep for a storm. Guess I gave you too much credit."

"I meant to," Cal said.

Aiden rolled his eyes and dropped what was left of the bag by the door.

"How's the apartment hunt going?" Rowan asked me.

"Nowhere," I said as Cal held open the door for her. Skye let out a bark and galloped toward me. I opened my arms and caught her when she leaped at my chest. "How's my girl?" I asked, nuzzling her ear. She licked my face and wiggled so much I had to put her down.

"You know," Aiden said, from the opposite side of the porch where he'd pressed himself against the railing. "If you bought a house, you wouldn't have to worry about pet policies and could get your own."

"You're letting out all the heat," Cal shouted as he flopped on the couch and pulled Rowan onto his lap. Skye shot off toward them and did a few circles before collapsing at Cal's feet with a contented sigh.

Aiden and I hung our coats in the closet by the door and kicked off our shoes. I liked that Cal never treated me as a guest in his house. Perhaps things would change once Rowan officially moved in, but I hoped not.

The coffee table was already set up with snacks and drinks. So far, the better food selection had been the only change to our game-watching nights since Rowan came into Cal's life. I wasn't complaining. The smell wafting from the kitchen made my mouth water. My stomach grumbled, and I realized I hadn't eaten anything except a protein bar all day.

Rowan had started making different flavors of sparkling water for me whenever I visited, and I had to admit, I was looking forward to trying something new. At home, I stuck with tap water, but it'd be rude not to drink what Rowan set out. I poured myself a glass from the pitcher on the coffee table.

"To Logan," Aiden said, raising his beer.

We all raised our drinks and sipped. The moment the water hit my tongue, I knew it was my new favorite.

"How is it?" Rowan asked as she slid off Cal's lap to the cushion beside me.

"It tastes like summer."

She smiled, and yet again, I was struck by the similarities between the Stevens sisters. Poppy didn't smile as often, but when she did, the resemblance between her and Rowan was uncanny.

"It's watermelon lime. I really love the flavor combination. I'm thinking of doing something in a custard."

"That sounds amazing," I said.

"Is that seven-layer dip?" Aiden asked, rubbing his hands together as he sank into his favorite chair.

"Yep," Rowan said. "I even found those blue tortilla chips you like. There are meatballs in the slow cooker for subs later."

"You didn't need to do all this for us," I said to cover the loud noise my stomach made.

"You know," Aiden said, grabbing a chip. "If you had a house, Theo, you could host sometimes."

"You have a house, and we still always end up here," Cal said.

"Yeah, but I can't cook for shit, and no one delivers that far out."

"We could pick up something on the way next week," Cal said grinning at me. "Right, Theo?"

It'd been almost two years since Aiden bought his farmhouse on the outskirts of town, and Cal and I had yet to be invited inside. Cal was offended until one of Aiden's sisters told him none of the O'Malleys had been allowed in either. It was odd, but I'd known Aiden long enough to figure he had his reasons. I worried he was hiding something. Of the three of us, he'd been the first to attempt to move on from the accident, but it seemed unhealthy to me that he chose to live next door to where Logan spent his last night alive. He even bought the neighboring farm and cleared a view to the barn where we partied before the accident.

Aiden shook his head. "It's still a construction zone. I keep getting sidelined by other projects. Like the house on Maple."

"What house on Maple?" Cal asked as I reached for a chip and loaded it with whatever heavenly concoction Rowan had put together.

73

"There's a little rancher for sale that I'd love to flip," Aiden said with his mouth full. "Only problem is most of my guys take off in the winter since work usually slows down. Damn, Rowan. That's good."

"Is it livable?" Cal asked.

Aiden nodded while he worked to swallow a huge mouthful of chips and dip. "Outdated as all get out, but it's built solid. Little old lady who lived there decided to go into a retirement community after her husband passed."

"Mrs. Jenkins?" Rowan asked.

Aiden nodded.

"That's the house right behind Principal Twillings. It's practically next door," Rowan said, gripping Cal's arm.

"You want to move?" he asked.

"Not me, Poppy," she said. "She wants a place of her own. Too bad Mrs. Jenkins is selling now. In a year or two it'd be perfect, but I doubt she could swing it yet."

"Maybe Theo could buy it," Cal said, avoiding eye contact. "Renovate it with Aiden and then sell it to Poppy in a few years."

They all paused. I looked between them. I finished chewing the chip and dip, which was delicious. Then I took another sip of water and let the silence settle around the room. "How many times did y'all practice that performance?" I asked once they all looked good and nervous.

Rowan winced. "A few times. But come on, Theo, it'd be perfect."

"We went over this last night," I said. "Banks don't like lending to felons."

"Max thought you could get a mortgage," Aiden said, leaning back in his chair. "He knows a couple bankers and said he'd write you a glowing letter of recommendation. We all know you don't spend shit on yourself, so I'm guessing you have enough for a pretty good down payment."

I did. But that didn't mean I wanted to buy a house. "When did you talk to Max?" I asked.

"Well," Aiden said, stretching even further back in the overstuffed chair. "After you ditched us last night and left little Max's picture behind, we decided to take a trip to your boss's house this morning to deliver it before we called you to bring back our keys."

"He loved the picture, by the way," Cal said. "T-Rex holding an umbrella."

"That was a T-Rex? I thought it was a gecko," Rowan said.

"Definitely a T-Rex," Aiden said. "My nephew draws them the same way."

"Did you go with them?" I asked Rowan.

"I drove. Plus, I had to make sure they behaved themselves. They got a little heated last night after you left. I told them they needed to give Max an opportunity to explain why he evicted you before they went all alpha hole on your behalf."

"As usual, you were right," Cal said, kissing her neck.

"To get to the point before kickoff," Aiden said. "We all agree it's time you got a decent place to live."

"Max didn't mention it," I said, rubbing my forehead. We'd worked hours together and talked about everything except the eviction. I'd even noticed the new dinosaur picture at his station, but figured it was a gift from one of his girls.

"My realtor showed me a few places today," Aiden said. "The one on Maple is the cheapest because it needs the most work. Plus, it's already vacant. It will take more than a few weeks to get a mortgage, but I'm sure Mrs. Jenkins would be OK with you renting for a bit while the paperwork goes through."

"She even left behind some furniture, so you wouldn't be starting from scratch," Cal said.

I frowned at the three of them. "Did all y'all go and look at it?"

"Well, it's basically next door," Cal said.

I wanted to ask if they'd dragged Poppy along as well but mentioning her would just unleash the usual ribbing about our friendship. "Thanks, but I doubt I'd get a decent rate from any bank willing to give me a mortgage. I just need to find somewhere to rent."

"Yeah," Aiden said, taking a sip of his beer. "I figured you'd say that, so I put in an offer this afternoon. Got the call right before I came over that Mrs. Jenkins accepted it. Now all I need is someone to rent it from me until I can do the flip."

"What the hell, Aiden?" I yelled. Cal and Rowan seemed genuinely surprised, so I assumed their involvement ended with the house tour. "What if I don't want to live there?"

"Then I rent it to someone else," Aiden said with a shrug. "It was too good of an opportunity to pass up."

"Bullshit," I said.

"I own a construction company, Theo. I buy houses and flip them all the time. It was a solid business decision for me. Period. If it helps you out, good. And if Hell Cat wants to buy it someday, even better."

"On that note," Rowan said, standing. "If you'll excuse me, I have a few hours of baking ahead of me."

"I'll walk you," I said as Cal started to stand. "I need some air."

Cal looked uncertain, but then settled back on the couch. "Thanks, brother. Kickoff is any minute, and I'd hate to miss it."

Skye whimpered when Rowan kissed her goodbye but then rested her head on Cal's knee.

Cal did love football, especially the playoffs, but I knew what he was doing. He wanted me to know he trusted me with the most precious person in his life, that I was worthy or some shit. I wasn't. I'd still make sure Rowan didn't fall.

"Thanks, Theo," Rowan said as we both pulled on our coats. "I'm glad you're coming to the house. I took a stab at baklava this afternoon and hoped you'd try it."

My stomach grumbled again. "I haven't had baklava since—" Instead of finishing that sentence, I threaded my arm in hers and pulled the front door shut. "I'm happy to try it."

"I think it got colder out here," Rowan said, shivering. She gripped the railing, and we walked slowly down the steps, which were thankfully clear.

"How's the back?" I asked as we inched down Cal's sidewalk. Ice hit my face like pin pricks. We both stopped at the curb and looked at the slick pavement.

Rowan glanced up the street toward her mother's house. "I'm not letting it get in my way," she said, stepping onto the grass. "I think we better cut across the yards and cross the street at my house."

"Yeah, if we go down, I don't want Cal to see," I said, glancing back at his house. Cal was pressed against the picture window, like I expected. Rowan and I waved at him.

"Positive thoughts only, Theo. We're not going down."

I tightened my grip on Rowan's arm and took a tiny step forward. Thankfully, we were both in boots and walking slightly uphill, but if we kept at this rate, it'd take half an hour to get to her house. The icy grass wasn't as slippery as I expected. Rowan let out a relieved breath and walked a little faster.

The ice pinged down, coating my beard. "Days like this, I wish I was in Greece," I said. I'm not sure where the thought came from, perhaps from painting Mana this morning or the mention of baklava, but it was out of my mouth before I could consider the conversation I'd invited.

"You haven't been in a while, right?" Rowan asked, trying to sound casual even though I'd never spoken about my family with her before. Everyone in Peace Falls knew what a mess my life became after the accident.

"Not since my senior year of high school. My passport expired a few years ago, and I've never tried to renew it."

"Why?" Rowan asked softly.

"No reason to," I said.

Rowan squeezed my arm but didn't say anything. We crossed another yard in silence, both of us focusing on our steps.

The front door to Rowan's house opened and Chris came out carrying a large disc. "Hold on, Ann," he shouted to Rowan. "Don't cross the street without me."

"Is that a sled?" she asked and laughed.

"Sure is," he said, just as his feet slipped on the road. In a show of impressive agility, he managed to catch himself before he fell.

"You expect me to sit on that?" Rowan asked, eyeing the blue plastic disc.

"Can't fall if you're already on the ground," Chris said. "I'll pull you to our driveway. I salted everything earlier, so this is the last part we need to worry about."

"This is ridiculous," she said.

I looked at the solid sheet of ice covering the street and gripped her arm tighter. "I think you should ride the rest of the way. Cal would never forgive himself if you hurt your back more, and neither would I."

She nodded and I helped her lower herself onto the sled after Chris pushed it to the pavement beside us.

"Hey, Theo," he said. "Mind holding onto me while I pull Ann? Might improve my chances of getting there without wiping out."

"Oh my gosh, I should have stayed at Cal's," Rowan said. "I'm sorry I put y'all through this."

"I bet your family is happy to have you home, and I needed some space from Aiden."

"What he do?" Chris asked as he gripped my arm with one hand and pulled the sled with the other.

"He bought a house because my boss evicted me."

"He bought you a house?" Chris asked.

"No," Rowan said. "He bought a house and offered to rent it to Theo, but only if he wants to live there."

"Where is it?" Chris asked.

"Behind Mr. Twillings." My boot slipped, and I pulled out of Chris's grip. If I was going down, I wasn't taking him with me. "Fuck, that was close," I said, straightening.

"How bad do you want to watch that game?" Rowan asked with a nervous laugh.

"Couldn't care less," I said, taking Chris's arm again. We'd made it halfway across the street, but a sheet of black ice stood between us and the Stevens's driveway.

"Well, I'm still sorry to be so much trouble," Rowan said. "I know you were looking forward to the game, Chris."

Chris shrugged. "I'll make sure you get in the house. Then I'm taking this for a spin down the street to Cal's since Poppy won't let me watch the game on the living room TV. Unless you want the sled, Theo?"

"You have half a chance of not going airborne in that thing. No way I'm making it."

"Great," Rowan said as Chris pulled her to the edge of the road. "You sled to Cal's and watch the game, and Theo can taste test the baklava. Hopefully, they'll plow or drop some salt before long."

Chris and I helped her stand on the driveway, which was starting to accumulate ice despite the salt. Once Rowan was safely on the porch, Chris started toward the road with the sled.

"Think about renting that house, Theo," Chris said. "It'd be nice to have you in the neighborhood."

I nodded and waved goodbye.

"I can't watch," Rowan said, turning to face the house as Chris shoved off down the street towards Cal's. He laughed as he picked up speed.

"Shit. How's he supposed to stop?" I asked.

Rowan turned and let out a gasp as Chris careened toward the intersection of Sullivan and Broad. Just as he reached my truck, he tucked and rolled off the sled. The plastic disc shot off through the stop sign, collided with the curb on the other side of Broad Street, and flew into someone's yard.

Chris stood and gave a loud whoop. Rowan sighed beside me.

"Come on," I said taking her elbow. "Let's get inside so you can text Cal before he tries to climb up the street."

Rowan swung open the front door just as Poppy appeared at the top of the steps in the smallest pair of pajamas I'd ever seen.

"Theo," she said and smiled.

Her shorts ended just below her ass and were loose enough I could see the creamy skin of her inner thighs as she walked down the stairs. Her thin top left little to the imagination. She shuddered when she reached the bottom of the steps and hugged herself, but not before I saw the outline of her pert nipples.

"Crap on a cracker, y'all must be freezing. Head to the kitchen. It's so hot back there I had to change."

I tried not to look at her ass as she walked past us, but I still dropped my boots on the wood floor before placing them on the doormat to dry.

Rowan stifled a giggle and held out her hand. "Give me your coat. I'll toss it in the dryer."

"That'd be great," I said, peeling off my thick winter jacket and handing it to her. The entryway had several puddles where the ice had dripped from us. "I'll grab a paper towel and clean this up."

"Thanks." She headed upstairs with our coats while I tried to brace myself for the smoke show in the kitchen.

"Sorry to leave you out there," Poppy said when I walked in. "It was colder than a witch's tit by the door."

"I, um, need to clean up some water," I said, turning my back to Poppy and tugging off half a roll of paper towels.

"Do you need a mop?" she asked as I practically ran from the kitchen.

"I'm good," I yelled. I wasn't. I needed to leave before I did something stupid, like lift Poppy onto that stainless-steel table and pull off those little shorts with my teeth.

"Fuck," I breathed, hitting my forehead against the front door.

"Don't worry," Rowan said, starting down the stairs. "I brought her a sweater. I don't want to see my sister's nips any more than you do. But for different reasons, obviously."

I could feel my face growing red, so I started wiping the water from the floor. As I finished cleaning up, Rowan's words sank in. Did she understand my reasons for not wanting to see so much of Poppy? Cal knew I hadn't been with anyone since committing to the straightedge lifestyle a few years back. I guess he'd told Rowan. Or maybe Poppy had. I'd never discussed my decision to abstain from sex, but I figured Poppy knew enough to interpret the Xs on my hands. What other reason could I possibly have for not asking her out yet? Anyone with eyes could see I was attracted to her. I balled up the soggy paper towels and squeezed them so hard I dripped water on the floor again. I was in for one hell of a wet dream tonight.

When I returned to the kitchen after cleaning up the hallway a second time, Poppy was wearing a thin gray sweater and humming as she put the finishing touches on a miniature cake. My dick throbbed to life in my jeans. Nope, the sweater didn't help. If anything, it made me imagine how it would feel to slip it off.

"Do you want coffee?" Rowan asked. "I don't usually drink caffeine this late, but I'm freezing."

"Sure," I said, looking around the kitchen for a place to sit while I got my body under control, but finding none.

"Sorry, there's no place to rest your ass in here," Poppy said, with a sigh. "We need a bigger space. We saw a shop on Main that would be ideal. Aiden even drew up a design, but Rowan is too chickenshit to pull the trigger."

"I think you meant fiscally responsible," Rowan said, dumping scoops of ground coffee into the machine on the counter.

I leaned on the table by Poppy. Why? Because I liked to test myself sometimes. Maybe torture myself a little. "Aiden had a busy week."

"Oh yeah?" she said, gripping an icing bag. It shouldn't look sexual, but as I watched her talented hands at work, my jeans got tighter. "What's he been doing other than helping us and bothering Lauren at Karma every morning? He said his business slowed in January."

"You don't know about the house on Maple?" I asked, doing my best to calm my body. Rowan's shoulders bunched around her ears.

"What house on Maple?" Poppy asked, putting down the icing bag, thank fuck.

I glanced at Rowan and waited for her to say something. Poppy glared at her sister who kept fiddling with the coffee maker like it was a delicate espresso machine and not a standard Mr. Coffee drip brew.

"Will someone tell me what's going on?" Poppy snapped.

"Aiden is buying the Jenkins's house on Maple. He wants Theo to rent it from him until he's ready to flip it," Rowan said in one breath.

"That's awesome," Poppy said, smiling at me. "You'll be right around the corner."

I shook my head.

The smile dropped from her face. "Unless you found something else?"

"No," I said, rubbing my forehead. "But I don't need Aiden's charity."

"Doesn't sound like charity to me," Poppy said, grabbing the icing bag again. "You'd be helping each other."

"He only bought it because I need a place to live."

"Sure, he did," Poppy said with a laugh. "Aiden is growing on me, but I doubt he'd buy a freaking house just because he's worried you might have to sleep in Max's guestroom a few weeks."

"He mentioned maybe selling it to you after it's fixed up," Rowan said, throwing herself into the conversation now that Poppy was clearly on her side, "Assuming Theo doesn't want to buy it."

"I'm not buying anything," I said.

"Shut the fuck up," Poppy said, her eyes wide. "Aiden did not say that."

"He did," Rowan said, bouncing on her feet.

Poppy slammed down the icing bag. Finally, someone other than me realized how idiotic this entire plan was. "Rowan, you know how I feel about getting my hopes up," she said, pointing her finger at her sister. "Now I'm imagining all my future little nieces and nephews darting to Aunt Poppy's house whenever they want. Do not dream dangle."

"I swear on my Kitchen Aid Stand Mixer. Aiden's offer was just accepted. Cal and I went to see the whole house today. It'll be cute as a button after a little cosmetic work. I bet you could pick out all the finishes. Theo, back me up."

I nodded.

Poppy let out a squeal and threw her arms around me. I patted her awkwardly on the back and stepped away as soon as I could. No way could I take anything from Poppy. If someone other than me rented the house, she wouldn't be able to plan the remodel the way she wanted since no other renter would let her in and out of the space anytime she liked. She looked up at me and frowned.

"Aiden didn't talk to you before he put in the offer?"

"No," I said, gripping the table to keep from reaching for her. Each time she read one of my silences correctly, I ached to hold her, to show her how she made me feel not only seen but understood. "I haven't even seen the place."

"Ok, that was a dick move," she said. "But honestly, it sounds like a decent solution to your problem, and I'm not just saying that because selfishly I want to live next door to my sister but can't afford it right now."

I blew out a breath. "You're right."

"Yes!" Poppy and Rowan screamed. Thankfully this time they hugged each other.

Rowan's cell started ringing on the counter at the same time mine vibrated in my pocket.

"Oh shoot," Rowan said, fumbling for her phone. "I forgot to call Cal. Do you want to give him the good news or should I?"

Chapter Nine

Poppy

"Be brutally honest," Rowan said, pressing her palms on the dining room table.

Theo picked up a piece of baklava and studied it before taking a bite. He closed his eyes and let out a soft moan, and thank the stars Rowan made me put on this sweater because there was no way my nipples were calming down before he opened his eyes.

I may or may not have suggested the baklava to my sister. Theo seemed so nostalgic this morning, and I thought maybe he'd like a taste of something from his childhood. If I'd known how hot he'd look eating a pastry, I might have spared myself.

"It's delicious," he said, licking a drop of honey from his full lips.

"Of course it is," I said. "Rowan threw out two batches before this one. She wasn't going to let you try anything that wasn't amazing."

"Be honest though," Rowan said. "Does it taste like what you've had in Greece?"

"Close," he said, putting the rest of the piece in his mouth and chewing it slowly. "It's a little too sweet. Did you use lemon or orange zest?"

"Neither," Rowan said, frowning.

I picked up a piece and shoved it in my mouth. My sister did the same.

"Yeah, I can see how zest would balance the flavor," she said after a few chews. "Which is better? Orange or lemon?"

Theo laughed, the sound so deep and rich I squirmed in my seat and crossed my legs to relieve some of the pressure that started building the moment he walked through the door.

"That's up for debate," he said. "Mana swears by oranges, but Thia Eleni always made it with lemon. She said you needed a bigger bite to cut the sweetness."

He looked at the plate of baklava and all the mirth drained from his face.

I wanted to pull him into a hug, but judging by how fast he'd jumped away from me in the kitchen, he didn't want me near him. I shot my sister a worried glance. Being the perfect person she was, she'd already reached over and grabbed his hand.

"How much zest would I use for a batch this size?" she asked softly, giving his hand a single squeeze and dropping it. Just enough to show she cared, but not enough to embarrass him.

"Mana used one orange. I suppose you'd use the same with a lemon, but I never watched Thia Eleni make hers."

"Which did you like better?" I asked.

"I've always preferred my sweets with a little bite."

The way he looked at me when he said it was so hot, I considered opening the window and sticking my head out into the ice storm to cool off.

"Um, so lemon then," Rowan said, her cheeks flushed. "More coffee, Theo? Poppy, come help me get Theo more coffee." She grabbed my arm and yanked me from my chair before he had time to answer.

"Holy pheromones," she said, grabbing an oven mitt as soon as we reached the kitchen and fanning herself. "No way you two aren't sleeping together. Why didn't you tell me?"

"Because there's nothing to tell. We're just friends."

"Who bang," she shouted.

I slapped my hand over her mouth. "Quiet. I don't need Mom or Theo hearing you. No one is banging except you and Cal. I mean, unless Lauren and Aiden have indulged in a hate fuck or two and kept it to themselves."

"Oh," Rowan said when I took my hand from her mouth. "Why not?"

"Just drop it, please." I pulled another mug from the cabinet since Rowan had failed to grab Theo's in her dash to the kitchen. I wished I knew why Theo didn't want to move from friends to more. Every reason I could think of felt like a kick to the crotch. Maybe he simply didn't find me attractive, though that little voice in my head was getting easier to ignore since everyone around us thought otherwise. More likely, he didn't see me as someone he could be in a committed relationship with, and since he was straightedge and didn't believe in friends with benefits, we were just friends. I got it. Sort of. I could be a bitch at times. I wouldn't want to date me either.

Just as I started to pour the coffee, something cracked outside, followed by a boom so loud the floor shook.

"Crap," I said, spilling hot coffee on my hand. The lights flickered and died.

Rowan grabbed my arm. "What was that?"

"Poppy, Rowan," Theo shouted in the other room. The swinging door creaked opened before either of us could answer.

"We're fine," I said. I fumbled around with my stinging hand to set down the coffee pot on the counter. A moment later I felt Theo's large hand on my shoulder.

"Girls, Chris," Mom yelled. We heard a thump and then a "son of biscuit" before the door swung open so hard it slammed into the wall.

As my eyes adjusted to the darkness, I could make out Mom's outline in the doorway, and Theo standing between my sister and me with a hand on each of our shoulders.

"We're OK," Rowan said.

"Oh, thank goodness," Mom yelled. She ran to Theo, threw her arms around his waist, and hugged him from behind.

Rowan and I started laughing.

"Cal?" Mom asked.

"It's Theo, Rose," he said. "Chris is at Cal's."

"Oh, I'm glad you're all OK," she said, finally dropping her arms. "I wasn't sure if the tree hit the house too."

"What else did it hit?" Rowan asked, but before Mom answered, I knew. I took off out the back door, ignoring the sting of the ice against my bare feet. Instead of fighting to keep my balance, I intentionally slid, the rough ice cutting my skin.

"Stop," Theo yelled behind me, but I kept going to edge of the yard where a large oak had crashed into the studio.

I lunged toward the wreckage, but a pair of arms wrapped around me. "Come inside, Poppy," he said, softly, pulling me against him.

"Let me go," I yelled.

"At least put these on," Rowan said, dropping a pair of boots at my feet. "I'll get your coat." She stumbled as she turned toward the house and Theo let go of me to grab her before she fell. I shot off toward the tree. I vaguely registered the ice-coated twigs scraping my arms as I pushed through the branches to the trunk, which had smashed through the studio, flattening the front wall to the ground.

"No, no, no," I said, stepping forward. Something sharp and solid pierced my foot. I hopped back on my other foot and sank onto the tree trunk to stare at the wreckage. Ice pinged off my sketches. My worktable had snapped in half and the turntable had lost its top. The failed piece in the corner was covered in a tarp, but it too would be ruined soon.

A strange noise burst from my chest. Something more feral than a shout. I'd heard it before. Rowan had made the same sound the night our dad died.

Somewhere behind me people were shouting my name while I watched the last of my art, those scraps of imagination, never fully realized, that I'd refused to trash, coat with ice, along with all my tools and supplies. I started to laugh when I realized the only thing that wouldn't be ruined was that damn lump of clay since I'd stored it in an airtight plastic bucket.

"Rowan Eloise Stevens," Mom yelled, which got my attention. "Do not go in there."

Oh shit. My sister was the only other person small and stupid enough to get to me without cutting a few limbs out of the way. She'd break what was left of her spine, and we'd have to close Red Blossoms since I still couldn't bake.

"Stop," I shouted. "I'm coming out." I felt the branches a lot more this time, but my feet were oddly numb despite having stepped on something so painful. It hurt a lot more when I stepped down on my injured foot, so I hopped on the other one. When I reached the edge of the branches, a large arm pulled me out just as I began to shake so hard my knees buckled.

"Call Cal," Theo said, sweeping me off my feet and hurrying toward the house. My teeth chattered so much they ached, and I could no longer feel my feet.

"What were you thinking, *kardoula mou*?" Theo said, elbowing the back door open. He shoved something off the counter by the kitchen sink and plopped me down.

"Is she OK?" Rowan asked, coming in the back door.

"I can't see a damn thing," Theo said.

I was shaking so bad I was afraid I'd fall off the counter.

"I've got the lantern," Mom said, calmly. She switched on the lamp we took camping and let out a cry when the light illuminated my feet.

"What?" I said, leaning forward. The last thing I saw before everything turned black was a nail the length of my finger stuck in the bottom of my beet red foot.

CHAPTER TEN

Theo

My arms and legs shook as I carried Poppy to the living room. Instead of laying her down on the sofa like a sane person, I lowered us both to the cushions and leaned against the armrest.

"Good idea," Rowan said, yanking my legs onto the couch and pulling Poppy's legs over mine. "Mom, put the lamp on the table and grab some blankets. We should start a fire."

The front door slammed open, and Aiden, Cal, and Chris rushed in. Cal had a gash on his face, probably from falling on the way over, and the other two didn't look much better.

"Is she unconscious?" Cal asked calmly despite his disheveled appearance.

"Fainted when she saw the nail in her foot," Rowan answered with enough panic in her voice to send my heart pounding more than it already was. "That's on brand for her, but I'm worried she might be hypothermic. This was all she had on outside."

"How long was she out there?" Cal asked.

"A few minutes," I said.

Poppy stirred, then began to shake. "Did I faint?" she asked in a weak voice.

"Yep," Chris said.

"Here," Rose said, covering us both with one blanket and then another.

"Leave her feet out," Rowan said. "Mom, take off her top."

"No," Poppy said.

"Yes, it's soaking wet," Rose said. "Boys turn around."

"Theo, take off your shirt too," Rowan yelled.

"Um, maybe you should switch places with him, Rowan," Cal said.

I reached behind my head and yanked off my shirt, then closed my eyes while Rose pulled the wet fabric from Poppy's skin.

"Good, Theo," Rowan said. "Now wrap your arms around her and hold her hands until Cal can look at them."

I brushed my hands across Poppy's stomach, praying I didn't accidentally cup a boob, until I found her hands and gripped them. They were ice cold, but she did her best to squeeze my fingers back. If I wasn't so worried about her, this position would be torture. Her entire naked back was pressed to my bare chest. I could feel every breath and shiver like they were my own. Hell, maybe they were. My breaths were coming in panicked bursts in time with the tremors racking Poppy's body.

"Can someone grab me a bowl of lukewarm water?" Cal asked.

"I'll get it," Chris said, turning on his phone's flashlight and running toward the kitchen.

"Should we call 911?" Rowan asked Cal.

"Maybe. I don't know what to do with the nail. But it would take them forever to get here with the ice. We should at least try to warm up her feet. I don't like how swollen they are."

"Let me take a look," Aiden said, shoving Cal aside. "I see stuff like this all the time. Take off Theo's socks and check his feet too since the big oaf won't notice if he's getting frostbite."

Cal yanked my wet socks from my stinging toes. "What were you idiots doing outside without shoes?" he asked, gripping my foot.

"Stop rubbing my feet and just get me a dry pair of socks," I said louder than I meant.

Cal dropped my foot, and I heard his own boots hit the floor before he slid a pair of warm socks on my aching skin. It felt too nice to give him shit about wearing his dirty socks. I pressed my face into Poppy's hair, breathing deep the lavender scent and trying to calm down while everyone worked around us.

"Good thing you got that tetanus shot, Pop," Chris said, bringing a bowl of water into the room.

"Don't talk about shots, Christopher," Rose snapped from the hearth where she already had a small fire burning. "We don't want her to faint again."

Everyone paused and looked at Poppy.

"Stop fussing, I'm fine," Poppy said, which would have been reassuring if her teeth weren't chattering. "Fudge nugget," she shouted and arched off my body.

"Got it," Aiden said, handing something to Cal. "Worst is over, Hell Cat. I don't think she needs stitches, do you?"

"Not tonight, assuming we can get the bleeding stopped," Cal said. "But I'm a physical therapist, not an ER doctor. Poppy, you should follow up with Dr. Evers tomorrow."

"I'll get the first aid kit," Rowan said and hustled out of the room.

"Don't rush," Cal shouted after her. "We need to soak her feet first anyway. Theo, can you sit up so her feet are hanging off the couch?"

I did as he asked, pulling Poppy tight against my chest and resting her legs between mine. She let out a hiss as Cal gently lowered her feet into the bowl on the floor. "Fuck, that burns. Sorry, Mom."

"It's OK, sweetie," Rose said before blowing on the small fire.

"Chris, see if you can find Poppy something warm to drink," Cal said. "It'll help raise her core temp."

"On it," he said, taking off again.

Rose and Aiden built up the fire in the hearth and soon the room filled with dancing light and heat. Slowly, Poppy stopped shaking. Cal swapped the bowl for one with slightly warmer water. As Poppy's skin warmed, my tense muscles softened against her. My body melted closer, the blankets capturing the building heat between us.

"It's all ruined," Poppy said after she'd downed the coffee Chris brought her. She started shaking again, only this time, I could hear the sobs she tried to muffle. I fought the urge to twist her around so I could hug her face-to-face. I rubbed my hand down her arms, but the feeling of her soft skin beneath my fingers was too much. I gave her back a couple pats, which only made her cry harder.

"What's ruined?" Aiden asked.

"The tree took out the front of Poppy's studio," Rowan said. "All her current projects and supplies were inside."

"Are there any downed lines out there?" Aiden asked.

Fuck. I didn't even think of that when Poppy disappeared into the branches. This could have been so much worse. "The lights went out right after the tree fell," I said, forcing down the wave of nausea that crashed over me.

"I couldn't see any lights anywhere in the area," Cal added.

"All right," Aiden said, clapping his hands together like he was on a job site and about to dole out tasks. "We need tarps and rope. Shower curtains work too, even trash bags if that's all we've got. I'm assuming you don't have a chainsaw, Rose?"

"Just an ax and a hedge trimmer," she said.

"That'll do," Aiden said. "I'm going outside to check for downed lines before we do anything. Anyone joining me needs boots and proper winter gear, no exceptions. Bonus points for eye protection."

Chris shot off again. Rose walked to the couch and brushed Poppy's short hair aside with gentle fingers. "Don't worry, baby. We'll save everything we can."

I started to shift Poppy off my lap. "I should—"

"Stay here and help me," Rowan said in a tone that left no room for discussion. "I want to move her closer to the fire once Cal finishes bandaging her foot, and it'd be easier if you lifted her."

I nodded and listened as Poppy continued to cry, wishing there was something I could do other than act as her personal heater. By the time Cal and Rowan finished with Poppy's feet, everyone else was outside. After he checked her hands, Cal joined them.

"Give me a second," Rowan said. "I want to grab something to put on the floor." She took the lantern and ran up the stairs, leaving Poppy and me completely alone.

I gripped Poppy tighter in the gentle glow from the fire. She turned slightly and laid her head on my shoulder, her breast brushing against my chest. My cock stirred to life, begging me to touch her, but I sat like a boulder, silent and unmoving. Poppy wrapped her arms around my neck and snuggled against me, and I fought like hell to get my body under control.

"Sorry that took so long," Rowan said when she returned several minutes later. "I had to stop in the bathroom and hurl."

"You OK?" I asked.

"I faint at blood," Poppy said. "Rowan pukes."

"Hey, at least I held it in until I'd taken care of you," Rowan said. "I think that earns me double sister points."

Poppy started laughing. The sound, coupled with the movement of her skin against mine, sent jolts of pleasure down my stomach, invigorating the erection I'd tried so hard to calm.

"You're going to make me wear pink at your wedding, aren't you?" she said.

"Obviously," Rowan said, rolling out a sheet of memory foam. "Grabbed this from your bed. I figured you should sleep down here since it'll be the warmest place in the house."

"Any chance you brought me sweats too?" Poppy said.

"Slipped my mind," Rowan said, with a hint of laughter in her voice. "Sorry. Just hold onto the blankets when Theo moves you."

"I'm not worried about that. I'm sure Theo has seen plenty of tits in his line of work, and mine are nothing to brag about. But I'd love to get out of these wet bottoms."

"He's probably seen plenty of bottoms too, haven't you, Theo?" Rowan said, with a smirk.

"I've seen plenty of everything, but no one as fine as Poppy."

They both sucked in a breath. Maybe *I* was hypothermic. I certainly wasn't thinking straight, saying shit like that. In one sentence I'd confessed my attraction to Poppy, something I'd never flat-out admitted to anyone. "Um, why don't I bring you over to the fire, Poppy, then you can have the blankets to yourself and just ditch the bottoms."

I felt her nod against my neck, so I stood and carried her across the room. She held the blankets close as I lowered her onto the foam "I'm going to help outside," I said, standing and reaching for my wet shirt.

"Please stay," Poppy said so softly my chest ached.

"OK, *kardoula mou.*"

Rowan patted my bare shoulder. "I'll see if I can find something of Chris's for you to wear and grab her sweats."

I should have kept my distance, but after Rowan left, I stretched out on the floor beside Poppy, facing her and the fire. Seeing her so hurt and upset made it impossible to deny myself the closeness I'd always craved with her.

"It doesn't matter what they salvage," she said, softly.

She began tracing the omega on my arm that surrounded Logan's name. It was one of the first tattoos I'd given myself and one of the most significant. I held my breath, enjoying the feel of her small fingers on my skin and waiting for her to say more. The fire crackled, bathing us in a warm glow. The rest of the house was dark, the silence rich and thick.

After a few moments she gripped my arm. "I've lost it."

"What have you lost?" I asked, brushing the soft, damp skin below her eyes with my thumbs.

"I haven't been able to sculpt in weeks. I've lost my art."

"Impossible. I saw the sketches you did the other day. Maybe you just need a break from sculpting until something inspires you, but you haven't lost your skill, your talent."

She nodded but her eyes looked so sad, I couldn't stop myself from inching closer and brushing a kiss on her forehead. A quick kiss wasn't out of line, especially after everything that had happened. But I lingered too long.

"Theo," she breathed, lifting her hands to my face when I didn't pull away. I leaned into her touch and lowered my mouth to kiss the tip of her nose. It'd been so long since I'd felt a woman's hands on me like this. Had it always felt this good, or was it because the fingers brushing gentle circles on my cheeks were hers? My feisty, talented Poppy who deserved so much more than I could ever give her. She lifted her face until our lips were so damn close.

I don't know if she erased the slim distance between us or if I did, but suddenly, our lips were touching and we were pressed together, leaving no doubt of the effect she had on me. She arched against my erection, and I buried my hand in her short hair, pulling her closer. I lowered my other hand beneath the blanket to her breast, caressing her smooth skin until my fingers found her nipple. She moaned, opening her mouth for me to explore. I wanted to crawl under the blankets and learn every inch of her beautiful body. I wanted her to touch me until I forgot all the reasons I'd kept us apart.

Her fingers skated down my torso to the waistband of my jeans and all the consequences of what was happening slammed into me. There'd be no stopping if she went further, and I had to stop. I pulled away and stumbled to my feet, shoving my hands in my pockets to keep myself from reaching for her again. I kept my eyes on the ground, my resolve too weak to look at her face.

"This might work," Rowan said as she walked into the room. I didn't bother looking at what she'd brought me or thanking her, I just grabbed the clothes and started for the front door where I'd left my boots.

While I dressed, the weight of the sisters' silence smothered all the thoughts in my head, so when I stepped outside without my jacket, I was numb to the cold, the sounds of activity in the backyard, numb to everything but the certainty that I should be alone.

CHAPTER ELEVEN

Poppy

"Do you think I made enough?" Mom asked as she moved the last piece of chicken from the oil-soaked paper towel to the cloth-lined basket on the counter. "There's two pounds in the fridge, but I was hoping to have that later this week."

"I could make another side," Rowan said, studying the basket of chicken like she was taking a crack at Einstein's theory of relativity.

"You made plenty," I said.

"Does Theo like green bean casserole, Poppy?" Mom asked.

I love my family. I love my family. I love my family.

"Oh, that's a great idea," Rowan said. "I'll just run to the store for some crispy onions." She reached for her purse on the counter, clearly ready to delay the visit I'd been dreading for the past two weeks another hour or more. I lost it.

"We're delivering this right now," I snapped. "Not in an hour. Not after Rowan realizes she should have made him baklava for dessert instead of brownies because he doesn't like chocolate. Now."

Mom and Rowan stared at me with wide eyes.

"The chicken will get cold," I added with a shrug.

"She's right," Rowan said, tucking another cloth over the chicken. "Plus, Cal texted that they'd already finished moving everything in."

"How is that possible?" Mom asked. "They've been gone less than an hour."

"Theo doesn't have a ton of stuff." I grabbed a stack of containers and tossed a Ziploc baggie of biscuits on top. "Come on, let's go. The chicken is cooling fast."

"I need to change first," Mom said, motioning to her frying shirt. Yes, my mom has a frying shirt. It's about ten years old and covered in oil stains, and even I wasn't a big enough bitch to insist she leave the house in it.

"We'll load the station wagon while you change," I said, heading for the door.

Rowan ran after me with the basket of chicken. "Do we need to drive? It's just around the corner."

I nodded toward the living room and the small jungle of plants Mom had gathered from her shop this morning. "You plan on carrying all the food and those?"

"Oh," Rowan said, frowning. "Maybe we went a little overboard?"

"You think?"

"You know Mom," Rowan said, opening the front door with her free hand. "She always goes above and beyond to welcome people to the neighborhood, but this is Theo."

Like I didn't know. Theo who had become so tangled in my life I couldn't avoid him even when I tried. It'd been two weeks since the ice storm, and even with using a freaking puncture wound to bail on some stuff, I'd already had to suffer through game night, three dinners, and two classes. I couldn't blame my family for the classes, but with my studio destroyed, they were the last link I had to any type of art that didn't involve fondant or modeling chocolate.

And not once in all those meetings had Theo and I discussed what happened. At least I'd managed to eliminate all alone time with him. I swung by the pharmacy to chat with Wilson while he closed so we'd arrive at class together. Then I booked it out the door the second the lesson ended.

Theo, of course, pretended everything was perfectly normal. Scrolling through our text exchanges, you'd think nothing had happened. He still sent me links to interesting art articles and shared stories of his more memorable clients. He'd even found an art show coming to Staunton in May and suggested we go together. I tried to respond with my usual sass, but every time I had to force myself to pretend nothing had changed when everything had.

I'd lost my studio and practically any hope of being with Theo in the same night. To add a cherry to the shit sundae of January, Theo now lived within a frisbee toss of my house. OK, maybe not a frisbee I'd throw, but I bet Chris could fling one as far as Twill's yard, and Theo's house was clearly visible from there.

"Poppy," Rowan said, and I realized I was still standing on the front porch with a tower of sides while she'd loaded the chicken and was coming back for plants. "Does your foot hurt? Let me take some of those."

I nodded, even though my foot felt pretty good, considering. She lifted the top container and the biscuits and probably would have grabbed more if I hadn't nudged her with my elbow to move on. I followed her to Mom's station wagon, where she'd already placed the basket on the floorboard of the backseat.

"I've been patient," Rowan said as she crawled in and tucked the container beside the chicken. "But something is clearly off between you and Theo, and I'm worried it's my fault."

I handed her the rest of the containers. "How? Nothing was ever on between us."

"Please," she said, checking the lid on the coleslaw. "It's clear to anyone with a pulse that you two like each other. And not 'just as friends,'" she added, air quotes and all.

If I'd done that, the coleslaw would have slid off my lap and splattered all over the backseat because that's the kind of month I was having.

"Not enough," I said.

"Nope," Rowan said, shaking her head. "I've never seen you so into someone."

"Fine. You're right, but he doesn't want to be with me. Happy? Want me to list all the reasons I've considered why he finds me undatable? We can start with personality traits and work back to physical."

"Oh, honey," Mom said, suddenly behind me. "You're perfect."

Crap on a cracker. Today just kept getting better. I turned to face Mom, who was staring at me between two potted plants. "Can you just pretend you didn't hear that? I'll grab the rest."

When I got back to the station wagon, Mom and Rowan were eerily quiet.

"Let's go," I said, shoving the last plant in the back. "The chicken's getting cold."

"He has a lot of baggage," Rowan said from the back seat as Mom reversed out of the driveway. I shot her a death glare via the rearview mirror, but she continued undeterred. "Way more than Caleb, and you remember how hard it was for him to work through his before we could be in a relationship."

Kind of hard to forget your sister sobbing her eyes out for two days straight because the man she'd fallen for was too broken to fall in love, or at least admit he had.

"Not to mention Theo's parents abandoned him," Mom added. "They should have supported him the most. That surely messed with his head."

"I pushed him too far with the whole topless snuggle," Rowan said softly. "I mean, looking back I realize you weren't in any real danger of hypothermia. The thought just popped in my head. I figured it couldn't hurt and might even inspire him to finally make a move."

"Wow, did you know she was doing that?" I asked Mom. "Or did you think I was freezing to death too."

Mom shrugged. "He didn't seem to mind."

I slapped my thighs. "Unbelievable."

"Cal says Theo hasn't dated anyone in years," Rowan continued. "And that he's still punishing himself for the accident. For what it's worth, I think he genuinely likes you, Poppy, but he doesn't think he deserves to be with you."

I laughed so hard I snorted. "Because I'm such a prize?"

Mom gripped the steering wheel but didn't say anything. I turned in the passenger seat to face Rowan. "Is she angry or sad?"

"Both," Mom shouted. "What kind of people disown their son because of a tragic accident? Logan Hendricks's mother testified on Theo's behalf, but his own parents scurried off to Greece because they were embarrassed. Who does that? And you, Poppy," she added, taking one hand from the wheel to jab a finger in my face. "Where did I go wrong raising you? How can you think so little of yourself?"

"Geeze, Mom," I said, as we turned onto Maple. "Reel it in. You raised Rowan and Chris into bright shiny stars of humanity. You did the best you could for me with what you had."

"She's kidding," Rowan chirped from the back seat.

Mom pressed her lips together and shook her head as we pulled up to the Jenkins's place.

I guess I had to start calling the rancher Theo's place since his black truck was in the driveway and would be from now on. Lauren's beater sat across the street. Aiden's beastly new truck was parked in front of us. This one was even bigger than the boat he drove when we started hanging out together last summer. He claimed he needed it to move his crew between construction sites, but no doubt he was compensating for something.

"Let's just treat Theo like anyone else who moves here," I said. "Give him dinner and a plant, or twelve, welcome him to the neighborhood, have a little chat, and leave."

"Fine," Mom said, slamming the station wagon into park. "But we are not done with this conversation, young lady. I will make you see the beautiful, amazing person you are if it kills me."

"Pretty sure I'll die of embarrassment first."

"Poppy!" Mom and Rowan shouted.

"Let's go," I said, flinging open the passenger door. "Any longer and the chicken will need to be zapped in the microwave."

Mom gasped, and Rowan did her best not to laugh. Before we could divvy up everything, Cal and Chris came running to help us.

"For heaven's sake," Rowan said, swatting Chris's hand. "I can carry the biscuits. You'll eat two before we get inside."

I sauntered up the walk empty-handed since I wasn't entering the pissing match between Cal and Chris to see who would carry more, and Mom would be mortified to enter the house without something to hand Theo.

"Hell Cat," Aiden shouted, when I walked in the open front door.

Mrs. Jenkins had left her couch, but there wasn't anything else in the room except a single box marked *Books* in Theo's neat handwriting. No rug. No lamps. The floral curtains were still on the windows, so at least the neighbors wouldn't be able to see Theo painting at night with his shirt off.

"Stop calling her that," Lauren snapped. She waved a burning sage stick in his face before passing it over the couch. "It's mean."

"Lighten up, Lauren. It's just a nickname," Aiden said, but his voice lacked its usual cockiness. If I didn't know any better, I'd say he was blushing.

"It's OK," I said. "I call him Hammer Dick." I didn't, but the name just popped in my head.

Aiden smirked and Lauren hurried down the hall, leaving a trail of smoke in her wake. "Great nickname."

"Don't get used to it."

Theo smiled at me from the arched doorway that led to the kitchen, which made me feel warm and miserable at the same time. Theo's smiles were rare, and I treasured every one he gave me, locking them in my memory like a miser guarded his gold.

"Come look at this," he said, grabbing my hand. My chest tightened; my stomach danced. I hated how my body reacted to him still. He pulled me through the large, dated kitchen to the glass sunroom Mr. Jenkins added to the house for his birds. The man was obsessed with cockatoos. I'd made a couple bucks bird sitting a time or two in high school, which had actually been pretty fun, despite Mr. Jenkins's three-page instruction guide. All the cages, plants, and toys were gone, leaving a room with three glass walls and a linoleum floor that had weathered a decade of bird droppings.

"What do you think?" he asked, dropping my hand and holding his arms wide.

"I think you may never get the smell of bird shit out of here."

Theo waved his hand. "Turpentine smells worse. It'll cover that up."

"You're making this your studio," I said, turning in a circle to admire the room with new appreciation. The light was fantastic. The floor easy to clean. The one interior wall even had built-in cabinets Mr. Jenkins had used to store his bird seed and whatever other crap birds needed. They'd be perfect for storing paint and brushes. Theo had already stacked several canvases in the corner beside a box labeled *Art*.

"We could add a sliding door to the back yard for ventilation. That space over there is directly behind the kitchen sink. Aiden said he could easily put in a utility sink and a counter so you wouldn't have to drag anything into the kitchen to clean."

"Theo, you just moved in. There's no rush for Aiden to renovate the house. It'll be years before I can buy it."

"But you need a place to work now. Why not here?"

"Because it's yours," I said, putting my hands on my hips. "You're right. This space would make a great studio *for you*."

"We can share it. It's twice as big as your shed, and I only had a tiny corner to work in before."

"You want me to stroll into your house at 2:00 am when I get an idea for something I want to sculpt?"

"Sure," Theo said. "If we put in a slider, I won't even know you're here. The door between the kitchen and this room is an exterior door. It's solid as a rock. I doubt I'd hear a thing."

"By the time Aiden puts the door in, I could rebuild the shed."

"That sounds like a challenge," Aiden said, stepping into the sunroom. "How far have you gotten with the insurance claim, Rose?"

Mom peered over his shoulder. "Nowhere. If y'all hadn't come over to cut up the tree and cart off the debris, it'd still be there. The insurance company says it was the town's tree. The town says it's mine. They're battling it out. I'd make a fuss, but I know several families dealing with the same problem, only the trees hit their homes. When you put it in perspective, our claim just isn't a priority. I doubt we'll have a decision for months."

"Yeah, that doesn't sound promising, Hell Cat," Aiden said wrapping his arm around me. "I got a door guy who needs work. I'll call him, assuming my new tenant doesn't mind the noise for a couple days."

"Don't mind at all," Theo said, staring at his boots.

"Well, we better eat before the chicken gets cold," Mom said with a smirk.

Aiden and Mom went inside, but when I turned to follow, Theo walked ahead of me and pulled the door closed.

"I've been meaning to talk to you," he said. He shoved his hands in his pockets and stepped away from the door as though giving me the option to leave.

I waited. He backed further from me until he'd wedged himself between one of the glass walls and his box of art supplies.

"More like apologize," he said, looking down at his boots again.

"To me or your shoes?"

"You, but I'll never get this out if I look at you."

"OK," I said. Because what else do you say to someone who apparently can't stand the sight of you but invites you to share their awesome new studio space?

"Your friendship means a lot to me, and I never want to do anything to risk it. I'm sorry I crossed the line. I promise to never let that happen again."

"Well, that sucks," I said.

He lifted his head and his eyes darkened when they met mine before he turned to face the glass wall. "You should know," he said, his voice so deep I swear I felt it roll through me from across the room. "We can never be anything more than friends."

I figured as much, but actually hearing him say it hurt. Bad. I wanted to ask him why. Was it something I did? An annoying quirk? Or several? I wasn't the easiest person to be around, but Theo never seemed to mind spending time with me.

Or was Rowan right. Had he taken some vow of celibacy to atone for the accident? Pretty sure sex wasn't involved in the crash, but I guess, maybe, it made sense in some fucked-up way. If Logan couldn't have a girlfriend, Theo wouldn't either.

"Yeah, all right," I said, trying to sound relaxed, even though I wanted to ugly cry so bad my stomach hurt. I wrapped my arms around my waist hoping to ease the ache. "We'd better get inside before my brother and your friends demolish all the food."

I flung open the door and stepped into the kitchen where everyone was hovering over the containers, since Theo apparently didn't own plates. A single plastic spoon rested in the mac and cheese. I'd be skipping that side. Ditto for the coleslaw, baked beans, and mashed potatoes. Since I'd taste tested a few of Rowan's brownies already today, I didn't want those either. So, I grabbed a drumstick and a biscuit before tucking myself between Chris and Lauren.

While I choked down enough food to not bring attention to myself, the others talked about the wedding, the bakery, and whether Cammie had shared any more details about her family, which, shocker, she hadn't. Aiden and Chris even snuck in some football stats. No one mentioned that Theo hadn't followed me inside. Or that he stayed in the glass room until Lauren shouted it was time for her to get back to Karma.

"Thank you, Lauren," Theo said, stepping into the kitchen as Mom added water to the devil's ivy she'd brought. "The place smells and feels great."

Instead of saying anything, Lauren hugged him, longer and harder than I'd ever seen her hug anyone. A stab of jealousy shot through me while they stood locked in each other's arms. Finally, she stepped away from him, grabbed my hand, and dragged me from the kitchen. I pulled myself free as soon as we were outside. "Is there something you want?" I asked.

"Get in the car." She walked ahead of me across the street and slid behind the wheel of her old sedan.

I could have turned around and gone back inside, but honestly, I appreciated how she'd gotten me out of the house without having to say goodbye to Theo. I huffed but joined her.

"That door to the sunroom isn't soundproof," she said as I buckled my seatbelt.

Well, wasn't that great? The only thing worse than being turned down was having an audience while it happened.

Lauren started the car but faced me as the engine groaned to life. "Believe what he told you, Poppy. Either accept what he's willing to give you or move on. He's a huge part of Cal's life, so he'll be part of Rowan's, but he doesn't have to have a place in yours. If it hurts too much to be his friend, let him go."

And now I understood the hug. Lauren believed in karma more than anyone I knew. In her mind, her little lovefest in the kitchen offset the pain she might cause Theo by suggesting I drop him from my life. No doubt, she'd keep hugging him like that forever if I took her advice.

I stared out the window, and we drove around the corner in silence. Lauren pulled up to the curb in front of my house and blew out a breath. "I get it, Poppy. More than you know. But sometimes loving someone isn't enough to save them. At some point, you have to protect yourself."

I raised my eyebrows and waited. Lauren never talked about her life before she came to live with her grandpa in middle school. From her silence, Rowan and I assumed Lauren's early childhood was bad, but after years of trying to learn more, we knew not to ask questions.

"Better go," she said, "so you have time to get a good cry in before your family comes home."

And that's exactly what I did.

Chapter Twelve

Theo

When I arrived at Marked on Aaron's first day, Max was already at his station with one of his regulars, George. "You settled in?" Max asked, pausing his needle above an outline of a sloth.

George already had representations of five of the seven deadly sins inked on his left arm: a mirror, a pile of money, an overflowing shopping cart, boxing gloves, and an outstretched hand in green ink. After today, he'd just need lust.

"Sure," I said, despite the fact I'd spent the night before sleeping on an air mattress and drank water straight from the faucet this morning since I didn't own a glass. I should have bought a bed and some basics, but I'd held on to the hope something would delay Aaron, and I could wait to move until the house sale went through. Instead, I was renting from Mrs. Jenkins for the next two weeks until the closing and sleeping on the floor. Not that I could call it rent. She'd charged me five dollars and a painting class at her retirement home. I was basically up half a month's rent on the exchange, and Aiden and I were still battling it out for a fair rental price. Fair for him, that is. He'd emailed me a lease with some bullshit amount that included a construction inconvenience credit.

"I picked up Aries yesterday and got him settled," Max said, pressing the needle down.

"Who's that?"

"Me," a guy said, stepping out of the supply closet. "You must be Theo."

He held out his hand, and I shook it while we assessed each other. You could learn a lot about a person from their tattoos. He had some decent ink, including a Japanese-style dragon in bold blue that wound around his left arm, but most of the rest were basic prison tats: barbed wire on his wrist, a spiderweb on his arm, both black and freestyled.

"Thought your name was Aaron," I said, dropping his hand.

He pointed to a large tattoo on his neck. "Changed it."

"To the Zodiac or the god?"

"Ain't they the same?" he said, laughing.

"How do you spell it?"

"A-r-i-e-s."

"That's the Zodiac."

"Theo's Greek," Max said, as if that explained why I was being a dick.

"Ah, got it man," Aries said, scratching his chest. "Didn't mean no disrespect. You speak English good." He laughed softly. "Probably better than me. I stopped going to school when I was thirteen."

Max shot me a look that made my balls shrivel. Growing up, I'd butted heads with my old man all the time and never felt an ounce of guilt, but the few occasions Max and I had gotten into it had left me feeling like a complete piece of shit. That look was an order to be the man he'd helped me become.

So instead of telling the dumbass who displaced me that I was born and raised in Peace Falls, I pointed to the partial sleeve on his right arm. "You do any of those yourself?"

"Yeah, this one," he said, pointing to the spiderweb.

"It's good," I said, because considering he'd probably done it with pen ink and a staple, it didn't look half bad. "Guess you're a leftie?"

Aries nodded. "You do any of yours?"

I held up the Xs on my hands. I had half a dozen more I'd done myself, including the Omega with Logan's name, but the Xs told him the most about me.

"You did both your hands?" he asked, his eyebrows raising in disbelief.

"I'm ambidextrous," I said as the bell rang to announce a client entering the waiting room.

"No shit," he said. "You're the first one of those I've met. I can't imagine being able to use both hands the same."

"It's why he's such a good art teacher. He can switch depending on who he's teaching."

If every muscle in my body tensed at the sound of her voice, they knotted as I watched Aries scan Poppy up and down. His eyes, which had looked a little bored while we talked, sparked to life. He flashed her a huge smile. "Good morning, how can I help you?"

I'm not sure what my face did, but he stepped back and held up his hands. "My bad, man. Seriously, no disrespect. Must happen all the time though, right?"

I braced myself and turned. Poppy had added a green streak to her hair that sharpened her moss-colored eyes to jade. Her shirt draped artfully off one shoulder, showing the strap of whatever black lacy thing she wore underneath. I swallowed, hard.

After Rose, Chris, and Rowan left yesterday, Cal and Aiden gave me enough shit about my conversation with Poppy to stink up Maple and Sullivan Streets. But it had to be done. Even if part of me had wanted to follow her into the kitchen and beg her to forget everything I'd just said. I'd planned to stay in the studio until I felt confident I wouldn't. If Lauren hadn't left, I'm not sure how long I'd have been there. But what I'd told Poppy was the truth. We could never be more than friends.

"What must happen all the time?" Poppy asked.

"Other guys checking out his girl."

Poppy shook her head. "We're just friends."

I'd be lying if I said I was relieved she sounded relaxed. A selfish part of me wanted her to be angry or even hurt, which basically proved I was not, and would never be, good enough for her.

"In that case," Aries said, stepping right into my space to stick his hand toward Poppy. "I'm Aries." She took one of her hands from the bakery boxes in her arms and shook his. He gave her delicate fingers two squeezes before he dropped them.

"A-r-i-e-s," I said.

"Poppy," she said. "I'm an Aries."

Her cheeks pinked, and my stomach plummeted to my boots. Was she flirting with him?

"I bet you are," Aries said. "I know a badass when I see one."

Poppy laughed. "Hardly. I'm here to deliver baklava and conquer my New Year's resolution to get over my fear of needles."

"You want a tattoo?" I asked. Poppy's gorgeous skin was a blank canvas I'd been dying to work with from the moment she walked into my life. If offering her body for me to ink was her idea of punishing me, she'd nailed it.

The pink in her cheeks deepened. "Maybe. For now, I'm just trying to be in the same room with a needle and not faint." She lifted her chin toward the station where Max continued to work, his needle buzzing a deeper pitch each time it connected with skin.

I reached for her instinctively. She responded by stepping back.

"I'm good. I'll tell you if I start to feel dizzy."

My chest tightened. She appeared cool and collected, but I could tell I'd hurt her, and she needed me to keep my distance.

"Hey, every journey begins with the first step," Aries said, taking a step closer to Poppy. "I'm starting one today too. I'm apprenticing with Max, so maybe by the time you're ready for ink, I can give it to you."

"I'll think about it," she said and smiled. She fucking smiled.

"Are those for me?" I asked, pointing to the Red Blossoms boxes.

"Yeah, Rowan went a little crazy with the zests. One is orange. The other is lemon. She cut one into triangles and the other into squares, but she made me swear not to tell you which was which. Try them out and let her know the shape you like best."

"Thanks, Poppy," I said taking the boxes. "But she shouldn't base her recipe on what I think."

"It's a lot of baklava, so feel free to share," she said, smiling at Aries again. "I know you don't like to eat sweets."

"Man, I'm a total sugar addict," Aries said, giving her a look that made me grip the boxes so hard they dented. "I can't get enough."

Among other things. Thankfully, I kept that part to myself. Pretty sure Max would have tossed me out by my gauges if I hadn't.

Max's client grunted in pain, and the pink drained from Poppy's cheeks. "Well, it was nice to meet you, Aries. See you in class, Theo."

She turned and Aries started walking out with her. "So, I'm new in town," I heard him say as the bell on the door rang. The rest of their conversation was muffled, even after I walked to the waiting room to put the pastry boxes on the counter. I watched him pull out his phone and hand it to her. Poppy typed something in it and smiled at him before she climbed into her hearse and drove away.

"Damn," Aries said, pushing through the door. "That's one badass bitch. And she drives a hearse. She ever get freaky in the back?" he asked me.

The needle stopped and before I could round the counter and beat the ever-loving shit out of Aries, Max gripped my shoulder, tight. I swear the man had wings in addition to the hearing and reflexes of an ex-con.

"Theo, I'm taking Aries outside to show him where Karma is, so he can get us some coffee to go with that dessert. Grab a twenty from the register and write down your order. Ask George if he wants anything."

I did as he said and watched while he instructed Aries far longer than necessary to point the guy in the direction of the one and only coffee shop on Main Street. Max stepped inside to grab the twenty and the order I'd scribbled down, which included his usual flat white and George's cinnamon toast latte. Max let out a disappointed sigh and added a double espresso to the list before he took it outside to Aries.

"Go ahead and grab a smoke, George," Max shouted to the back while we stared each other down.

George lumbered past us to the door. "Back in five."

"Take your time. We both need a break."

George nodded and headed to the sidewalk, already pulling his cigarettes and lighter from his jeans.

"You hate when people smoke out front," I said.

"I hate it more when someone doesn't give a person a chance," he said, crossing his arms over his chest. "I'd think you would too."

I rubbed my forehead. "Sorry."

"Don't apologize to me. And so we're clear, I don't expect you to apologize to Aries either. Just stop being a dick to the kid."

"You heard what he said about Poppy."

"I did, and he and I had a little chat about how we treat women in this town, whether they're within earshot or not. But you were being a dick before Poppy got here."

"There's something about him I don't like."

"Look, Theo," Max said, gripping my shoulder. "I get that change is hard for you. But you have the opportunity to be a great role model for Aries, if you're willing to look past his rough edges. The guy's had a hard life from the start. Yours only went to hell when you were eighteen. And even then, you've had friends in your corner every step of the way."

I blew out a breath. "And I've never had to fight addiction."

Max nodded. "If we want to help Aries become a better man, we have to meet him where he is now. Having said that, if he disrespects your girl again, I'll look the other way while you kick his ass."

"She's not my girl."

Max laughed. The kind of laugh that had him bending at the knees and wheezing.

"I'm serious."

"I know you are," Max said, straightening. He gripped my shoulder again and all the humor left his face. "That's been your problem for a while now, son. It's long past time you started enjoying your life again."

"You done, Dr. Phil?"

Max smiled at me. "Not yet, but soon, I hope."

CHAPTER THIRTEEN

Poppy

I ARRIVED AT KARMA twenty minutes before my date with Aries. He'd texted not long after I left Marked to ask if I wanted to meet up. I didn't hesitate. If I was the kind of person who kept track of New Year's resolutions, I'd be kicking ass in all but one: Stop lusting after Theo Makris. Aries looked like every guy I'd ever dated, so I figured why not?

Lauren was wrong. I couldn't accept that Theo and I would never be more than friends, but I also couldn't cut him from my life, no matter how much it hurt. For one thing, Peace Falls was the size of a postage stamp. And if Theo was part of Rowan's life, he'd be part of mine unless I limited my time with my sister and every other human I actually liked.

Which was why I stole Rowan's baklava while she was in the shower and strutted my ass into Marked this morning. Theo didn't want more. Fine. No sense letting my hurt fester until I saw him in class. I ripped the Band-Aid off my heart and got a date at the same time.

"She's here," Cammie shouted when I stepped inside.

Lauren burst through the stockroom door with a huge smile on her face. "Did you show her?"

"She hasn't even shut the door yet," Cammie said.

119

I pulled the door closed behind me and walked to the coffee bar. "What's going on?" I asked.

Cammie and Lauren pointed up at the menu board along the back wall, which now advertised a lavender-vanilla macchiato called The Poppy. I put my hands over my face and burst into tears. The next thing I knew, Cammie and Lauren had dragged me into Lauren's tiny office and plopped me in the desk chair.

"Here," Lauren said, handing me a tissue. "Your eyeliner is running."

"I hate you both," I said, sniffling into the tissue. "I'm going on my first date in over a year, and you had to show me that. What did you think would happen?"

"Um, not this," Cammie said, rubbing my back.

Lauren shrugged. "I figured it was 50/50 she'd cry."

Cammie's mouth fell open.

"Congratulations on tricking everyone into thinking you're nice," I said to Lauren.

Lauren smiled. "I am nice. I figured you still had some emotions to let out."

"Maybe," I sniffed. "But this isn't the best time."

"Oh, I think it is," Lauren said. "Bet you're not nervous about your date now."

"I was never nervous about my date."

Cammie nodded. "Which means you don't really like him."

"I don't know if I like him or not. Isn't that the point of a date?"

"Yeah, about that," Cammie said hopping onto Lauren's desk. She grabbed my hands, snotty tissue and all. "I did a little digging into Aries, and there are some things in his record you should know about."

This time Lauren's mouth fell open. "Cam, that's—"

"Smart," Cammie said, her kind blue eyes hardening. "I know you're all about second chances, Lauren, and that's great, but a woman should be aware of who she's dealing with."

"How did you even know I was going on a date with him?" I asked.

"I didn't, but thanks for confirming. When he came in earlier, he said he was new in town, so I figured I needed to know about him. You can never be too careful. Plus, the name Aries sounded totally fake. It took a while, but I finally teased his full name out of him. Aaron Piro, by the way. Then I did a little research."

"Spill it, bitch," I said. "It took me ten minutes to do this eyeliner. No telling how long it will take to fix it."

"Did you know he was just released from prison?" Cammie asked.

"I kind of figured since Theo said Max wanted the apartment to help someone, and that's how Theo ended up there."

Cammie nodded. "Aries is not like Theo. Let's just put that on the table now."

"Kind of the point, Cam," I snapped.

"Fair," she said, squeezing my hands. "From what I've read, Theo went to prison for an accident."

"Wait. If you researched Theo, you should have known he was a felon that night at Church."

Cammie shook her head. "I looked up his story after. I don't research everyone when I meet them. Cal trusts Theo, and I trust Cal." She blushed slightly. "After I did a background check on him."

"Wow, you really have trust issues, don't you?" I said.

"Obviously," she said, giving my hands another squeeze. "Anyway, Aries has a long record. He's got charges for dealing oxy going back to his late teens, probably further but his juvie record was sealed. Then there's petty theft and a handful of other misdemeanors, most having to do with using. But the thing that worries me is an assault and battery conviction."

"Oh," I said. Lauren bustled over with another tissue and wiped at my face, which was no doubt covered in black streaks.

"It was a bar fight, not domestic," Cammie continued. "But in my experience, that kind of violence can follow a man."

"Your experience?" I asked. All I knew of Cammie's life before Peace Falls was something happened that made her afraid of most men, and her dad was serving a life sentence somewhere.

Cammie cleared her throat. "Just be a little guarded. If for no other reason, he's been inside a few years. He probably wants to sleep with you as fast as humanly possible and will say anything to make that happen."

"What if all I want is hot sex with someone who has enough pent-up frustration to go all night?"

Lauren laughed.

"I mean, if that's what you want," Cammie said. "No judgment here. I just wanted you to be informed."

"Oh shit," Lauren said, getting herself under control. "You're serious?"

I shrugged.

"Don't," Lauren said with a steel-edge to her voice I'd only ever heard her use with Aiden.

Cammie gave Lauren a puzzled look. "Not to get too personal, Lauren, but are you really one to judge her?"

"I'm not the one saving my virginity for someone I love," Lauren said.

Cammie's eyes widened. "Wait, what?"

"Thanks, Lauren," I said. Not even my sister knew that little nugget. Leave it to "let's take a few shots" Lauren to pry the info out of me after my last boyfriend ditched me for not putting out.

"You're almost twenty-four," Cammie said.

"I'm aware," I said. "It's not that weird. Rowan was twenty-two her first time, and she ended up marrying the dick."

"Yes, but you're you," Cammie said, as though that made any sense.

"What the hell does that mean?" I snapped.

"It's just you don't seem like the type who'd be timid about sex," she said, blushing.

"I'm not. I've done plenty of *things* with plenty of guys. I'm just saving the p in the v part for someone worth the pain of breaking my hymen."

"You know, that's just something they tell girls in health class to make them afraid of sex. It doesn't always hurt the first time. Many women break their hymen with tampons," Lauren said, a slow smile on her face. "Or falling on a fence post while cow tipping."

"Bite me, Lauren. We don't speak of that night." But yeah, it was totally possible I didn't have a hymen left.

"Oh, my goodness," Cammie said softly, putting a hand over her heart. "Poppy Stevens, you're a romantic."

I stood up. "I need to fix my war paint. Thanks for the heads up, Cammie. Lauren, you're top of my shit list until further notice."

"You're welcome by the way," Lauren called after me as I stormed toward the bathroom in the café. "I'll have two Poppies ready when your date gets here. Let's see how he likes it."

She did, in fact, have two steaming mugs on the table moments after Aries arrived.

"What's this?" he asked, draping his leather jacket on the back of a chair.

"The drink we named after Poppy," Lauren said with her best customer-service smile. "Enjoy. I'll grab you a couple cookies to go with it."

He pulled out the chair and sat down, spreading out his arms and legs to take up as much space as possible in the crowded cafe. I wasn't sure if I admired him for it, or if it made him look obnoxious. Theo had several inches on Aries, but I'd seen the way he softened his voice and stooped his shoulders whenever small children seemed afraid of him. He never gave a shit what the adults thought, which I appreciated, but he also didn't claim as much space as he could.

"Pretty cool you have a drink named after you," Aries said. When he lifted the mug to his face, he crinkled his nose.

"Smells like air freshener," I said.

"Glad you said it." He winked at me, and my stomach gave a promising wiggle. He took a sip and nodded. "Not bad. I'm not used to fancy drinks like this, but it's nice."

Lauren set down a plate of snowflake cookies. No doubt in my mind she'd waited to approach the table until she could hear his reaction to the drink. "Poppy decorated these herself," she said.

I shot her a look to get lost, but she just smiled at me like a psycho.

"How'd you make them so detailed?" he asked, holding one closer to his face.

"A lot of patience and time," I said.

"Lauren," Cammie shouted, "the espresso machine is acting up."

I was starting to like the perky blonde more and more.

"They taste as good as they look," Aries said around a mouth full of cookie as Lauren headed for the counter.

"My sister, Rowan, is the baker. I do all the decorating. Most of my work is custom cakes."

"You're talented."

My face warmed at the compliment. Aries scooted his chair closer, but kept his knees spread, so his leg brushed mine.

"So, you want to become a tattoo artist?" I asked, trying to decide if I liked his leg touching mine or just tolerated it.

He nodded. "I've done a few on my own already, but Max is helping me work toward a license."

"That's great," I said. "Do you paint or sketch?"

"A little," Aries said, his eyes downcast. "I'm not an artist or anything. Not like Max or Theo. Definitely not like Theo. That guy has sick skills."

"I bet you're more talented than you think," I said, smiling at him despite the ache in my chest. "You should join Theo's class at the community center. We meet every Thursday."

Aries shook his head. "Nah, that's his thing. He sees enough of me as it is."

Something about the way he said it, like being around him was a burden, made me link my fingers with his. "Trust me, most of the class are grumpy retirees. You'd be a welcomed addition."

"I'm glad to hear you say that," he said, rubbing his thumb across the back of my hand. We talked for a while about Peace Falls, his new job, my sculpting, holding hands the entire time. He never mentioned his past, and I didn't ask any questions I knew would lead there. After we finished our coffee, which was delicious despite smelling like my favorite fabric softener, he leaned toward me.

"This place closes soon," he said. "But I don't want our night to end. How'd you like to walk down to Church for a drink?"

"You drink?" I asked.

"You don't?"

"I do. I just figured—" I didn't know how to finish that sentence without revealing I knew he was an addict and newly released felon. Do drug addicts drink? Was alcohol a gateway drug or was that pot? I wished I'd paid more attention to those D.A.R.E lessons in middle school.

Aries dropped my hand. "It's cool. This was just a coffee date, right?"

"Yes," I said, relieved he'd come up with a better excuse than I could. "But I had a really great time."

The tension melted from his forehead, and he smiled. "Yeah, me too. We could grab dinner next week. Things are a little tight for me right now, but I'd like to take you out after I get my first paycheck."

"Sounds great," I said.

We pushed away from the table, Lauren and Cammie watching our every move.

"I'll walk you to your car," Aries said, pulling on his jacket while I shuffled into mine. "I mean hearse. Awesome ride by the way."

"Tallulah's the best."

"I like that," he said softly as he held the door open for me. "Did you name her after Tallulah Bankhead?"

"Um, yeah, but no one has ever made that connection."

"I'm a huge Hitchcock fan," he said, grabbing my hand again when we stepped onto the sidewalk. "It's a new thing. I've, um, watched all of his films a few times. *Lifeboat* is one of my favorites."

"Mine is *Psycho* unless I'm in the mood for a laugh, then it's *The Birds*."

"You can see the damn strings," he said, a huge smile breaking across his face, making him look younger, closer to my age than Theo's. "That settles it. You, me, dinner, and *The Birds* next week."

"Sounds great," I said, smiling back at him. Because it did sound great. But honestly, I'd have jumped at the opportunity to watch the movie if Aiden had asked me, and for an obnoxiously attractive man, I had zero interest in him.

Aries cleared his throat and started to lean forward just as Lauren ran out from Karma.

"Don't forget you're giving me a ride to your house," she said. "I'm helping Rowan narrow down ideas for the centerpieces."

I tilted my head at her. She hadn't asked me for a ride anywhere. I gave it less than a twenty-five percent chance my sister was even home and not at Cal's, but I knew Lauren. She had her reasons, and I trusted her enough to go with it.

"Well, come on then," I said.

Aries let out a breath and dropped my hand. "I'll text you later, Poppy."

"Sounds good." I waved and he started down the sidewalk in the direction of Marked.

"Well?" I asked Lauren.

"Get in the hearse," she said, flinging open my passenger door. The inside light came on, illuminating the art supplies we'd salvaged from the shed. There wasn't much, but it was more than we had room for in the house. Thankfully most of my chisels weren't damaged, but nearly all my paints and sketch pads were wrecked. The damn ball of clay survived as expected, as well as quite a few brushes.

"I didn't know you were coming over," I said, throwing Tallulah into drive.

"I hadn't planned on it, but I didn't think you were ready to kiss him," she said, pulling out her phone and texting furiously.

"Kiss who?"

"Aries, you idiot. What do you think happens when a guy walks you to your car?"

"Um, you say good night and leave?"

Lauren shoved her phone in her apron pocket, but the streetlamps gave me just enough light to see her pinch the bridge of her nose. "What kind of Neanderthals have you dated?"

"The kind who don't walk me to my car, apparently."

"Half my hookups get started when the guy walks me to my car. That's when he makes his move, and I either tell him to get lost or get naked."

"I think Aries got the hint I didn't want to get naked tonight when I didn't go to Church with him for a drink. But more to the point, why would you lip block me? Maybe I wanted him to kiss me goodnight."

Lauren shook her head. "You don't."

I didn't, but I hated when Lauren read my emotions as if I walked around with little flashcards on my forehead: Angry, happy, PMSing,

127

horny. Not that she'd ever called me out on that last one, but I'm sure she'd seen it.

"Face it, Poppy. He's a good-looking guy, and you had some things in common, but the chemistry is tepid at best."

"How do I know that unless I kiss him?"

"Please. The sparks between you and Theo could burn down Peace Falls."

"Doubtful," I said, pulling into my driveway and throwing the hearse into park.

"Yes," she said simply. "Look, I just didn't want you rushing into something with Aries to try to get over Theo. I know I'm being overprotective, but I don't want you hurting any more than you already are."

Cammie's car pulled to a stop in front of my house. "What's Cam doing here?" I asked.

"Giving me a ride back to Karma," Lauren said, climbing out of the hearse.

"You're a pain in my ass, Lauren Arnaud. I'm bringing Aiden to the café tomorrow, and we're sitting right by the counter for at least an hour."

"That's cold," Cammie shouted from her rolled-down window. "Come on Lauren, before someone realizes there's no one working."

"Love you, Poppy," Lauren shouted as she ran to the car.

I rolled down my window and flipped them off after Cammie did a three-point turn and headed back to Main.

"What a nightmare," I said resting my head on the steering wheel. My phone vibrated in my purse. Lauren had probably sent Rowan a play-by-play of my date all evening. I grabbed my phone, expecting a text from my sister. Instead, it was a picture of the studio at Theo's house, which now had a couple free-standing lights, an impressive table, and a rotating modeling stand on wheels. My phone buzzed again with a text from him.

Ready whenever you are

Time for another round of exposure therapy. As I reversed out of the driveway, I told the butterflies in my stomach to simmer. I'd prove to everyone, myself included, that I wasn't hung up on Theo. Not one bit.

CHAPTER FOURTEEN

Theo

Mana

Pos eisai?

Kalo. Pos eisai?

Kalo

Patera?

Kalo

Na se kala

Na se kala agapi mia

THAT WAS NEW. SHE hadn't called me *my love* since she went back to Greece. That, coupled with the fact it was 4:00 am her time made me uneasy. Mana often texted late at night my time, but not before 6:00 am hers.

My phone buzzed again but instead of Mana I had a group text from Lauren, Cammie, and Rowan.

Lauren

> *Theo, did you know Poppy is on a date with that new guy at Marked?*

I didn't want to be part of this conversation. I felt sick when Aries told me he was meeting Poppy for coffee tonight. Max seemed excited that Aries was making friends and gave him another twenty. He gave me a stern look until I unclenched my fists and headed to the back to lose myself in a custom sketch for one of my regulars.

Cammie

> *Did you know he did time for A&B?*

Now, I did. My hands started to sweat as I typed.

> *Yes to the date. No to the A&B. Domestic?*

The muscles in my neck and shoulders bunched as I waited for Cam to reply.

Lauren

> *WTF! You knew she was going on a date and you didn't stop her?*

Cammie

> *If he won't date her, he can't stop her from dating other people*

> *Why are you texting each other? Aren't you together?*

Lauren

Focus, Theo. Poppy, your Poppy, is on a date with a guy who checks all her boxes. He's a bad boy with an actual rap sheet. The girl is attracted to toxic like a moth to flame. She'll be putty in his hands

Rowan

Agreed. She has never once expressed interest in anyone decent until Theo

Lauren

Thanks for finally joining us. If they try to leave together, should I stop her?

Rowan

Yes

No

Cammie

So, you don't think Aries is dangerous?

Lauren

<Picture of Aries and Poppy>

They were sitting together at one of Karma's small bistro tables. Poppy looked gorgeous with her bold eyeliner. I'd never seen her wear that sweater before. It dipped just low enough to give a peek at the tops of her perky tits. She'd clearly put in some effort for the date, and Aries looked like he'd ironed his shirt with the iron I'd never used in the apartment. They were so close their thighs touched, and my stomach soured when I saw their hands entwined.

Rowan

That's a definite yes, Lauren

Lauren

Rodger

I left the chat. I never should have been part of it to begin with, and if I saw another picture of Poppy and Aries together, I might break my promise to Cal and Aiden and hurt myself. Sometimes the only way to dull the pain in my chest was to pull it from my skin. I cut, tattooed, or pierced away the ache until I was a walking testament to it, my scars as real on the outside as they were inside.

I paced from one end of the house to the other and finally ended up in the studio. Aiden and I had spent the better part of the afternoon searching for a table to replace the one Poppy lost. I'd also bought a couple floor lights since the one overhead sucked. The studio was ready for her to move in. I pulled my phone from my pocket and snapped a picture. I was just being a good friend, letting her know she had a place to work whenever she wanted. I typed a quick text, but my thumb hovered over the send button for one minute, five minutes, as I debated why I was sending it now. I finally broke and hit send.

I knew I was torturing myself. The longer the text went unanswered, the more I let my imagination wreck me. I'd just started picturing them kissing when someone knocked on the front door. I expected to find Rowan or Cal on the other side, but instead Poppy stood on my porch with a huge cardboard box. I'd never felt more relieved in my life.

"You sure you want all this in your house?" she asked, squeezing past me, her flowery scent jolting my cock to life.

"Of course," I said. "Is there more in the hearse?"

"Yeah," she shouted, still walking toward the studio.

I ran outside and sucked in a lungful of frigid air, forcing my body to calm down. I pulled two more boxes from the back and stacked them.

"I'll get the rest," she said as she held open the front door for me. I set everything down and returned to the living room as she came back with a large plastic bucket hooked to her arm. I shut the door behind her and followed her to the studio, admiring the curve of her shapely ass in the leggings she wore and the sliver of pale skin where her sweater rose up.

"I've always wanted one like this," she said with a huge smile as she spun the sculpture modeling stand I'd bought for her. "But I never had the floor space. This is perfect."

She was perfect, the best mixture of sass and sweet, strong, yet delicate. Not that I could ever tell her that. "You're welcome anytime. Aiden ordered the door. It should go in next week."

"Thanks, Theo," she said, aiming that powerful smile at me like a cannon.

"So, um, how was your date?"

Damn it, I really was a masochist. That was the last thing I wanted to talk about with her.

"You knew about it?" she asked, something like hurt sneaking into her expression before she squashed it down.

"Aries wouldn't shut up about it."

"I like him. We're—"

And that's when I lost my damn mind. Before I registered what was happening, I'd taken her face in my hands and crashed my lips to hers. She tasted like lavender and sugar, impossibly sweet. Poppy let out a shocked yelp before she started kissing me back.

The thought of anyone else touching her made me crazy. Her lips were made for mine. And the rest of her body. Fuck. I lowered my hands to her ass, finally gripping it like I've wanted to for so long. She gasped into my mouth when I lifted her, but quickly wrapped her legs around my waist.

I pressed her against the only real wall in the studio to free my hands, the need to touch her more desperate than taking my next breath.

When I broke the kiss, both of us were panting. "I want to make you feel good," I said, my voice strained.

She nodded. I ran my hands down her body, gripping her breast with one and dipping past the waistband of her leggings with the other. My fingers slid across her soft, wet skin until I found the bundle of nerves that had her moaning my name.

She gripped my shoulders, arching against my touch, taking her pleasure. I kept my thumb on her clit and pushed two fingers inside her in time with her movements. She squeezed her eyes closed and her grip on my shoulders tightened just before she found her release. I'd never seen anything more beautiful than when she shattered in my arms.

Her green eyes locked with mine when they opened, and she said my name with such tenderness my heart clenched. I loved her. I had from the moment she walked into my class. I loved her, but I couldn't let her look at me with affection I'd never deserve.

"I'm sorry," I said, pulling away and lowering her gently to the ground. "I shouldn't have done that. It won't happen again."

"Don't you dare," she said, smacking my chest. "You give me the best orgasm of my life and ruin it with an apology?"

"Because I am sorry," I said. My chest grew heavy with an overwhelming sadness. "I can't be with you. Not like this, no matter how much I want to."

"That doesn't make fucking sense. Why not?"

"Because I can't be with anyone." The ache in my chest deepened. What had I done? She should walk out of my life forever after what just happen. But being a selfish prick, I let the panic of never seeing her again take over my mouth. "Please, Poppy, I don't want to lose you as a friend."

She studied me a moment, the hurt and confusion raw on her face, then nodded. "On one condition. You have to kiss me again. Then I'll leave, and we'll pretend this never happened."

"And you'll still come to class and use this studio to work?"

"I promise. But you better make it good. No peck on the lips. Kiss me like it's the last time."

I stepped closer and gripped her waist. She placed her slender hands on my chest. I wasn't sure if we were holding each other or keeping the distance between us, suspended in the moment before we crossed the line for the last time. Her eyes found mine and she nodded. I lowered my lips to taste her once more. The kiss was agonizingly gentle until she parted her soft lips for me. I dipped into her mouth, savoring every caress of her tongue. I released her hips and buried my hands in her hair, pulling her close until every inch of her body rested against mine, her hands twisting the fabric of my shirt. I kissed her until the second before my hunger for her took control, then I pulled away, rested my forehead on hers, and closed my eyes. "Go."

She sucked in a stuttering breath and my entire body ached as her heated skin left mine. I kept my eyes shut and listened to her footsteps as she left, waiting for the front door to close before I walked to the kitchen and washed her from my hands. Like it never happened. If only I could rid my heart of her as easily as I could her scent.

I walked back to the studio, sank to the floor, and stretched out by the wall where I'd held her. I was still there, staring at the colorless ceiling, when the front door opened and moments later Skye ran in. She whimpered when she saw me and laid her soft head on my chest.

"You OK?" Cal asked, taking a seat beside me.

I nodded and ran my fingers through Skye's fur as I pulled myself up to sitting. She rolled onto her back for a belly rub. Her tail twitched with measured excitement when I complied. "Poppy went to your house?"

Cal nodded. We'd been friends since kindergarten when he started talking my ear off and never stopped. He only got quiet when something upset him.

"I fucked up," I said.

Cal nodded again.

My stomach lurched. "How upset was she?"

"Not my place to tell you."

"Then why are you here?"

"Figured you needed Skye."

Skye gave a huff and wiggled her head under my hands until I took the hint and started petting her again.

"Thanks," I said.

"Not to make this about me, but I'm not sure what to do right now. I'm so mad I don't want to be in the same room as you, but I'm so worried, I can't imagine leaving you alone. Your cutting scares the shit out me, you know."

"I know," I said. "And I get why you're mad. You care about Poppy, and I hurt her." It felt like tiny pieces of glass were lodged inside my chest, trying to work their way to the surface.

"Yeah," he said, pulling at his hair. "But it's more than that. I'm pissed because I don't know what else I can do. You need someone who can help you more than I can. A therapist or something. Maybe then you could really move on with your life. I know you think you don't deserve Poppy. I also know you're in love with her."

I let the silence confirm it.

"Damn it, Theo," Cal said, his voice hoarse. "What happens now?"

I shrugged. "She moves on. Hopefully not with Aries."

"I take it you don't like him."

I let out a bitter laugh. "I didn't trust him before he went out with Poppy."

"She's going to date other people," Cal said softly. "Maybe even get married one day and have kids. Do you really think you can just watch that happen?"

I nodded. "If she's happy. If she ends up with someone good like Aiden."

Cal looked at me like I'd sprouted two extra heads. "You know Aiden wouldn't touch Poppy with a ten-foot pole."

"Why not? They get along. He pretends to be an asshole, but we both know he'd give the shirt off his back to anyone who needed it. He's generous and loyal and—"

"One of your best friends. He'd rather cut off a nut than date the woman you love."

"He doesn't know how I feel."

Cal shook his head. "He's not blind. If I could see it, so could he. Why do you think he's working so hard to help Rowan and Poppy find a place for their bakery?"

"You're marrying Rowan. That's reason enough for him. But I've seen the way he teases her. He likes her."

"Aiden separates women into two categories: Those he can fuck and those he can't. Poppy is one hundred percent the latter. He treats every woman he won't sleep with like one of his sisters, which means helping them whenever he can and teasing them every chance he gets."

Fuck. Cal was right. Aiden may banter with Poppy but when it came down to it, I couldn't see him actually making a move, which means some other dickhead would. "Can we change the subject, please?"

Cal rubbed his forehead. "Well, apart from you and Poppy, I have two topics on my mind. What to give Rowan for Valentine's Day and who to ask to be my best man."

"That last one is easy. Chris."

Cal shook his head. "He's nervous about being in the wedding. He hasn't been to many, and he quote 'Doesn't want to screw it up.' I had a hard enough time convincing him to be a groomsman. There's no way he'd be the best man, so that leaves you or Aiden."

"Well, that's a no-brainer too. Aiden will give a better speech and throw an epic bachelor party."

"True," Cal said, staring off at the blackened glass walls. "But he's not you. Logan and Aiden were best friends before we met them. You've always been mine."

"By default," I said.

"Maybe," Cal said. "But you're my brother now. You have been for years."

I gripped his shoulder to show I felt the same, but said, "All the more reason you should ask Aiden. He'll never get to be Logan's best man."

Cal let out a sigh but nodded. "So, what do I give Rowan for Valentine's Day?"

"You finally realized camping gear isn't an appropriate gift for your fiancée?"

Cal shoved my hand off his shoulder and twisted me into a head lock, giving me the noogies of all noogies. "It was the perfect birthday gift, asshole. We're hiking part of the Appalachian trail for our honeymoon."

"Can't spring for a tropical vacation, doc?" I said, shoving him off me.

"It's what she wanted," Cal said. "And I've made it my mission in life to give her everything she wants."

"Good thing Rowan is low maintenance."

"Yeah," Cal said, frowning. "But is she too low maintenance? Does she only want the bare minimum because she thinks that's what she deserves?"

Skye whimpered again and glanced between Cal and me. Poor dog didn't know who needed her more. Cal petted her, either to make her feel better or to ease the tension that had gathered around his eyes.

"That's a terrible way to look at it," I said, my stomach twisting. Rowan's ex was a douche, but she seemed to have moved on from the marriage with her self-esteem intact. She called Cal on his shit when needed. She genuinely loved hiking and gave up a lucrative career because she valued her friends and family above money. But Cal was a worrier, which was in no small part thanks to me. I cleared my throat. "She's not me."

Cal chuckled. "Thank goodness for that. I don't think I could handle two of you."

I shoved his shoulder. "Look, I was kidding about the camping honeymoon. It's perfect for you and Rowan."

"Yeah, but I don't want to get her a water purifier for our first Valentine's Day after giving her a mixer for Christmas."

"What if you made her something?"

"Like at one of those paint-a-mug places?"

"Are you five?"

"No, but my artistic skills haven't improved since elementary school."

"Even if they haven't, you could make her a necklace. All you need is silicone to carve the mold, a crucible, and some silver or gold. Max has a blow torch and all the safety gear."

"Pretty sure anything involving a blow torch is beyond my skill set."

"It's not beyond mine. I've helped Max make a few custom piercings for clients. How cool would it be to give Rowan jewelry you designed and made yourself?"

"You just want to help me because you feel guilty for refusing to be my best man."

"Technically, you never asked."

"Theo, will you be my best man?" he asked with the enthusiasm of someone asking for the salt.

"No, brother," I said, slapping his back. "But I'll help you make Rowan a kick-ass gift. Who knows, maybe you'll like it and smelt your own wedding rings."

"That's a hard no."

"You underestimate yourself."

His eyes looked sad as he nodded and said, "Same, brother. Same."

Chapter Fifteen

Poppy

"Can you see it, Poppy?" Rowan asked, pressing her hands together and spinning in a circle. It was difficult to look past the chipped tiles the color of pea soup, the water stains on the drop ceiling, and the walls riddled with nail holes and smoke stains, but I could. I could see everything we'd ever dreamed Red Blossoms Bakery could be, and a few things Aiden had dreamed up himself.

"We'll put up new sheetrock, of course," Aiden said. "I was thinking we could save a small space by the front windows for consultations and make the rest workspace. Do you want it open, or would you like a wall between you and the customers, Hell Cat?"

"Whatever you and Rowan think."

Aiden narrowed his eyes. "Theo's an idiot."

"Agreed," Rowan said, clearing her throat, "but we're not talking about it."

My sister really was perfect, which meant I needed to be fully in the moment for her, not replaying everything that happened at Theo's the other night and trying to figure out what went wrong, again.

"Maybe we could have a half wall with a door," I said. "I'd like to have the sunlight from the front windows, but I don't want people creeping into my work area."

"Are you OK with them seeing you work?" Rowan asked.

I shrugged. "I don't like people breathing down my neck when I'm sculpting serious art, but I don't mind when I'm decorating."

"I like the idea of a half wall," Aiden said. "This wall here," he said, thumping the plaster, "isn't load bearing, so we can knock it down."

"I have to check the lease first," Rowan said, ruffling through her color-coded file folders.

"Shouldn't be a problem," Aiden said, clearing his throat and looking everywhere but at us.

Son of a bitch.

I'd wondered why the rent had mysteriously gone down five-hundred dollars per month for the perfect space. "You'd know, wouldn't you?"

He grabbed my arm. "Poppy and I are going to discuss her worktable while you read through the lease," he said to my sister.

"OK," Rowan said, not even bothering to look up from the stack of papers in her hands as Aiden pulled me into the worn commercial kitchen.

"You bought the building," I hissed.

"Keep your voice down," he said, shifting his feet like a toddler who needed the potty. I'd never seen Aiden O'Malley flustered. It was almost adorable.

"Explain," I said, crossing my arms.

"I knew this was the right space before I showed it to you, so I made the owner an offer and bought it with an LLC."

"What if we'd hated it?"

"Then I'd have fixed it up and rented it to someone else. This is a great location."

"It is, which is why you'd have had no problem getting the rent the original owner wanted," I said poking his chest as hard as I could. He didn't even flinch. Pretty sure it hurt my finger more.

"Don't tell Rowan," he said, gripping my shoulders. "Please. She'll tell Cal, and he'll have questions I don't want to answer."

"If I'm going to lie to my sister by omission, I need a good reason."

Aiden nodded. "Fine. But this stays between us."

"Obviously."

He released my shoulders and took a step back as if giving himself space for my potentially violent reaction. "I got money from the accident to start my construction business, which has been doing really well for a while now. I'm a lot better off than anyone knows."

"You sued Theo?" I said louder than I meant. I cringed and we both waited for Rowan to storm into the back, but all we heard was the frantic flipping of papers in the other room.

"Of course not," he said in an angry whisper. "But my parents sued his parents' insurance company. And Cal's. I had a ton of medical bills we couldn't pay."

"Makes sense," I said, softly. "But why be so secretive about it?"

"Because," he said leaning against one of the pocked walls, "it felt wrong. Still does. I think that suit was the last straw for Theo's parents. They left for Greece right after the case settled. My parents gave me all the money left over after they paid my bills. I felt like a dirtbag taking it, but without my scholarship I couldn't afford college, and I had to start my career somehow. Theo and Cal never talked about the lawsuit. I doubt they even know about it. Theo was in jail when it happened, and Cal was focused on PT and school. But it's never set right with me. I'm just trying to pay it back however I can."

I got it. Helping Rowan was helping Cal, and helping my sister and me build our dream bakery and slashing the rent was likely the only way Aiden would ever be able to gift Cal any of the money he'd gotten. No doubt it was the same reason he'd bought the house on Maple when Theo needed a place to live.

"So, we good?" he asked.

"Yeah. Now please say something obnoxious. I'm dangerously close to thinking you're decent."

"Should I make the wall waist height so your customers can admire that great rack of yours?"

"Wow, that didn't take long."

He held up his hands. "It's a gift."

"I honestly don't care how tall you make the wall, just so it lets the light in and keeps the people out."

Aiden nodded and scribbled something in the notepad he'd carried around in his back pocket all morning. "For what it's worth," he said without looking up, "I'm still rooting for you and Theo."

"Yeah, well don't hold your breath. All I need to work is our prep table, so let Rowan take the lead with the kitchen design. I have a fuck-ton of hearts-and-flowers cookies to decorate, so I'll see you around."

To his credit, Aiden didn't try to stop me. I slipped past Rowan, who had her nose buried in the lease agreement, and out the door, climbing into Tallulah and speeding away before my sister realized I'd gone.

At least I really did have a fuck-ton of hearts-and-flowers cookie pops to keep me occupied. Rowan had this idea for custom cookie bouquets for Valentine's Day, and I needed to decorate a sample to figure out how long each would take before we set a price and popped the order form on the website. The sample was going to have the names of everyone who worked at Karma and would sit on the café counter with a stack of order forms.

Thankfully, Chris was still at school and Mom was still at work, so I had the house to myself. I cranked my emo punk playlist and lost myself in AFI, My Chemical Romance, and royal icing. The stainless-steel table was littered with piping bags in various shades of pink and red when I finished. In all, I had a dozen flower cookies and five hearts attached to colorful cake pop sticks. Each heart had a name piped in pretty script: Lauren, Cammie, and Wyatt—who'd started at Karma after I left—plus the Karma Cats, Desdemona and Medusa. I stuffed a foam block into one of the heart-shaped pots I'd found for cheap online and arranged the cookies. Once I finished, I noted how long it'd taken me and stepped back to admire my work. I decided we should include a cake pop add-on for anyone who wanted to take the bouquet to the next level.

I'd never admit it, but I loved Valentine's Day. It started when I was a kid, making handmade cards for everyone in my classroom. The number of cards I made got smaller and smaller each year as kids broke off into cliques that didn't include me, but the card designs became more intricate, part watercolor, part three-dimensional cutouts. Last year, I only made them for Mom, Rowan, Chris, Wilson, and Lauren. I suppose this year I should make ones for Cal and Cammie. Probably Aiden too since he's done so much for Red Blossoms Bakery. Which meant I couldn't not make one for Theo.

Talk about emotional whiplash. I vacillated between wanting to cry for Theo, yell at Theo, and just plain wanting Theo so often I should have been curled in a ball mumbling to myself. It would be easy to hate him for what he did. For a moment, I thought he was finally ready to be more. He'd kissed me with so much passion, gave me the most satisfying orgasm of my life, and then apologized like he'd stepped on my hurt foot and not my heart. The worst part of the evening I had to own: Making him kiss me one last time. Like he'd change his mind once he felt my lips again. Nope. What's worse, that kiss broke me. He'd poured himself into it, and I got a taste of what it'd be like to be adored by a man like Theo. I've been choking on it ever since.

I wanted to skip class tonight, give myself more time before I faced him again, but I promised. I just needed to keep busy for the next few hours and then attach myself to Wilson like a barnacle.

I grabbed one of the sketch pads I used for custom cakes and settled on the couch to start my card designs. I usually went the funny route with cards for my friends. Since I wasn't in a laughing mood, I'd have to figure out Cammie's, Lauren's, and Wilson's later. I drew a garden scene for Mom, a mountain scape for Rowan, various football accouterments for Chris, which could probably work for Aiden as well. For Cal, I went full sappy with a picture of him and Skye with the rest of our family. I'd brainstorm later for something sentimental to cut into 3-D letters.

So far, I'd succeeded in making at least one person cry every year when we exchanged cards, and this year, I had my sights set on my future brother-in-law. Mom and Rowan were the sure bets, but I was never one to back down from a challenge. Valentine's 2021 will hold a special place in my heart as the year I made Chris bawl like a baby.

I looked over the sketches, satisfied. I could go the humorous route with Theo's card as well, but I wouldn't. That'd be too easy. I started messing around with tattoo-like designs around the border and stopped. Something about it wasn't right. I flipped to a fresh sheet and a clear image popped in my mind. After a few minutes of drawing, I realized I wasn't sketching a card design, but an idea for a sculpture.

My pencil moved without pausing, and the image started to form on the page. I kept going, adding details and layers until everything was there. I dropped the pencil and massaged my hand. Could I make this? Or more to the point, should I?

I was so lost in the sketch, I hadn't realized Rowan was watching me until I looked up from the page and found her leaning on the wall by the couch.

"How long have you been there?" I asked, shuffling the card designs on the coffee table, so she wouldn't see them, like those were what had her staring at me with her mouth open.

She plucked the sketchbook from my lap, and for the first time, I didn't hate that she was seeing something so unfinished.

"You need to take this to class tonight," she said in a firm voice.

"Hell no," I said, leaning forward to grab the sketch book. She pivoted with surprising ease for a woman with a serious spinal injury.

"I already have my sketch for class," I huffed.

Rowan shook her head. "It's a nice picture of Chris, but no. This is the one you need to take."

"I can't," I said and bit my tongue to keep from crying.

"This," Rowan said, holding up the sketch, "is real and raw and—"

"Personal. Which is why I can't take it to class."

"Ah, sis," Rowan said, sitting on the couch beside me and wrapping me in a hug. "That's exactly why you should."

CHAPTER SIXTEEN

Theo

"I can't wait for tomorrow," Aries said, drumming his hands at a jarring staccato on the counter.

"Big plans for the weekend?" I asked. My first client couldn't get here fast enough. I wanted to slam Aries's hands against the wood to quiet the cutting flick of his wrists. It was too early for so much energy, especially after lying awake for hours worrying if I'd see Poppy in class tonight. She'd left my apology text on read for days, which I understood. She needed space. If she showed tonight, it meant I had a chance at keeping her friendship. If she didn't, I'd know I'd lost the brightest part of my life.

"Yeah," Aries said, his hands finally resting on the counter. "So, um, what's Poppy's favorite restaurant in town that won't eat half my paycheck?"

"What?"

I'd heard him fine, but I needed him to repeat it while I pinched my forearm hard enough to bruise, just in case I was still asleep and had slipped into my worst nightmare. The pain released some of the tension in my chest, but as soon as Aries opened his mouth and started talking, my lungs felt like they were being squeezed in a vise.

"I'm taking her to dinner tomorrow. I told her we were getting takeout and watching a Hitchcock film, but that feels a little too friend zone, you know what I mean? Plus, I realized I don't have a TV. Inviting myself over to her house didn't feel right. So, I figured we'd eat at a restaurant and see where the night takes us. That Church place looks nice. Is it any good?"

"It's a bar," I gritted out.

"Yeah, but they serve food, right? The only other place within walking distance looks pricey. White tablecloths and shit."

"Poppy has a car," Max said, stepping into the front and joining the conversation. He'd clearly been listening while he set up his station.

"Yeah," Aries said, scratching his neck like he'd just gotten stung by a mosquito in the middle of winter. "But I want to do this right. Having the girl drive on a date doesn't sit well with me."

"That's fucking stupid," I snapped.

Max cleared his throat. "What Theo means is a woman like Poppy doesn't care about that. She loves driving her hearse."

Aries nodded, but then asked, "Is the food that bad at Church?"

"No," Max said, blowing out a breath. "But it's a bar, son."

Well, that hurt. In all the years I'd known him, Max had never called someone else son. I shouldn't feel like I owned the word, but now I wondered what it really meant to Max if he'd attach it to Aries after only knowing him a short time. Guess it's just a word he used with anyone he mentored.

"So what?" Aries said, drawing himself up.

"You're still new in your recovery. It's best to avoid temptation."

"Bet Theo went there when he got out."

I did. The first night, actually. None of us were twenty-one, but Aiden's big sister Fiona bought enough pitchers to get him and Cal hammered. When I didn't drink, they accepted it without comment. I ate my weight in fried food before making sure they had sober rides home since my license had been revoked. Then I texted a girl I'd known in high school and spent the rest of the night and the morning releasing a year's worth of sexual tension before Max arrived at Marked.

"See those Xs on his hands," Max said, pointing at me.

"So, if I scribble some straight-edged shit on me I can take a date to Church?"

"I have them so people don't ask why I don't drink." And, when I first got them, to remind myself not to screw around when I wanted to let off steam.

"Yeah, I get that, but what does that have to do with me and Poppy?"

Hearing him put their names together broke something inside me. "Because I was never an addict, you fucking tweaker."

"Outside," Max said, grabbing my arm and dragging me out the door just as my one o'clock arrived for his session. "He'll be right back," Max shouted over his shoulder.

"Thanks for the great first impression with a new client," I said once he released me.

He took a few steps back. That wasn't normal. Max leaned into conflict, at least with me. He recognized, early on, that sometimes all I needed was a hand on my shoulder to calm down. Either he wanted to beat the crap out of me, or he figured whatever he was about to say would set me off. He looked up at the gray sky and took a deep breath like he was trying to channel the Holy Spirit. "You need to man up," he said finally.

"What does that mean?"

"The way I see it, you've got two problems. Let's get the easy one out of the way. You're acting like a firstborn brat. Mia couldn't stand Charlotte when we brought her home from the hospital."

"Are you really comparing me to a three-year-old?"

"It fits," Max said. "Mia's anger was really fear. Fear that we didn't love her as much. Fear that she wasn't the center of our universe anymore."

"She wasn't," I said with a shrug. "I'm sure that hurt like hell."

"Spoken like an only child," Max said with a laugh. "My point is, eventually Mia realized Charlotte wasn't going anywhere. So, she adapted. She grew. Now she takes pride in being the best big sister she can. It brings tears to my eyes when I see her being so patient with Charlotte. And Charlotte tests that patience on the regular. Toddlers ain't for the weak, man. But Mia keeps growing, keeps treating her the way she wants to be treated."

"You want me to stop being a dick to Aries. Got it."

"No," he said. "I want you to recognize that Aries isn't a threat. He can't replace you. Not with me, not with anyone. And if you just took your head out of your ass, you'd realize you have something to give that kid."

"Then why are you standing ten feet away like I'm contagious or something?"

Max seemed to deflate right there on the sidewalk. His shoulders curled down, and he stared at the cement instead of me. "Because what you said to Aries felt personal. To me. I know that's not what you meant, but being an addict is something I'll carry for the rest of my life. You judged him. And it felt like you were judging me. My temper threatened to get the better of me."

"I wasn't," I said. "I—"

"Need to deal with your second problem," he said, straightening. "Man up and tell Poppy you're in love with her or step aside."

"It's not about manning up, Max. You know why I live the way I do."

Max nodded. "For the record, I've never agreed with it. But it's your life, your journey. I'd have let you stay in that dump upstairs another decade if Aries didn't need the place. Sure, I wanted you to live somewhere nicer, but more than that I wanted you to stop hating yourself enough to want it. A better place. A better life. But you're not just hurting yourself anymore, Theo. It stops being noble when your pain hurts someone else. It's plain wrong. You're better than that. So, drop the guilt and love that girl with everything you have or step aside so someone else can. Now get over here."

I erased the space between us and pulled him into a crushing hug. He pounded my back a few times, cleared his throat, and stepped back.

"I wasn't thinking about you when I said that to Aries," I said. "I'm sorry, and I know it was out of line. I'll apologize to him."

Max nodded. "And for future reference, Aries was a pill popper. I was the tweaker. We're both alcoholics though, so drunk jabs are a two-for-one." He smirked, and I knew he'd already started to forgive me. I, on the other hand, would feel like a piece of shit for a while.

Max wiped at his eyes. "Client's waiting. I'll get him settled. Say what you need to say to Aries first. Everything you need to say."

He walked inside without elaborating and ushered my client to the back. I shuffled over to the counter where Aries was laser-focused on neatening a stack of after-care sheets.

"I owe you an apology," I said.

He nodded, still not meeting my eyes.

"And an explanation."

That got his attention. He looked up and leaned against the counter, crossing his arms. "I'm listening."

"My feelings for Poppy aren't platonic."

Aries laughed, sharp and loud. "No shit," he said, once he'd gotten himself under control. "So, which was it? Were you two a thing and stayed friends after or did she friend zone you?"

"Neither," I said. "The truth is, I thought we should only be friends."

"You friend zoned her?" he said, raising his eyebrows. "Dude, she's got to be the hottest chick in this town."

I nod. "And one of the nicest," I said. "She's also talented and unique and bold."

"So your type is an ugly, basic bitch, extra heavy on the bitch?"

"I said I thought we should be friends. Not that I didn't want to be more."

Aries nodded. "I see how it is. You realized you wanted her after I made a move. Well, sorry, my man, but you snooze you lose."

No. I'd wanted her the moment I saw her. Her friendship was more than I deserved, and I'd treasured every moment of it. I could handle being in love with her without being with her, barely. But Max was right. If only being friends hurt her, I couldn't justify my place in her life.

I'd been lying to myself thinking we could go back to the way things were after we'd sampled what we could be together. We could only be more or nothing at all. The thought of losing her filled me with a pain so big, I couldn't imagine a way through it. And I didn't want to. "Shouldn't that be for Poppy to decide?"

Aries shrugged. "Honestly, I don't mind sharing. I'm just looking to have fun, if you know what I mean."

The mere suggestion of her being with someone like Aries filled me with an intense anger I'd never experienced before. I imagined how satisfying it would be to smash his face against the counter.

"Your client is ready," Max shouted from the back, startling us both. I unclenched my fists and took a deep breath. "Poppy is not someone you mess around with, Aries. If all you want is a good time, find someone else."

"Or what?" he said, stepping around the counter and into my space.

The guy had balls; I'd give him that. I was at least half a foot taller than him and had a good thirty more pounds of muscle. "Or I tell Max and ask him if he wants to beat your ass or if I can have the privilege."

Aries stepped back, but his face was still red with rage. "Like you said, it's not up to us. Let's see who Poppy wants. You stay out of my way, and I'll stay out of yours."

"Smartest thing you've said all day." I stormed to the back before I said or did something that would disappoint Max again.

Chapter Seventeen

Poppy

Despite being late, Wilson shuffled down the hall toward the classroom at a leisurely pace.

"Is your hip bothering you?" I asked. "We could have grabbed a walker at the pharmacy."

He stopped and leaned against the cinderblock wall. "I'm fine. I was just giving you more time to tell me what's bothering you."

"Oh," I said, looking down at my boots. "Is it that obvious?"

"It is to me," he said, kindly. He placed his weathered hand under my chin and tipped my face up, so we were eye to eye. "Now tell me what's wrong."

I fought the tears blurring my vision and sucked in a shaky breath. "I wish I knew. I've been going over and over it in my mind, but I don't understand why Theo doesn't want to be more than friends. Something's wrong with me, Wilson."

"Balderdash. Don't you think that for a minute, sweetie." He opened his arms, and I snuggled in for one of his bear hugs. He smelled like the pharmacy, a unique blend of peppermint, something antiseptic, and the man himself. I immediately felt better.

"What happened to bring all this on?" he asked, holding me at arm's length.

Instead of going into detail, I pulled the sketch from my bag.

He nodded. "Are you showing Theo that in class or after?"

"Never," I said, shoving the paper back in my bag.

Wilson shook his head. "I've never known you to be chickenshit."

"Wilson!" I said, smacking his chest. "What would the town council think if they heard that language? You'll never be citizen of the year again."

"I'd cuss enough to make the devil blush if it meant you'd show Theo that sketch."

I tugged his arm. "Come on, we're already late."

When Wilson and I opened the door, the rest of the class stared at us from their usual seats. Theo stood at the front of the room, watching us as well. I made a point to lock eyes with him and smirk. The creases on his forehead melted.

That smirk cost me every ounce of my limited social graces. Luckily, Wilson acted like a shield, nodding hello to everyone as I trailed him to the back table.

"All right, y'all," Theo said, clapping his hands. "Now that we're all here, let's start by showing the sketches you did for homework. Who wants to go first?"

Wilson elbowed me in the ribs. I elbowed him back hard enough to shift his body on the stool. He shook his head and centered himself.

Gladys scooted her walker toward Theo when no one else volunteered. She hacked some phlegm from her throat and pulled a sheet of paper from the little basket attached to her scoot 'n sit. She wiggled closer and held out her elbow for Theo to hold. "Get a good grip," she said, flashing him a worn smile. "I'm better on my back than my feet."

The other members of Theo's Fan Club snickered, and he blushed an adorable pink. Whenever young women flirted with him, which let's face it, happened all the time, he ignored them. But these old biddies made his cheeks burn every class. I sometimes wondered if he could make himself blush at will. A small gift for the women who looked forward to seeing him all week. It's exactly the kind of thing Theo would do. And one of the million reasons why I couldn't find it in me to stop wanting him.

"If you're not showing that sketch, what are you showing?" Wilson whispered as Gladys shared a rather phallic looking still life of a vegetable garden.

"One of Chris," I whispered back.

"Lovely. Can I see it?"

I pulled out the sketch I'd done of my brother and slid it to Wilson. He picked it up and ripped it in two. Gladys stopped mid-sentence and everyone but Esther turned in their seats to stare at us.

"Oops," Wilson said, and then proceeded to tear the two halves in half again.

"If you're done, Gladys," Esther shouted. "I'll go next."

Gladys wasn't, but she nodded and shuffled back to her chair as Esther groaned out of her seat with the grace of a front loader lifting a dumpster.

"Wilson," I whisper yelled once everyone had turned their attention back to the front. "I thought we were friends."

"We are," Wilson said, his eyes twinkling with mischief. "Sometimes we need our friends to nudge us in the right direction when we're scared."

"I'm not scared."

Wilson shrugged. "Hurt, then. Embarrassed. Whatever negative emotion you choose that's keeping you from showing that picture."

I glared at him, unwilling to admit it was all of the above, and turned my attention to Esther, who'd made a decent attempt at a self-portrait. When Esther finished, we all clapped and Wilson raised his hand.

"You're up, Mr. Wilson," Theo said with a smile.

"Oh no," Wilson said. "I forgot to do the assignment, but my friend Poppy here is ready to present hers."

Really, Wilson? He couldn't even let me sit in abject panic until everyone else had gone before I made a fool of myself. More likely he'd figured I'd realize I could make another sketch of Chris while everyone went before me.

"You're evil," I hissed before taking *the* sketch from my messenger bag. Wilson smiled like I'd given him the greatest compliment on Earth and made little shooing motions with his hands.

I pressed the sketch to my chest to hide it and purposefully stopped before I reached Theo. He'd have to walk past me to see it, but everyone else had an up-close view. I turned the sketch to face them, but didn't say anything.

Theo started to walk forward, but Mrs. Adams held out her hand to stop him. "If she wanted you to see it, she'd have walked closer."

"He should see it," Wilson shouted from the back.

Mr. Fitzwilliam and Twill nodded.

"She doesn't need any of you old farts telling her what to do," Millie hollered. "Or forcing her to do something she doesn't want to do." She aimed a death glare at Wilson, and he had the decency to look a little ashamed.

"Come on, Millie," Mr. Fitzwilliam said. "You've been trying to get them together for over a year now. Aren't you the one who brought Poppy to class?"

"That was me," Wilson said, raising his hand.

This time Gladys and Mrs. Adams glared at him, and he lowered his head like a puppy who'd just piddled on the living room rug.

"Well, Millie's the one who keeps drawing all the dirty pictures to get them in the mood for romance," Mr. Fitzwilliam said. "Heck, we all have. I haven't doodled this many peckers since high school."

Theo said my name and everyone hushed. He pointed to the paper in my hand. I stood as tall as I could and turned toward him. I watched him take in every detail: My hands reaching for his, my fingers grasping the air. His hands balled in a fighter's pose with the Xs facing out, creating a rigid end to the empty space between us. I'd drawn it from several angles, like a rendering of a sculpture, recreating his intricate tattoos with each. My hands aren't as distinctive, but anyone who knew me would see them and know.

Theo stared at the sketch for a good thirty seconds before he cleared his throat, the sound booming like a firework in the quiet room. "Excellent work, Poppy."

"For the love of Pete," Twill said, throwing his hands in the air. "What's the problem, Theo? I know we're not supposed to assume things, but I caught you with enough girls under the bleachers to figure you like women. And Poppy is perfect for you."

Theo took a deep breath. "Does anyone else want to share their work?"

Everyone glared at him.

"OK," he said, walking to the front. "Tonight, we're going to work on color mixing for shading."

"Red and yellow makes orange," Gladys shouted. "We got it. Now what do you have to say for yourself, Theo?"

"Enough," I said. "I've presented my sketch. Let's move on."

"Is that what you want, Theo," Wilson said from the back. "For Poppy to move on?"

Theo gripped the table in front of him so hard his fingers whitened.

"Of course, he doesn't," Esther shouted. "I can't hear half the time, but I've got the eyesight of an eagle. That boy is beyond smitten. We've all seen the way he looks at her."

"Then what's the problem?" Mr. Fitzwilliam asked.

"Right now, seven seniors who can't mind their damn business," I snapped, storming to the back of the room where I grabbed my bag, tossed the sketch at Wilson, and stomped out.

I ignored everyone I passed in the hallway and pushed through the glass front door. The frigid night air stole the breath from my lungs but did little to cool the full-body flush of embarrassment. I climbed into Tallulah, slammed the door closed, and threw my bag into the passenger seat. I banged my head on the steering wheel and took a few deep breaths to slow my heart rate before I drove.

A gentle tap on my window interrupted any hope I had of finding my Zen.

"What!" I yelled, looking up. Theo stood beside the hearse, my sketch in his hands. I lowered the window and waited.

"This is a plan for a sculpture," he said, surprising me.

"It is," I replied.

"It's brilliant," he said. "Evocative."

"Um, thanks."

"It's also wrong," he said, leaning into the window and handing me the sketch. "It looks like I'm fighting you."

"Aren't you?"

He shook his head. "Can I sit with you for a minute?"

I shrugged like my heart wasn't about to beat out of my chest and tossed my bag into the back.

Once he'd folded his tall frame into the passenger seat and closed the door, he gripped his knees and blew out a breath. "I don't want you to leave," he said to the windshield.

"For fuck's sake, Theo. I stormed off. I can't go back inside now. First rule of storming off is to stay gone until whoever you left has time to think about what they did."

"I don't want you to leave me," he said, finally turning to face me, his eyes soft. "Ever."

Oh.

He wrapped his long fingers around mine and gently pried them from the sketch so he could clasp my hand. I watched the paper flutter to my lap.

"I've been fighting myself," Theo said, and I lifted my eyes to his. "I thought I was doing the right thing, keeping us apart. I thought you'd be better off with someone else, anyone else. The truth is I've had feelings for you for a long time, and if you'd let me, I want us to be more. To be us. Just you and me and no more lines to cross."

I felt my head nodding, but I couldn't find the words I wanted to answer him. "OK, sure." OK sure? What the hell was wrong with me? After a year of waiting for this man to leave the friend zone, all I had was OK sure? "I mean, I'd like that too."

Theo's grip on my hand tightened, and his eyes filled with the heat I'd come to crave. Both of us started breathing like we'd just run for miles. "Will you go to my house?" he asked in a tight voice. "Aiden put a key under the garden gnome in the flowerbed. I need to smooth things over here, but I won't be long." He lifted his chin toward the classroom window where the entire class had their aged faces pressed to the rapidly fogging glass.

My stomach squeezed at the thought of being alone with Theo, knowing he would touch me in ways I'd never known, if I wanted. "OK sure." I guess I left half my brain in the community center. I glanced at the window again, like I'd find part of my IQ there and winced. "Good luck."

"They might let me leave faster if I kissed you. Otherwise, there's no telling what they'll do to me when I get inside."

I fought the smile tugging at my lips. Just like that, he'd made me feel completely at ease. "Theo Makis, are you afraid of a bunch of senior citizens?"

163

"Yes," he said, without hesitation. "I also can't wait another second to kiss you."

I grabbed the front of his shirt and pulled him close. We kissed to the sounds of muffled cheers and clapping, his hand cradling my face like something precious.

"See you soon," he said. The smile he gave me would have stolen my heart, if he didn't own it already.

CHAPTER EIGHTEEN

Theo

THE LIGHTS WERE ON inside when I arrived home. I grabbed the paper bag from the passenger seat and opened it. Condoms. Mr. Wilson had handed me a 12-count box of condoms in front of everyone. Apparently, he'd had them in his bookbag for months, waiting for me to break. No wonder there were so many smirks and raspy laughs when he handed me the bag at the community center. My first instinct was to laugh as well, but then I realized what they meant.

Since I hadn't bought condoms from the pharmacy in years, Mr. Wilson had made the correct assumption that the single rubber in my wallet was long expired. I opened the new box and shoved the ribbon of condoms in my pocket. It'd be a miracle if I lasted long enough to get inside Poppy tonight, assuming things went that far. At least I might have more than one chance to be a decent partner.

I walked inside, more nervous and excited than I'd been my first time. Poppy wasn't in the living room, but a bang from the studio led me to the back of the house.

She was so intent on organizing her tools, she didn't notice me in the doorway. Her salvaged supplies had sat untouched since she brought them over. I'd worried she'd never use them again, at least not here. She looked adorable, placing each chisel and wire brush on the worktable like a surgeon preparing for an operation. I leaned against the doorframe, admiring her graceful hands, the slight flush in the cheeks, until she saw me.

"How long have you been there?" she asked, the red in her face deepening.

"Not long," I said, pushing off the door frame and walking toward her. I stopped short when she crossed her arms over her stomach. Shit. Maybe she'd changed her mind. Maybe she liked Aries enough not to start something with me.

I reached out, not realizing I was recreating her sketch in reverse, until she did the same. I quickly stepped closer and laced her fingers in mine.

"Sorry," she said. "I don't know why I'm making this awkward."

"We both are," I said, dropping one of her hands to push her green strand of hair behind her ear, so I could see her eyes. "Want to go to the living room and talk?"

"Good idea," she said and took off so fast, she ended up yanking my arm with her. She dropped my hand completely when she settled on the far side of the couch, her tiny body pressed tight against the frayed armrest.

I'd cage her in if I sat right next to her, but sitting on the opposite side of the couch was something I'd have done before, when I needed to be as far from her as possible. I sat smack in the middle of the couch, far enough away she had room to breathe, but close enough she knew I wanted to be near her.

"I have a confession to make," I started.

Her gaze snapped to mine, and she seemed to melt further into the sofa. She nodded, the lovely pink draining from her face.

Great. Now I really was the one making this awkward as fuck. "I got into it with Aries today," I said quickly. "He told me about your plans for tomorrow, and I realized I might lose you. Which, now that I'm saying it out loud makes me a massive jerk. I wanted you long before he showed up, it's just that I—" Didn't think I deserved to be happy. Didn't want to saddle you with my truckload of issues. Because you're so young and vibrant and perfect that I didn't want to ruin you like I ruined my family, my friends.

"I understand," she said with a small smile. "I'll call him later and cancel."

My stomach churned. Was I really any better for her than Aries? They were closer in age. Doubt he'd ever had a panic attack that left him helpless on the floor. Of course, he'd be better for her, I heard my father's voice say.

"I—"

"You changed your mind," she said, her eyes filling with tears.

"Never," I said in a rush. "You're the first person I think of in the morning and the last when I fall asleep. It used to be Logan. But now, it's you, and part of me is relieved and part of me feels so guilty. Not just because I'm not thinking about Logan, but because I don't deserve you. I'm a fucking mess and always will be."

Poppy launched herself from the armrest and straddled me. She kissed me with so much hunger my dick tried to punch through my jeans to get to her. I wrapped my arms around her and pulled her close. She gasped when my hard length pressed against her. Fuck, she felt good.

"Are you sure?" I asked pulling away.

"Yes. Are you?"

When I nodded, she took my face in both hands. "Say it."

"I want you, Poppy."

The relief on her face made my stomach bottom out. I'd hurt her more than I'd realized. I needed to show her how much I'd wanted this, wanted her.

I grabbed the hem of her sweater dress and pulled it over her head, revealing the most delicate pale pink bra I'd ever seen. It was so unlike the harsh black clothing she wore every day and yet so perfectly Poppy. I lowered my mouth and sucked one of her tight nipples through the lace. She moaned and rocked against me.

I was going to lose it before we even got started if she kept moving like that. I stood and she wrapped her legs around me, peppering my neck with kisses that tightened my balls. I practically ran to the bedroom, but when I got there, I looked at the air mattress and frowned.

"What's wrong?" she asked, placing her hand on my cheek and forcing me to look her in the eyes.

"I just remembered I don't have a real bed."

She twisted in my arms and took in the air mattress sitting in the narrow beam of light from the hallway. "It'll do."

I laid her down gently and froze. This wasn't a dream. She was here, just as turned on as I was. Her chest moved in rapid bursts, her skin flushed in anticipation, lips swollen from my kiss, more beautiful than anything my subconscious concocted to tortured me.

"Theo?"

"You're exquisite."

She gave me a soft smile, and I couldn't wait a moment longer to feel every inch of her. When I reached for the waistband of her leggings, she lifted up to help me roll the black fabric from her shapely legs, leaving her in nothing but a pair of sexy lace shorts that matched her pink bra. I took a step back to admire her as best I could with only the light from the hallway, willing my body to cool long enough to sink inside her before I blew. I wanted to flip on the overhead light and study every curve, but then she'd be able to see all of me.

"Sorry, I'm not a thong girl," she said, biting her lip and looking vulnerable. "I know they're sexy but I can't walk around with a wedgie all day."

"You're perfect," I said and the little tension lines in her forehead disappeared.

"Pretty sure talking about wedgies right now makes me less than perfect."

I leaned down, so I could whisper in her ear. "I've never been this turned on."

A shiver ran through her body before she started fumbling with my shirt. I leaned back and pulled it over my head. Her eyes roamed the ink on my chest and arms before she rose on her knees and placed her hands on my heated skin.

"They're incredible," she said, tracing one of the larger tats on my shoulder. She took her time, letting her fingers roam over every design, gentle, almost reverent. My heartbeat slowed as I relaxed into her touch. Every inch of my torso was inked, except a small patch on my chest.

"You left the skin over your heart blank."

I nodded.

"Why?"

"I've thought about what to put there, but nothing seemed important enough." Instead, I'd left it, the blank skin like a note of silence in a song, the emptiness holding a weight of its own.

She rubbed her fingers across my unmarked skin before trailing them down my abs to my fly. A surged of panic rushed through me. I grabbed her wrist. She tensed, and I realized I was holding her too tight.

"It's been a while," I said, rubbing gentle circles on her wrist. And you can't see me. Not yet. Not without an explanation for the scars that would taint our first time together. "Probably better you don't touch me if you want me inside you."

She swallowed, hard, and nodded, her eyes fixed on the bulge in my jeans.

"Hey," I said, squeezing her hand. "You set the pace, Poppy. If you're not ready, we can slow down. We don't have to have sex tonight."

She cleared her throat. "Is that what you want?"

"I want whatever you're comfortable with."

"If we have sex," she said, finally looking up at me. "What does it mean?"

"What do you want it to mean?" I asked, suddenly worried I'd misread her sketch. Maybe she only wanted to be friends with benefits. Maybe she still wanted to have dinner with Aries, if not tomorrow, another time.

"Everything," she said softly.

"And you'd be mine?" I asked, my heart pounding in my chest at the thought of her being with anyone else. "I don't want to share you." Every bit of calm I'd felt before evaporated as a desperate need to take her filled me.

"I'm already yours," she said, wrapping her arms around my neck. I kissed her as I unclasped her bra with one flick. Then, I rolled us on our sides, so I could use both hands to explore every inch of her beautiful skin without crushing her. She seemed to understand that I'd detonate with one touch and kept her fingers gripped in my hair, her breath becoming more erratic as my fingers roamed everywhere except the juncture of her thighs.

"Theo, please," she panted. "I need you."

I ran my hand down her stomach and lower, feeling the drenched fabric that separated her most intimate parts from me. My balls were already so tight they ached. "I'm going to make you come first," I said, working my way to the edge of the bed and tugging the delicate lace down her legs. I wanted this to be good for her even if I couldn't last, but I almost came when I finally tasted her and she moaned my name. I took my time, slowly circling her clit with my tongue before I plunged a finger into her tight heat and rubbed her front wall. I pressed my other hand on the soft stretch of skin beneath her bellybutton and mimicked the increasing rhythm of my tongue against her salty sweetness. I kept the speed of my finger constant and considered adding another when she arched closer.

"Oh. Wow, that's—"

Her legs started to shake on either side of my head. I slid a second finger inside her, matching the quick rhythm of my hands, and she fell apart with a scream that echoed off the walls of the near-empty room.

I grabbed the ribbon of condoms and unzipped enough to free my aching cock. She bit her bottom lip and watched me sheaf myself. I leaned forward, my tip brushing against her soft skin. She nodded and I sank into her in one thrust. She was so wet, so tight, I squeezed my eyes shut and took a deep breath.

"Fuck," I hissed, looking down at her.

Poppy stared back at me with startled eyes.

"You OK?" I asked. "Did I hurt you?"

"I'm good," she said, but her voice sounded tight.

I pulled out an inch and her face twisted in pain. I knew better. I was bigger than average and usually took my time when I was with someone new, especially a woman as small as Poppy. "*Kardoula mou*," I said, but she wrapped her legs around me and pulled me closer until I bottomed out again.

"Move, Theo," she said, running her nails down my back.

I pumped in and out as slowly as possible until I was certain her gasps were from pleasure, not pain.

"I'm not going to last," I said, gritting my teeth. I propped myself up with one arm and lowered my other hand to her clit, rubbing it in time with my thrusts. She bounced back into me on the over-inflated mattress, tightening more each time. Within moments, we came together, the release unlike anything I'd ever felt.

I pulled out and rolled off her but drew her close while my breathing slowed. "That was incredible," I said.

"Is it always like that?" she asked breathlessly.

Something in the way she said it made my heart stop. "With me or with anyone?" I asked carefully.

"Um, with you, of course," she said, the beautiful glow in her cheeks deepening to scarlet.

"Poppy," I said, taking her face in my hands. "Be honest with me. Was this your first time?"

She nodded and all the blood in my head drained to my stomach like a pile of bricks. "You let me take your virginity on an air mattress? Without telling me?"

Her eyes filled with tears.

"Don't cry," I said, pulling her tight. She pressed her face to my chest, her tears leaving a trail of searing guilt down my skin. "Please don't cry. I'm just worried I hurt you. If I'd known, I would have been gentler, especially at the beginning. Why didn't you tell me?"

She laughed and then hiccupped, the sound wet and pained. "If I told you, you wouldn't have touched me."

"That's not—"

"That's exactly what would have happened," she said, looking up at me. "You're regretting it now. Aren't you?"

"Being with you, no. Hurting you, absolutely."

"I'm fine. I promise. Are you mad at me?" The tears made her eyes impossibly greener. They were so beautiful and utterly focused on me. A feeling I've never experienced filled my chest, warm and painful. I was so in love with this woman it hurt.

"Myself," I said, brushing away her tears with my thumbs. "I'm only angry at myself."

"Well, stop then," she said, smacking my chest. "That was fucking amazing. In case you missed it, I came twice. Pretty sure most women can't say the same for their first time."

"You did, didn't you?" I said, smiling.

"So, what happens now?" she asked.

"I take you home," I said and kissed her wrist, where her pulse fluttered in rapid beats. "You're not spending the night on this crappy mattress."

"I don't mind, as long as I'm with you."

I shook my head. "I'll walk you home." I pulled off the condom, knotted it, and shoved it in my pocket before tucking myself back in my jeans. I wanted her to stay, probably needed her to stay, but the pressure was building. There was only one way to let it out, and I couldn't do it with her here.

"Fine," she huffed. "But you need to buy a real mattress ASAP."

"Anything for you," I said, kissing her hand.

Her eyes were sad as she stroked my face, and I worried I'd hurt her more than she let on.

"You sure you're all right?" I asked, my chest tightening.

She nodded. "One of these days," she said, caressing me with a tenderness that stole my breath, "you're going to realize your worth."

I closed my eyes, enjoying her touch as long as I could before the guilt forced me to my feet and away from her. When I returned after walking her home, I went straight to the bathroom closet and grabbed the first aid kit with the razor blade hidden inside.

Chapter Nineteen

Poppy

CAMMIE ABANDONED HER CUSTOMER mid-order when I walked into Karma. "Wyatt, can you take over?" she shouted, weaving through the crowded café before the guy had a chance to reply. She grabbed my arm and tugged me to the leather sofa in the bookstore portion of Karma and shoved me down.

"I need details," she said in a voice two octaves higher than her usual squeal as she sat entirely too close to me.

"You need to relax," I said, taking off my oversized bag, which contained all of Rowan's notes for this bridal meeting from hell. I loved my sister, but I'd rather resurrect my career as a barista than discuss dress colors and shoe options one more time.

"Fine," Cammie said, flicking her long blonde hair over her shoulder. "I'll just wait until Rowan gets here to ask if Theo's a good kisser."

Lauren sank into one of the club chairs flanking the sofa with a steaming mug of coffee. The woman must run on good vibes and caffeine since she usually slept four hours a night and still looked perky. "I heard he's phenomenal in bed."

"You heard or you know?" I asked, my stomach twisting. Theo went to high school with Lauren, who for all her wonderful qualities, was the female equivalent of a fuckboy. No judgment. But the likelihood of her crossing genitals with Theo was higher than I'd like.

Lauren's lips curled up in a mischievous smile. "Someone looks jealous."

"You slept with Theo," Cammie said, glaring at Lauren, which reminded me why I was starting to think of her as a friend and not just some chick Rowan and Lauren dragged into my life. "I know Peace Falls is small but come on. Even a one-and-doner like yourself has options. He's one of Aiden's best friends."

That caught my attention. "Wait. You and Aiden?"

"There is no me and Aiden," Lauren said, straightening in her seat. "I *heard* Theo is phenomenal in bed from multiple sources. I don't have first-hand information. Do you, Poppy?"

My face burned despite my best effort to maintain my resting bitch face.

"Well butter my butt and call me a biscuit," Cammie said.

Lauren laughed so hard she snorted.

"Can we go back to Lauren and Aiden?" I asked.

That stopped Lauren's cackling, but Cammie wouldn't take the bait. "All I heard about was a kiss in front of the community center. And you and I both know Mr. Fitzwilliam can't see worth a damn. Come on, Poppy. Details."

"Well," I said, picking at one of the artfully placed holes in my jeans. "I have nothing to compare the bed stuff with, but it seemed pretty phenomenal to me. He's definitely the best kisser, hands down."

"He's hung, isn't he?" Lauren asked.

"How would she know?" Cammie snapped. "Plus, that's not exactly a good thing your first time. On a scale of one to ten, how sore are you today?"

"Eight," I answered honestly. "But it's not a bad sore, if that makes sense. He didn't know it was my first time until after, and then he was really upset that he might have hurt me."

Lauren fanned her face. "Packing and sensitive. No wonder all those women complained when he locked his dick down a few years back."

"Yeah, why is that?" Cammie asked me.

I shrugged. "Why did you lock your vag down?"

Cammie nodded. "He's even more messed up than Cal was before Rowan. You know what this means, right?" she said smiling.

"What?" Lauren and I asked together.

"He has real feelings for you."

My face warmed again. "Yeah. I guess so."

Lauren shook her head. "You guess so. That man has been head over heels in love with you since he met you."

If that's true, why did it take Aries showing interest for Theo to finally act? Lauren must have sensed how uncomfortable the conversation made me because she slammed her coffee mug on the table and said, "Yes, I slept with Aiden once. A long time ago."

"I knew it," Rowan squealed, coming around the corner of a tall bookcase.

"Who cares what happened years ago," Cammie said. "I'd rather hear about Theo and Poppy."

"Me too," Rowan said, sinking into the empty club chair closest to me while I kicked Cammie's shin.

"Got it," she said, rubbing her leg. "Don't do that again. Those boots could break something."

"Mrs. Adams told me that you and Theo kissed," Rowan said.

"For fudge sake. Does everyone in town know?" I yelled.

"Probably," Rowan answered with a shrug. "So, what does this mean? Are you two together finally?"

I nodded.

Rowan squealed and leaped out of her chair, tackling me in a hug. She pulled back and looked at me. "You slept with him, didn't you?"

"How would you know that?"

Rowan shrugged. "Sisterly intuition."

"Bullshit."

"Fine, I was listening in the stacks. I can't believe you were still a virgin. How was it?"

"Kind of weird but wonderful."

"Ok, it was with Theo, so I get the wonderful part," Rowan said, squeezing onto the sofa beside me. I felt like thin-sliced bologna sandwiched between two slices of bread with boundary issues. "What made it weird?"

"He's pierced, isn't he?" Lauren asked. "Does he have one or a whole Jacob's ladder going on? Or was it just because it was your first time?"

There was no way I was getting out of this conversation. Plus, part of me kind of wanted to know if I was being too sensitive, if it was normal for people in a relationship to do the deed and then chuck the other person out of their space. "Well, for starters, it was on an air mattress. I worried we might bounce off a couple times, and he was already close to impaling my stomach."

All three of those bitches burst out laughing.

"I'm sorry," Cammie said, wiping a tear from her eye. "So, you were fibbing about the good sore part."

"A little. And before you ask again, Lauren, I have no idea if his dick's pierced or not. I didn't spend a lot of time staring at it and have nothing to compare the feeling of it too. So even if it was, that's not what made it weird."

All three of them became solemn and Rowan grabbed my hand. "Go on," she said.

"Well," I said, taking a deep breath. "It happened so fast. He barely got undressed and then he walked me home right after. He said he didn't want me to sleep on an air mattress, but it felt odd to leave so soon. Does that make me sound clingy?"

"Definitely not," Lauren said. "That sounds pretty dickish to me. I should spit in his espresso next time he comes in."

"No," Cammie, Rowan, and I said together.

"I don't think it had anything to do with me," I said.

"I agree," Cammie said. "Maybe he felt a panic attack coming and didn't want you to see it."

"Can you feel a panic attack coming?" Lauren asked, whipping out her phone.

"Wait? Have you seen him have one?" I asked Cammie.

She nodded. "Normally, I wouldn't tell you this, because it's not my story to tell, but a few months ago something triggered him when he came to the office to meet Cal. I'd never seen anything like it. It brought Theo to his knees. I was afraid he'd pass out he was breathing so hard. Cal handled it like a champ, but even he looked worried. It broke my heart, to be honest."

"Yeah," I said. "They're pretty scary."

"It fits," Lauren said, nodding at her phone. "He probably thought he was at risk of having one once the orgasm endorphins wore off and the reality of what happened set in. He didn't want you to think less of him."

"Why would suffering a panic attack make me think less of him?" I snapped. "It's not like I haven't seen it before."

"You'd just slept together," Rowan said, placing a gentle hand on my arm. "Theo might have worried you'd take it personally."

I crossed my arms over my chest. "Well, that's just insulting."

"I saw his panic attack months ago, and he still seems embarrassed every time I see him," Cammie said. "It's kind of endearing, actually, which is why I stopped being nervous around him, despite how big he is."

"Yeah, how big is he?" Lauren said, leaning forward. "Your penile experience may be limited, but you're an artist. I'm sure you can eye up a measurement just fine."

"Can we talk about the d—urn dresses now?" I asked, throwing my hands in the air. "Rowan, I promise to wear whatever color you want and heels to match if you end this conversation."

Rowan smiled and clapped her hands together. "So, I'm thinking pink for the dresses. A subtle shade, like rose petal or blush. With nude or rose gold sparkling heels."

"That would look so good with your natural hair color, Poppy," Lauren said.

"Absolutely not," I said. "The only redhead at the alter will be Rowan. I'll find a color that goes with whatever you choose, sis."

"I saved a few dresses on Pinterest." Rowan pulled out her phone, and we all huddled around the small screen. "Which do you like, Maid of Honor?" she asked me.

I shrugged. "I told you. I'd wear a garbage bag if that's what you wanted, but I like the dusty rose Pnina Tornai with the long lace sleeves. It's going to be freezing on top of that mountain in early April. You could swap the satin bow for a beaded rose gold belt and then wear nude heels, since those will be easier for Lauren to find with her huge feet."

"She's not wrong," Lauren said, glancing down at her canoe-like appendages.

"The dress would complement yours, Rowan," Cammie said.

"I love it," Rowan said. "Let's figure out sizing, and I'll place the order. Mom insisted on paying for all the bridesmaid outfits, and this one is reasonable."

"She doesn't have to do that," Cammie said, shifting in her seat.

"Don't even try to argue with that woman," I said. "She's paying off mom guilt from the years Rowan had to be Mom 2.0 for me and Chris after our dad died. Just say thank you."

"Plus, I'm her favorite," Rowan said, winking at me.

She thought she was joking, but Chris and I both knew Mom had a special place in her heart for Rowan. Luckily, Rowan was too perfect a sister for us to feel bad about it.

"What are the groomsmen wearing?" Cammie asked.

"Gray suits," Rowan said. "Speaking of the groomsmen," she said looking at me. "Did you know Cal asked Theo to be his best man, and he refused."

"He did?" That was even weirder than Theo kicking me out right after we bounced on his air mattress. Cal and Theo were just as close as Rowan and me, more brothers than friends.

Rowan nodded. "He said to ask Chris, but we both know that was a hard pass. So, I guess it's Aiden."

"Poor Aiden," I said.

"You mean poor Cal," Lauren said with a huff.

"No," I said, with an edge to my voice. "Poor Aiden. I never realized until now that he's kind of the odd man out."

"The bromance between Cal and Theo is pretty strong," Rowan said.

Lauren frowned. "Yeah, I guess Aiden was closer to Logan."

"He's the one who died in the crash?" Cammie asked gently.

Rowan, Lauren, and I nodded.

"Poor Aiden," Cammie said. "Now I feel bad for running away from him every time he says hello."

"No, that's still a good idea," Lauren said. "He's an asshole."

"New plan," I said, clapping my hands together. "Let's get Lauren so shitfaced at the bachelorette party she answers all our questions about her Aiden fling. All in favor?"

Cammie and Rowan raised their hands.

"We've left Wyatt alone in the front too long," Lauren said standing. "I'll start looking for nude heels."

"That reminds me," Rowan said, digging into her small purse. We'd finally convinced her to stop lugging around a bag big enough to carry a small child to spare her back, but she still packed her purse as tight as possible. "Here," she said, handing Lauren and Cammie Visa gift cards. "Mom wouldn't tell me what she put on them, but it's probably more than enough for shoes."

"Where's mine?" I asked like a spoiled brat.

"Mom said the two of you could go shoe shopping together since, and I quote, 'She never spends enough time with Poppy.'"

"Wow, you weren't kidding about the mom guilt," Cammie said looking at her card.

"Nope," Rowan and I said together.

"Guilt is a powerful thing," Lauren said.

I immediately thought of Theo and wondered whether he'd ever be able to let his go or let me in enough to share the weight.

Chapter Twenty

Theo

I ARRIVED AT THE barn before Aiden or Cal. Usually, I'd have picked up Cal on the way, but he was out buying the supplies he needed to make Rowan's gift this afternoon. It gave me time alone to walk around the place where Logan spent his last hours. The barn always pulled my guilt and grief to the surface. It never left me, but usually I had it under control enough to fucking breathe. As I stomped through the dead grass, my jeans rubbed against the tender wound on my inner thigh, the sharp pain fighting for attention against all the feelings that threatened to consume me. I relaxed into the ache.

If I had a therapist, they'd probably tell me I was making progress. I'd spent over ten minutes beside the dilapidated barn without hyperventilating. No doubt, they wouldn't approve of my coping mechanism, but at least I was still on my feet when Cal and Aiden arrived.

"Explain to me again why we have to do this now?" I asked, blowing on my hands. I should have worn gloves. My fingers were red and painful by the time they showed up.

"Because now is when I have time for projects like this," Aiden said. "Plus, we'll all be busy with Cal's wedding soon. Speaking of which, what are the plans for the bachelor party, Theo?"

I glanced at Cal, but he just stared at the frozen ground.

"We can have that conversation later when we're not freezing our nuts off," Cal said to his shoes.

"Might as well have it now. We're still waiting for someone," Aiden said, looking across the field toward the road.

"Is someone from your crew helping out?" I asked.

"My whole crew volunteered to help," Aiden said, a rare look of embarrassment on his face.

"Wow, that's incredible," Cal said. "Most of them didn't even know Logan."

He might be my best friend/brother, but Cal had the emotional IQ of a slug sometimes. "But they all know Aiden," I said. "You must be one hell of a boss."

Aiden shrugged. "I overpay them. So, bachelor party. Is Rowan down for you going to a strip club or are you thinking more along the lines of paint ball and beer?"

"No strip club," Cal said. "If we go to one, the girls will too."

All three of us shuddered.

"Rowan and I were talking about doing a combo bachelor-bachelorette camping trip," Cal said.

"You're crazy," Aiden said shaking his head. "You think this is cold, try camping out in March. But a combo trip somewhere warm sounds great. What do you think, Theo?"

I looked at Cal long enough for Aiden to narrow his eyes. "What am I missing?" he asked.

"I'm not the best man," I said finally.

Aiden's mouth dropped open. "What?"

"He said no," Cal said.

"It should be Chris," I said, shrugging my shoulders. "He's Rowan's brother."

"Bullshit," Aiden said. "Of course, it should be you. You're the one Cal calls brother."

"Chris is nervous enough," Cal said. "I was hoping you'd be my best man, Aiden."

"Hell no," Aiden said. "Chris and I would only be fill-ins. It has to be you, Theo."

I shook my head.

"I'm just going to put all your names in a hat and pull one out," Cal said.

Aiden rubbed his forehead. "I'll plan the bachelor/bachelorette party because Chris is underage, and Theo hasn't known a good time in years, but I refuse to be the best man."

"Y'all really know how to make a guy feel loved," Cal said, looking genuinely hurt.

Aiden glared at me. "Whatever bullshit reason you had for saying no, forget it, Theo."

"It wasn't bullshit," I mumbled.

"Of course, it was," Aiden said throwing his arms in the air. "Either you're worried about having a panic attack at the altar, which could still happen if you're just a groomsman, or you think you don't deserve the title. Both are bullshit reasons."

Of all the places to have this conversation, the site of Logan's future memorial was the last I'd have chosen.

"Did he tell you why?" Aiden asked Cal.

"He said you should be my best man because you'd never be Logan's," Cal said quietly.

Aiden sucked in a breath and released it slowly. "Fine, let's make a deal. Theo, you're Cal's best man. I'll be Theo's, and Cal can be Chris's."

"Chris isn't even here, and he's still in high school," I said.

Aiden pulled his phone from his pocket and made a call. "Hey kid," he said. "You cool with asking Cal to be your best man when and if you ever get married, so Theo will stop making excuses and be Cal's?" He listened and said, "Thanks. Go back to sleep."

"You're assuming I'm getting married someday," I said.

"Well, maybe not in the traditional sense," Aiden said, rubbing his scruff. "But I'll stand up for you in whatever goth ceremony you and Hell Cat figure out. I heard you finally kissed her Thursday night."

"He did?" Cal said, staring at me in pretend shock. Aiden smirked.

"Cut the shit," I said, shoving Cal's shoulder. I wasn't surprised one or both of them had heard about that kiss at the community center. Peace Falls was small, and everyone knew how long Poppy and I had been circling each other.

Cal grinned at me. "I might have heard about it from one of my patients yesterday."

Which meant he hadn't heard it from Rowan, who likely knew what happened after.

"What's that look for?" Aiden asked, glaring at me again. "There's no reason to look so guilty for kissing a woman you like who likes you back."

I shoved my hands in my pockets.

"What did you do?" Cal asked, sounding exasperated.

Aiden studied me a moment and burst out laughing. "Her. He did her and now he feels guilty for breaking his monkhood."

"Did you?" Cal asked. He looked surprised and oddly proud.

"Do you really want to have this conversation about your sister-in-law?" I asked. "Here?"

"She's not his sister yet," Aiden said. "Besides, we don't want the details. Just tell us if you're finally with her or not."

"Yeah, that's all I want to know," Cal added.

"We're together," I said.

"I'm happy for you man," Aiden said, slapping my back. "Even if I owe Lauren a Benjamin. I figured it would take you until after the wedding to grow a pair."

"Didn't know you were on betting terms with Lauren," I said.

Aiden shrugged. "She hates to lose, and anything I can do to piss her off is fun for me. This bet had 50/50 odds of going my way, and 100% odds of making me happy."

Aiden did look genuinely thrilled. Cal did not, which meant he probably suspected what I'd done after taking Poppy home. For as out of tune as he could be with everyone else, he was hyper-aware of me. Most of that laser focus had shifted to Rowan, but he knew me well enough to know when I was at risk of doing something he'd never understand.

"Walk," Cal said, an edge to his voice that ripped the smile from Aiden's face.

"Leave it, brother," I said. "I'm fine, and I'd be honored to be your best man." It still felt wrong, but accepting the title would hopefully be enough to get him off my case, for now.

Cal nodded, but I knew it wouldn't be the end of it. As a PT, Cal studied people's gaits to understand their injuries. The only cuts he'd ever failed to notice were ones on my torso, which I didn't like to make because they damaged my ink, or my arms, which were too visible. My refusal to walk was enough confirmation for him. I wasn't looking forward to the conversation we'd be having this afternoon.

"So," I said, "if we're not meeting one of your guys, who are we meeting, Aiden?"

"Does Poppy know about the cutting?" Aiden asked. He never called her by her actual name, and the seriousness of his tone meant he wouldn't stop until I answered him or left.

"Not yet," I said.

"How is that possible? Were the lights off?" Cal asked.

"Dude," Aiden said. "No details, remember. Hell Cat feels like a sister to me already, and I don't need that mental image."

"I kept my legs covered," I said.

"Again," Aiden said, "I don't want that picture in my head. But that's weird as shit, Theo."

"Weird is explaining all those scars to the first woman he's slept with in years," Cal said.

"She wasn't some chick from Church," Aiden said. "She deserved that conversation before they fucked. Forget that, she deserved it months ago before she got her feelings all twisted in him."

"Wow," I said. "You really have gone full brother mode with her."

"Damn right," Aiden said. "And based on your not-so-subtle conversation with Cal, I'm guessing you're cutting again? You promised us you'd stop. Remember?"

Of course, I remembered. It was just after the tenth anniversary of the accident. We'd all talked about what we thought we needed to move past it. Me: Nothing. I'd carry the guilt the rest of my life. But Aiden and Cal had surprised me when they said they needed me to stop cutting myself. It scared them. Clearly, it still did.

"For what it's worth, Thursday was the first time I'd done it since I made that promise."

"Which is all the more messed up," Cal said. "It should have been one of the best nights of your life."

"It was," I said around the lump in my throat.

I hadn't seen Poppy since Thursday night because first I was working and then she had a rush custom order. At least, I hoped she did and wasn't avoiding me. We'd texted back and forth but neither of us mentioned what had happened between us.

"I'm so confused," Aiden said, shaking his head. "Maybe I really am as dumb as everyone thinks."

"No one thinks you're dumb," Cal said. "And I doubt anyone but Theo understands why he does what he does. It certainly doesn't make sense to me."

"It was just—a lot," I said. "You know I love her."

"Yes," they both said.

"Who do you love?" asked a soft voice. I turned and watched Everly Hendricks cross the final feet of frozen ground to where we stood beside the barn.

"Hey there, Ev," Aiden said, pulling her into a tight hug. "He has it bad for Poppy Stevens."

"I met her at Karma when she worked there," Everly said with a bright smile. "She's beautiful, Theo."

I cleared my throat. "She is."

Shit. Everly Hendricks was here. In the field where we all partied before my buzzed ass got behind the wheel and drove. The last patch of earth where Logan danced and laughed like he had decades left to live, because he should have, would have, if not for me.

"Good to see you, Everly," Cal said, pulling her into a hug.

No way in hell could I hug Logan's sister. I'd rather cut off my arms. I waved at her and shoved my hands in my pockets.

"Theo has a cold," Aiden lied. "He's not being a dick on purpose."

"Oh, I'm sorry," Everly said. "I had a terrible one a couple weeks back. They're never fun. So," she said, clapping her gloved hands together, "you want to build a memorial for Logan?"

"Well, Aiden is technically building it," Cal said. "We're hoping Theo might paint a mural or something. I'm just here for moral support."

"I'm not sure the barn could handle another coat of paint," I said. "It looks ready to fall in at any moment."

"Agreed," Aiden said. "Which is why I think you should make a sculpture."

"What makes you think I can do that?" I asked.

"Fine, work with Hell Cat and make a sculpture," he amended.

Cal turned to Everly. "That's what he calls Poppy."

"It doesn't have to be massive," Aiden said. "Then I wanted to build something in honor of Logan. There's the usual bench or gazebo, but that feels kind of boring, which is why you're here, Ev."

"A tree house," she blurted out, pointing to the large oak beside the barn. "Something big enough you could sleep in."

The muscles in Aiden's jaw clenched. Without a word, he started toward his house, which sat directly next door. Cal looked as confused as I felt, but Everly wiped a tear from her cheek.

"When we were little," she said, "Logan and Aiden built this amazing tree house. It was supposed to be a place where they could go to get away from us girls, but every time Aiden slept over, we'd all end up crammed inside. Some of the best memories I have of my brother were made in that tree house. We told ghost stories and sang stupid songs off-key and talked for hours."

"I remember it now," Cal said. "I don't remember sleeping in it though."

"You didn't. Aiden was the only one of Logan's friends Mom allowed to sleep over because they'd been hopping back and forth from our house to his since they were three. Logan always said he was going to live in a full-sized tree house when he grew up. Should we go after Aiden or give him space?"

Cal and I both shook our heads.

"A tree house is a great idea, Everly," Cal said. "Theo, you could paint a mural inside or work with Poppy on a sculpture or both."

"Yeah," I said, kicking at the hard earth with the toe of my combat boot. "It's perfect."

"You sure?" Everly asked. "I mean Aiden didn't say anything. That's not like him."

"He didn't want to lose it in front of us," I said. "The only time I've seen him cry was at Logan's funeral."

"Same," Everly said. We stood in silence until off in the distance Aiden opened his front door and disappeared inside. "So, Theo," she said, turning to me. "I've been looking into the expungement laws. Our first step would be to petition to have your conviction reduced since you can't expunge vehicular manslaughter. After that—"

I shook my head. "I appreciate the offer, Everly, but I deserved that conviction and every day of my sentence."

"The fact you think that makes you an excellent candidate for expungement. You're a good person, Theo. There's no reason you should still have restrictions on your life, but as long as you're a felon, you always will."

"Because of me, Logan is dead," I said, placing my hand gently on her shoulder. "I am a felon. Even if you're successful, nothing will ever change that for me."

"Just think about it, OK," she said. She looked so much like Logan. The same warm brown eyes. The same easy smile. She was tall like him as well, strong. Seeing her made me miss her brother, which sometimes got lost in all the guilt. "My parents and my sister want this too. If not for yourself, consider doing it for us. Mom got thrown out of the grocery store once because she overheard someone calling you a criminal and lost it on them. As her attorney, I cannot comment on the details, but let's just say the bakery department suffered casualties. Rolls everywhere."

Cal threw his head back and laughed. "Do you remember that time my dad told a prospective client to kiss his ass when he called you something?"

"Degenerate," I said, fighting the urge to laugh. "He called me a hopeless degenerate."

"Yeah, well, he got half of it right," Cal said, rubbing his forehead.

"Please, Theo," Everly said, clutching her gloved hands together. "Promise me you'll think about it."

Cal stared at me until I nodded. I'd think about it for however long it took Everly to walk back to her car and drive off, then I'd text her to tell her no.

"It was great seeing y'all," she said, pulling Cal into another hug. She waved at me and started back for her car.

"She reminds me of Logan," Cal said once Everly was far enough away not to hear.

"Yeah," I said, shoving my hands back in my pockets. They'd gone completely numb. "We should get going before my fingers freeze off, and I can't help you."

"He would have hated it," Cal said, his eyes going glassy.

"The tree house idea?" I asked. The cold wind whistled through the bare branches of the large oak. I could see it. An elevated house with real windows to keep the chill out in winter and screens to block the bugs in summer. Maybe a narrow porch all around to enjoy the view of the mountains and the rolling farmland. Chairs with a fire pit below for roasting marshmallows. Logan would have loved it.

"No, that's perfect," Cal said, staring off at the tree. "He'd hate how you keep punishing yourself. He also wouldn't want you to live the rest of your life as a felon if you could help it. It's bad enough you did time and lost your parents. Logan would have hated that too. But the self-harm," he said, turning to face me. "That would have pissed him the fuck off. You know that, right?"

"Logan is dead. We'll never know what he would have thought or not thought. And that's because of me."

"Fine," Cal snapped. "I hate it. Aiden hates it. And when you finally man up and tell Poppy, she'll hate it. I promise you that. You know you have to tell her. She'll see the scars eventually, and Aiden's right. She deserves to know."

I pulled him close in a tight hug. "I'll tell her tonight, brother," I said.

"Good," he said, pounding my back. He stepped away and wiped at his eyes. "I'm starting to think she's the only one with a fighting chance of saving you from yourself."

CHAPTER TWENTY-ONE

Poppy

I SHOOK THE CRAMP from my hand and picked up the piping bag again. Valentine's Day couldn't get here fast enough. The local paper had included Red Blossoms Bakery's cookie bouquet in an article titled "Skip the Overpriced Roses for Your Sweetheart with These Fresh Gifts." Not the best story for Mom's flower shop, but a huge win for us. Though based on how frazzled she looked, Mom was doing fine.

As excited as I was to grow the bakery, I worried we wouldn't be able to fill all the orders. The cookies had a decent shelf life, but we could only make them so far in advance. The free advertising had also brought in some non-Valentine's business, like the massive cookie centerpiece I'd been working on all afternoon for a baby shower.

Too bad it wasn't the type of work that erased every other thought in my head. Ice a cookie. Think of all the reasons Theo wouldn't want me to sleep over. Refill the piping bag. Think of all the reasons I wouldn't want to date me. Drop a cookie on the floor. Curse, then think of all the prettier women in Peace Falls with charming dispositions who Theo could choose instead of me.

We'd texted on and off since Thursday night, but anyone scrolling through our messages wouldn't think anything had happened. It's not like I was expecting late night sexting or booty calls, but a small acknowledgement of our transition from friends to more would have made me feel a lot better.

"Oh, my word," Rowan squealed behind me. "Those stork cookies are adorable."

"They start to lose their appeal after twenty," I said, shoving the last cookie in the florist foam and standing back to admire my work. I pulled out my phone and snapped a picture to post on our socials later, much later, like February 15th later. We were about to be a hearts-and-flowers-only operation.

The doorbell rang. "I'll get it," I said, desperate to escape the kitchen I hadn't left all afternoon. I ran to the front door and opened it without looking.

"Hey," Theo said, giving me one of those rare smiles that made me want to melt into a puddle at his feet.

"Hi."

Of course, I was a hot mess the first time he saw me after we had sex. He looked sexy as hell in a pair of gray slacks and a black button-down shirt with the sleeves rolled to show his inked forearms. I'd never seen him in anything so fancy. We stared at each other a beat. Should I hug him? Jump on him and wrap my legs around him koala style? He reached out and placed his hands on my face before bending to kiss me. Koala style sounded pretty good right now, but just as I relaxed into the kiss, he pulled away.

"Do you have a minute?" he asked. "I probably should have texted before coming over."

"Please," I said, opening the door wider. "You're saving me from clean-up duty. Rowan can't stand a dirty kitchen. She won't wait for me to washup."

"You sure?" he asked, wiping his boots on the welcome mat.

Something clanged in the kitchen. "Oh, I'm sure. Don't worry," I said, flopping onto the couch. "I've already worked a couple hours more than her today."

He sat right beside me, our thighs brushing. My core clenched like he'd touched something far more sensitive than my jean-clad leg. I blamed his cologne or body wash or whatever it was that smelled like a forest after a rainstorm. The fresh scent had tortured me for a year.

"So, does that mean you're finished for the day?" he asked.

Not really. There was always something I could do. Instead, I said, "I am."

"Great. Would you like to go to dinner with me?"

I looked down at my icing-covered shirt. "Right now?"

"Whenever you're ready. If we can't get into Antonia's, we can just grab a bite at Church."

"You want to take me to Antonia's?"

"You don't like their food?"

"I do, but it's really nice. We could just get take out and head back to your place. I'd kind of like to talk about the other night."

He started bouncing his knee. "We should talk now and then go to Antonia's. It's where I've always imagined taking you on our first date. We skipped ahead a few steps, but technically we haven't had our first date."

I wondered how long he'd been imagining our first date and why the thought of going on it made him so nervous. Maybe he wanted to pull back again now that we'd released all that pent-up sexual energy?

Fuck that.

"As long as I don't have to wait two dates more to get a return invite to your air mattress."

His knee bounced harder. Shit. That wasn't a good sign.

"Theo," I said, placing my hand on his knee. "Is everything all right?"

He didn't say anything and my heart sank. Something was definitely wrong. Maybe he had second thoughts about us, and the date was his way of feeling out if he wanted to be with me. Those old geezers did put a lot of pressure on him. My sketch wasn't exactly subtle either. A slight tremor started in my fingers. Theo noticed and grabbed my hand.

"Just say it," I said, pushing out the words like they were made of needles.

"There's something you should know about me," he said, squeezing my hand. "Something I should have told you a long time ago, but I was afraid you'd think less of me."

I thought I knew Theo better than anyone outside my family. The fact he'd kept a big secret from me made my stomach ache. My mind swirled through all the possibilities. Maybe he had an online girlfriend. Maybe he had a kid from the brief time he slept around. Maybe he had a super weird fetish and was embarrassed to tell me about it.

"Spit it out, Theo, before I puke," I said, pulling my hand from his.

He blew out a breath. "So, you've seen my tats and piercings."

I nodded.

"They're not entirely aesthetic. Sometimes I do them because I want to feel the pain."

"Crap on a cracker," I said. "OK. Well, I've never tried BDSM but if that's what you're into, I guess I could give it a whirl. I mean clearly, I've never tried it since you're the first man I've been with all the way. You'd have to tell me what to do. Wait, if you like feeling pain would that make me the Domme? You kind of took charge the other night, so I'm a little confused. But I guess it's like acting, right? It might take me a couple weeks to get ready. No way am I buying a whip in person anywhere around here."

Theo's lips quirked.

"You're not talking about being a sub, are you?" I asked, burying my face in my hands.

He gently pulled my fingers from my face and held both my hands in his. "It's more like a pressure release for me than something pleasurable."

"Oh. That's um—"

"Not normal," he said, his knee bouncing again. "Neither is the cutting."

"Cutting?"

He nodded.

"You cut yourself?"

He nodded again. His hands suddenly felt clammy in mine, or maybe mine were the one's sweating.

"It's not what you think," he said. "I'm not suicidal. Even after Logan died and I went to prison, I never once wanted to take my life."

"Just hurt yourself?"

"Exactly," he said.

Like someone admitting to double-dipping at a party because otherwise the chip to dip ratio was off. Like hurting himself was no big deal and might even make sense if you stopped to think about it.

"That's messed up, Theo," I said, my voice breaking. I dropped his hands and wrapped my arms around my stomach.

"Come here, *kardoula* mou," he said, pulling me close. "I wanted to tell you before you saw the scars."

"So, you haven't done it in a while then," I said.

He tensed.

"Just tell me, Theo," I said, lifting my face from his shirt.

"I hadn't in a while. But the other night—"

I nodded. After we had sex. He couldn't wait to get me out of his bed, out of his house, so he could punish himself for being with me.

I sucked in a deep breath, straightened my spine, and gently pulled away from him. "If you ever do that again, we're finished. I won't be the reason you hurt yourself. It makes me sick to think I already was."

Harsh? Yes, but as much as I wanted Theo, I drew a hard line at being an excuse for him to self-harm. I had no problem being an ice-cold bitch if it prevented Theo from hurting himself.

"I'm so sorry, *kardoula mou*," he said, pulling me to his chest again. His heart pounded against my ear, strong and fast. "I'd understand if you want to take some time to think."

"What does that really mean? I google translated Poppy or poppies, and it didn't sound anything like it." Because of course I googled it the second I left his apartment that day. Even with all the extra vowels, the word still began with a *p* sound.

"It's just something my mom used to call me," he said, kissing my forehead.

"Do you know what it means?" I asked, looking up at him.

He nodded.

"But you're not going to tell me?"

"What do you think it means?"

"Pain in my ass?"

He flashed me another smile. "I promise. It doesn't mean that."

"Well, then I guess I can go to dinner with you."

"You're sure?" he asked, looking equally hopeful and terrified.

"I am if you are."

"Great," he said, standing and lifting me with him. He set me down gently and pulled something from his pocket. "I should probably wait to give you this until after Cal gives Rowan his Valentine's gift, or at least until I have a chain, but I'd love for you to wear it tonight, if you can."

He handed me something small and shiny. I brought my palm closer to my face and gasped. It was a delicate silver flower. The petals curled around a small heart nestled on a bed of stamen where the pistil would have been. "It's a poppy," I said.

"There's a loop on the back of one of the petals where you can thread a chain through."

"I've never seen anything like it," I said, holding it closer to admire the intricate details on each petal. "Where'd you find it?"

"I made it," he said with obvious pride. It's something I loved about Theo. Art was the only area of his life where he allowed himself to feel accomplished.

"It's beautiful," I said, rising on my toes to kiss his cheek.

"If Rowan asks, tell her I found it on Etsy. I don't want to ruin Cal's gift."

"Did he make her a spring of Rowan?" I asked, slightly shocked. I mean, Cal was cool and all, but I couldn't see him making something anywhere near as detailed as this.

"He made her a C out of gold. I'd never made a pendant before, so I played around with some sterling silver first."

"I love it," I said. "I have a chain upstairs. Let me get changed, and we can go."

"Take however long you need," he said, settling back on the couch.

As I ran up the stairs, it hit me. Though he'd apologized for making me feel sick, he hadn't promised not to hurt himself again.

Chapter Twenty-Two

Theo

WE'D TALKED EVERY DAY for over a year. I'd seen her naked. I knew what her face looked like when she came. Taking Poppy on a date was nothing to worry about. Or it shouldn't be. My palms sweated as I waited for her to change, my knee bouncing with the same hurried rhythm as my heart.

"When you're nervous, your body feels similar to how it feels when you're excited," Rowan said, slipping beside me on the couch. "Telling yourself you're excited can help reframe your feelings from something negative to something positive."

I wish it was that easy to get my mind and body under control. It was sweet she wanted to help, but no amount of positivity was going to calm me down. "Thanks, Rowan," I said and forced myself to smile at her.

"Oh, you are so faking that smile," she said and giggled.

"Distraction sometimes helps," I said, my knee slowing.

She nodded. "No wonder you're friends with Cal. He could talk to a fence post."

The look on her face when she spoke about Cal put a genuine smile on mine.

"Let's go before Antonia's fills up," Poppy said, running down the stairs with a pair of black heels in her hand.

She was so beautiful I couldn't speak. In the span of five minutes, she'd somehow managed to apply makeup that made her green eyes pop and turned her lips a bold red. She'd changed into a black dress that hugged her hips then flowed out in a puff of tulle. It was edgy and feminine. Just like Poppy.

"I usually wear this with combat boots, but would you mind if I borrowed these?" she asked Rowan.

"Please," Rowan said. "My poor heels haven't been worn since the accident."

Poppy bent and slipped the shoes on her feet, giving me a flash of her cleavage beneath the pendent I'd made. I no longer felt nervous, but I was at high risk of embarrassing myself when I stood up. Rowan got up first and fussed around with Poppy's choppy hair while I took a couple breaths to get my body under control. Though they were the same height, the spiky heels made Poppy tower over her sister.

I stood and crossed the room to them. Poppy still only came to my chest, but our height difference had shrunk considerably. "You look incredible," I said.

She blushed and fidgeted with the tulle on her skirt. "Mind giving me your arm?" she asked. "I'm not sure I can walk on these toothpicks."

I took her hand and kissed it before I wove her arm through mine. We headed for the door with Rowan following us like a mom sending the kids off to prom. I half expected her to demand a picture. She pulled out her cell as she closed the door behind us, and I had a feeling Cal was getting a moment-by-moment recap.

"Holy crap, I didn't think about the weather," Poppy said, snuggling up to me. I was roasting in my jacket, so I let go of her long enough to remove it and draped it around her narrow shoulders.

"The truck should still be warm," I said and opened the passenger door. Poppy had climbed into my truck many times, but never in shoes like these. Somehow, she managed to hoist herself up, her fine ass level with my hands. It took everything in me not to grab it before she wiggled into the cab.

"Aiden finished the sliding door on Friday," I said as I climbed into the driver's seat. "I have a key for you back at the house. It opens the front door as well."

"First date and you're already giving me a key," she said with mock surprise.

"Not your typical first date." I reached my hand over the center console and laid it on the bare skin where her dress ended in a puff of fabric. She started to squirm as I rubbed lazy circles on her thigh.

"You made your point," she said pulling my hand from her leg and locking her fingers with mine. "I'm starving, but if you keep touching me like that, I'm going to need a detour to the air mattress."

"No more air mattress."

"Oh," she said in a small voice. "OK."

"Cal and I picked up a real bed earlier today. So, if you wanted to stay over—" I was a grown man for fuck's sake. When I was younger, I had no problem telling a woman exactly what I wanted to do with her. With Poppy, I sounded like a high schooler hoping to score for the first time.

"I'd like that," she said, giving my hand a squeeze. The trip to the restaurant wasn't long enough. There was something so peaceful about driving with Poppy beside me, like we were still in the world, but insulated from it. Part of me wanted to blow off dinner and just ride around in the calm. Instead, I pulled into a spot near the pharmacy, just down from the restaurant, and tightened my grip on her hand. "I know you can do it on your own, but I'd like to open your door and help you down."

"Would you believe you're the first date I've ever had who offered to do that?" she said with a small smile.

Hopefully, this was the last first date for both of us. The thought popped into my head with such conviction, I almost said it out loud. "Well, there's a first time for everything," I said before climbing out of the truck and hurrying to her side.

After I helped her to the sidewalk, I wrapped my arm around her waist and pulled her close. "In case there's ice," I said.

"And here I thought you just wanted to cop a feel," she said as an older couple passed us on the sidewalk. The lady let out a little gasp, but the older gentleman winked at me.

I laughed and gave Poppy a squeeze before opening the door to Antonia's for her. I honestly hadn't been on many dates. Most of my hook ups had been the friends-with-benefits variety, though when the benefits ended, the friendships faded one by one. But with Poppy, I wanted more, which meant showing her we were firmly out of the friend zone.

"I feel like I have to whisper in here," Poppy said as the hostess led us to a secluded table in the back. I pulled out her chair, and the shocked look on her face almost made me laugh.

"I'm guessing no one did that either," I said, taking a seat across from her.

She shook her head. "I always went for the rebel types. Social graces weren't exactly top of the list."

"What was?" I asked, pushing the wine menu across the white tablecloth to her.

She shrugged. "Shocking people, I guess. Which was why I dated them."

"Well, you're in luck. I shock people daily. I think it's the lobe gauging."

"Pretty sure it's the overall hotness," she said, without taking her eyes from the dinner menu. "It certainly shocks me daily."

"I know the feeling," I said, taking a sip of the ice water the waiter dropped at the table.

She glanced up at me and blushed before looking down at the menu again. "Well, that, and the fact you're so kind. You're like a marshmallow wrapped in a bad boy shell. No, not a marshmallow. They're gross. Maybe peanut butter."

"I'm not sure this is going to work. Marshmallows are not gross."

This time she put down the menu and locked eyes with me. "The only acceptable uses for marshmallows are in fondant, Rice Krispies Treats, or s'mores."

"Well, as long as you'll eat s'mores." I reached across the table, took her hand, and ran my thumb across her knuckles. Her eyes grew dark.

The server chose that moment to approach the table for our orders. Poppy jumped at the sound of his voice but recovered quickly. All my tension evaporated before the appetizers arrived. We talked about the upcoming art exhibit. The pink bridesmaid dresses Rowan selected for the wedding. Their construction plans for the bakery. The portrait class I was designing for next fall and the likelihood of finding models in our small town. All the museums I wanted to visit with her that'd require a long drive and an overnight stay. It was similar to all the conversations we'd ever had, except actual touch replaced the constant tension I'd felt whenever we were together. I scooted my chair close to her and held her hand as much as possible while eating.

"Don't tell my mom, but that was the best chicken parm I've ever eaten," Poppy said as we stepped into the cold night.

"Your secret is safe with me."

As we approached my truck, a car sped down Main Street. A moment later, it slammed on its brakes when it came up on a minivan waiting to make a left turn. The smell of tires burning, followed by the sound of metal crunching, pulled me right back into the nightmarish memory that had plagued me for years.

"I can't believe Avery dumped me," Cal slurred in the passenger seat beside me.

"You're better off, man," Aiden yelled from the back. "Now you can go wild when you get to campus. You'll forget all about her as soon as you get your dick wet again."

"And this is why you can never date my sisters," Logan said and laughed.

"Dude, I can't date your sisters because they might as well be my sisters." Aiden made a convincing gagging sound, and I glanced in the rearview mirror to make sure he hadn't hurled all over the back seat of Cal's car.

My heart felt like it was about to burst from my chest, and I couldn't catch my breath. The streetlamps faded as my vision tunneled. I bent at the waist and took deep breaths that quickly turned to pants. I felt myself sway and sank to my knees.

"Do you think she'd planned to dump me all summer?" Cal asked, slamming his head against the headrest.

"Yes," I answered. "Which is why you're better off without her, brother."

"Thanks, Theo," Cal said. "You're the best."

"Didn't I just say that?" Aiden yelled.

"But Theo stopped drinking so I could get trashed. That's why he's the best," Cal said, trying to pat my shoulder. He ended up patting the back of my seat before slumping against the door. "Why not just dump me? Why keep pretending she cared about me all summer?"

"Guess she wanted the D until the last minute," Aiden said. "Oh, I should text her that."

"Don't text her that," Logan said. "You'll only stir her up."

I glanced in the rearview mirror again. Aiden had pulled out his phone and was jabbing at the screen with his thick fingers. "Done," he said. "I can't wait to see what she writes back."

"I don't want to know," Cal said.

I accelerated as we reached the stretch of country road nicknamed "roller-coaster hill." Cal, Aiden, and Logan raised their arms and yelped as the car dipped, then rose quickly, a sensation that always made my stomach flip.

"I'm going to miss that hill when I'm at college," Logan said.

"Oh, shit," Aiden said, laughing. "Dude, you have to read this."

"No, I don't," Cal said pressing the heels of his hands to his eyes.

"Yes, you do," Aiden said, flinging off his seatbelt and leaning into the front seat with his phone.

"Sit down, asshole," I snapped.

"Read it," Aiden yelled.

"I don't want to," Cal said, pressing himself against the door.

"Cut it out, Aid," Logan said yanking the back of Aiden's shirt.

Aiden slithered in between the front seats until half his body rested on the center console. "Look, Cal."

I heard Logan's seatbelt unlock just before his huge arms wrapped around Aiden and pulled him back to his seat. I entered a blind turn. A seatbelt clicked.

"You can show him tomorrow," I heard Logan say just as a deer darted into the road.

"Shit," I yelled, slamming on the brakes and swerving toward the edge of the road. The car skidded, the acrid smell of rubber pouring into the interior. It happened so fast. The deer. The slide. The sickening crunch as the car wrapped around a tree on the passenger side.

The air bags deployed, saving my head from the steering wheel, pillow-like clouds exploding all around the front seat. I looked over at Cal, my heart hammering. He was limp against the side of the car, the air bag deflating fast, too fast. I flung off my seatbelt and crawled over the console to him.

"Cal," I yelled. Blood covered the side of his face. His arm bent at an odd angle. I couldn't even see his legs through the wreckage. "Brother," I yelled. He still didn't answer me, but his chest moved up and down.

I turned to look in the back seat. Aiden was slumped against the crumbled door, just as bloodied and broken as Cal. I reached into the back seat and grabbed his left wrist. A surge of relief crashed through me when I felt his steady pulse. Then I realized, he was alone.

The seat where Logan had been moments before was empty. My heart rate accelerated when I saw the broken glass littered across the back seat. Had I passed out? Did he climb out already and call 911? Logan would know we needed help, but why didn't he check on everyone first? He had to have climbed out.

I pushed down the air bag and opened my door, which was surprisingly undamaged. I rolled out of the car and smacked my knee on the asphalt, the pain soothing some of the panic filling my chest.

"Logan," I yelled, rising to my feet. I looked up and down the deserted road. Nothing. "Logan," I yelled again, my voice raw with fear. The moon was covered in clouds and without streetlights, the night lay dark and thick. I fumbled in my pocket for my cell and turned on the flashlight. I crossed the road and scanned the field. The reflective decal on Logan's shoes flashed back at me from a sweep of long grass. I ran and dropped to my knees beside him.

I knew he was gone the moment I saw him. His neck twisted in a way no one could survive. I rolled away from him and gagged; the beer I drank earlier made sour puddles on the grass. Then with shaking hands, I grabbed his wrist, hoping I was wrong. I wasn't.

A sound like a hurt animal filled the quiet night. It took me a moment to realize the animal was me.

A gentle hand touched my chest, and I was surrounded by Poppy's lavender scent.

"Look at me, Theo."

I raised my eyes to Poppy's soft green ones.

"Here," another voice said, and something cold and wet pressed against my neck.

"Let's sit," Poppy said, grabbing my hands and sinking onto the freezing sidewalk. I flopped onto my ass beside her, and she ran her fingers through my hair in soothing strokes. I leaned against her, filling my lungs with the sweetest air.

My vision sharpened, and I took in the spectacle I'd created. Poppy beside me with her dress spread across the filthy concrete. Mr. Wilson hovering nearby with a water bottle. A small crowd gathering around us.

"Drink," Mr. Wilson said, handing me the bottle. "Small sips."

Poppy glared at the crowd. "He's fine. You can move along now."

No one moved.

"We've got it under control," she yelled. "Get the hell out of here."

Everyone listened except Mr. Wilson. "Where are you parked?" he asked.

"Thanks for your help, Wilson, but Theo and I can manage."

"I'm sure you can," he said. "But I've been where he's sitting, and I want to help."

Poppy nodded and Wilson crouched down, his knees popping as he lowered himself until he could look me in the eyes. "All right, Theo, let's get you up, if you're ready."

I raised my arms, and he lifted me to my feet with surprising strength. "I'm fine," I said, though my legs shook.

"That's right," Mr. Wilson said. "We're going to take a few steps. Then rest a minute." He gripped my elbow on one side, and Poppy held the other. It felt like it took half an hour to reach my truck, even though it was right there.

"Keys," Poppy said.

"Jacket," I answered.

She'd slipped into my leather coat when we left the restaurant. I remember hoping it would smell like her when she gave it back. She dug in my pockets until she found the keys. After unlocking the door, she reached for me, but Mr. Wilson waved her off.

"I'll get him settled, Poppy. Just get in and warm up the engine."

"Thank you," I said as he guided me into the passenger seat.

He gripped my shoulder after I'd buckled my seatbelt. "Panic attacks are the worst, ain't they?"

I nodded and rested my head against the seat. Poppy took one of my sweaty hands.

"Thanks, Wilson," Poppy said, her eyes still wide.

"Glad to help. Call if you need anything, sweetie. You too, Theo. I've had more than my share of those, and I'm here to talk anytime you want."

I nodded and closed my eyes. I kept them closed while Poppy drove us back to my house. The better my body felt, the more my embarrassment grew. The truck slowed to a stop, and I heard her set the parking brake.

"Do you want to sit here a minute or are you good to go inside?" she asked.

"Are you coming with me?"

"Of course, I'm coming with you," she snapped. "I'm going to help you onto that new mattress and then I'm going to take off this dress because this tulle is itchy as fuck and then I'm going to cuddle the shit out of you."

I nodded and this time, she escorted me inside.

CHAPTER TWENTY-THREE

Poppy

I KEPT MY ARM around Theo as we walked through the living room. His shirt was drenched with sweat. Though he wasn't leaning on me like he had on Main Street, he still seemed unsteady. Whatever panic attacks I thought I'd witnessed before were nothing compared to the one that just happened. It was like he'd gotten so locked in his mind, he wasn't even aware of me or anyone else around him. All the color had drained from his face, and his breathing was so erratic, I don't know how he hadn't passed out.

"I'm going to hop in the shower," he said.

"I'm coming with you." I darted past him into the 1970s bathroom. Whoever decided mustard yellow was a good color for wall tiles should have their eyes checked. The busy pattern on the floor tiles was an equal sin.

Theo leaned against the sink while I turned on the shower. "You don't have to babysit me, Poppy. I promise, I'm fine."

"Well, I'm not," I snapped. "Fifteen minutes ago, you looked like you were having a heart attack. Plus, I think there's gum stuck to my leg. Not to mention all the ice melt. I'm taking a shower with you."

I contorted and groped until I found the zipper on my back and yanked it down. I kicked off Rowan's torture shoes and wiggled out of my dress.

213

Even though I'd already sat on the gross sidewalk, I hung it carefully on the empty hook on the back of the door.

When I turned back around, I caught Theo staring at my ass, his gaze heated. Well, at least he bounced back fast. I slid off my bra, then my panties, his eyes following my every move.

"You going to shower in your clothes?" I asked walking to him.

He started fumbling with the buttons on his shirt, getting nowhere fast. I placed my hand over his and took over. His chest moved up and down, and for a second, I worried he was starting another attack before he reached out and brushed his thumb across my nipple, sending a throb of need between my legs.

I slid his shirt off and ran my hands down his abs to the waistband of his pants. He sucked in a breath as I undid the button and slipped down his fly. He was already hard, his cock bobbing up to meet my hands when I reached inside his boxers. Definitely not pierced.

He closed his eyes and threw his head back. Good. I wanted him distracted when I saw his scars for the first time. I kept pumping him in slow strokes while I pushed his pants to the floor.

My hand stilled. Thin scars covered his legs. There was no pattern, no apparent design other than to inflict pain. All the marks had healed over to shiny white or pink scars but one. A long, angry gash on his inner thigh that looked hot and painfully red.

"Please, don't cry," I heard him say. I hadn't realized I was until he brushed the tears from my cheeks.

I let go of him and pulled back the shower curtain. "Get in."

"Poppy—"

"In," I snapped because I was one second from losing my shit. I wasn't sure if I wanted to scream at him or sob my eyes out. Probably both. He stepped under the shower head, the water sluicing down his toned body. I climbed into the yellow tub and yanked the curtain closed.

He grabbed my hands and pulled me under the water with him before wrapping his arms around me. We stood pressed together while the water ran down our skin. When I no longer felt like yelling or crying, I dropped my arms and stepped back. I grabbed a bar of soap from the built-in holder on the wall and lathered it in my hands.

Theo squirted some shampoo in his hand but froze when I started rubbing suds on his stomach. "You don't have to do that," he said, even as he leaned into my touch.

"I want to," I said, rubbing my sudsy hands over his perfect ass.

He let the water wash away the shampoo on his hand and watched me lather his shoulders, then arms, then torso again. He let out a groan when I lowered my hands to his dick. He reached for me, but I dropped to my knees, running my soapy fingers over the raised skin on his legs. He started to step back, either because I was touching his scars or because there was a real threat his impressive erection would poke me in the eye. I dropped the bar of soap and wrapped my hand around his cock.

I looked up at him while the water washed the last of the soap away and placed a gentle kiss on his crown. He watched me take him into my mouth before he closed his eyes and groaned.

Since I'd held onto my v-card until Theo, I considered myself somewhat of an expert at giving head. When I opened my throat and sucked his entire shaft into my mouth, his eyes popped open.

"Holy shit," he panted.

I smirked and hummed, my tongue caressing his delicate skin as I bobbed my head back and forth. He gripped my hair. "Poppy," he said as his legs started to shake. "No one has ever been able to—" His grip tightened. "Touch yourself," he ordered in a voice that made heat pool between my legs.

I slid one of my hands to my clit and moaned.

I worked both of us into a frenzy until Theo finally started thrusting into my mouth. "I'm going to come. You don't have to—fuck," he yelled, when I started massaging his balls with my free hand.

He let out a feral groan, and I swallowed around him, his hot cum sliding down my throat.

I sat back on my heels and took a few deep breaths. He lifted me to my feet, spun me around and placed my hands on the tile wall. Before I could ask what he was doing, his soapy hands began to roam over my body. Once I was clean, he kneaded my breasts before sliding his hand between my legs where I ached for release. The orgasm I'd started to build with my own fingers felt much closer with his.

"Come for me," he growled in my ear. Pleasure ripped through me with such intensity my vision darkened. He kept touching me, drawing out my orgasm until I sagged against the shower wall, spent. He turned me back to face him and wrapped me in his arms. We stood like that until the water began to cool.

"I'm making Aiden install one of those endless hot water heaters," he said when the water became icy. He turned off the faucet and opened the curtain, both of us shaking.

There was only one bath towel in sight. He yanked it from the bar, wrapped it around me, and dried my skin with the nubby fabric while goosebumps erupted over his entire body. Only after I was dry and wrapped in the towel did he reach into the closet and pull out an equally ratty towel for himself. He grabbed my hand and rubbed the water from his skin as he pulled me out the bathroom and down the hall toward the bedroom, leaving puddles on the hardwood floors the whole way.

If it weren't for the mauve carpet, I wouldn't have recognized Theo's room. The air mattress was gone. In its place was a queen-sized bed with soft gray bedding. It even had a black headboard. He'd taken down the floral drapes and swapped the mini blinds for sleek roller shades. A pair of nightstands with matching silver lamps completed the new furnishings. The room still looked as personal as a mid-range hotel, but at least he wasn't sleeping on the floor.

He tossed his towel on the pink carpet, pulled back the covers, and motioned for me to climb in. I dropped my towel next to his and lay down, still slightly damp from the shower. Once he was beside me, he wrapped the comforter around us and drew me close.

"Ready for me to cuddle the shit out of you," I said laying my head on his chest. His heart pounded beneath my ear. He didn't answer me, but he kissed my wet hair. I placed my hand on his stomach and felt the tip of his erection.

I lifted my head and smirked at him. "Doesn't take you long to rally, does it?"

"I need to feel you come around my cock at least twice before we cuddle," he said, running his hands down my back.

Woah. OK. Wasn't expecting Theo to be a dirty talker, but I liked it. "Oh yeah," I said. "Pretty sure of yourself, aren't you?"

He smiled down at me before lowering his mouth to mine. The kiss was gentle, his tongue caressing with languid strokes that put every nerve in my body on alert. In one swift move, he flipped me onto my back. He lifted my arms above my head and wove his fingers in mine while he sucked a sensitive spot on my neck. I arched off the bed when he ran his stubble across my nipples. He let go of my hands and moved down my body, kissing and stroking every inch with his equally skilled hands, his pace achingly slow. By the time he reached my waist, I was panting.

"Don't come," he said in that deep voice that made my core clench. "Not until I'm inside you. Tell me to stop when you get close." Then he pushed my legs apart and lowered his mouth to me. I gripped his hair and pulled. If he repeated the magic thing he did with his tongue and his hands on Thursday, I'd be a goner.

"That close, huh," he chuckled and then blew on my clit. When I didn't yank his hair, he swirled his tongue against me. I clenched and let out a strangled cry. I was right there. One more swipe was all I needed. He pulled away. I groaned in frustration.

"Are you always this responsive?" he asked, rubbing lazy circles on my inner thighs with his thumbs.

I shook my head. Honestly, I was lucky if the guys I'd dated could find my clit. None had been able to pull pleasure from my body like Theo. None had even tried.

"I could keep going if you want me to edge you," he said, dipping his hands between my legs. "But you have to promise not to come."

"Yeah, can't promise that," I said and arched against his fingers.

He flashed me a boyish smile, and I realized I'd never seen him like this. Playful. He reached into the nightstand and pulled out a condom. When he gave himself a hard stroke, I almost came. I'd just had an orgasm, yet I'd never felt this turned on before, like I'd combust and burn to ash if I didn't get relief soon. He rolled the condom down his length and rubbed his shaft across my throbbing center. I gripped the sheets, fighting my release while he positioned himself at my entrance.

"We're taking it slow this time," he said. He kissed me as he pressed his crown inside. I tightened around him, the need to come so strong it was almost painful.

"How far in do you need to be to consider yourself inside me?" I panted.

He smiled and withdrew, then pushed forward another inch.

I wrapped my legs around him and pressed my heels against his ass, urging him on. I fought my orgasm for a couple inches and then exploded. He thrust deep and groaned as I tightened around him. As I started to come down, he began to move, slowly at first, his hips rolling in a way that stretched me to accommodate him.

He threaded his hands with mine again and kissed me, all heat and tongue. Each thrust a little faster until he started a rhythm that had me moaning into his mouth. My orgasm started to build again from my toes up my body, and before long, I was clenching around him and calling his name. He let go then. Fucking me with powerful thrusts that kept the waves rolling through me, one orgasm bleeding into another until he found his release, his cock pulsing inside me.

We broke apart, panting.

"I'll be right back," he said, rising from the bed and walking out of the room in all his naked glory.

My stomach dropped. I wanted to run after him to make sure he wasn't hurting himself, but I forced myself to stay in the bed until he returned a moment later with a washcloth.

Condom. He had to get rid of the condom. He pressed the warm cloth against me, soothing the ache I hadn't realize was there.

"You all right?" he asked, looking at me with concern. "I got a little rough there at the end."

I nodded.

"You sure?" he asked, small lines appearing between his eyes.

"Yeah. I just need to pee. I heard somewhere it prevents UTIs."

UTIs. What the heck was coming out of my mouth? I mean, Rowan had told me that, but it wasn't exactly something you said to a guy right after you had sex. Then again, most guys didn't cut themselves either.

He handed me the washcloth. I hopped out of bed, scooped up the wet towels, and wrapped one around me before I scurried to the bathroom and shut the door.

"Stop being weird," I told my reflection in the mirror above the sink, which pretty much cemented my weirdo status. I draped the washcloth on the side of the tub and hung the towels on the bar next to the sink. With a huff, I went ahead and tinkled because might as well. After I flushed and washed my hands, I contemplated putting on a towel again, but a badass bitch would strut back to the room like a runway model, so that's exactly what I did.

Theo was propped against the headboard, waiting. He looked exhausted, and I felt a stab of guilt for taking so much from him before he'd had time to recover from the panic attack. He smiled and flipped back the covers like it was the most natural thing in the world to welcome me into his bed. I slid in beside him, and he pulled me close, my head on his chest, his arm resting low on my bare back.

"If I didn't hurt you, what's on your mind?" he asked. "And don't say you just had to pee. I know that's a lie."

"How?" I asked, raising my head from his chest. His eyes looked sad. All the playfulness of earlier gone.

"You scrunch here when you fib," he said, running a finger down the bridge of my nose. "And you bite your lip when you're worried," he added, tugging my bottom lip free from my teeth.

"Pretty sure you already know," I said.

He nodded.

I propped myself up, so we were eye to eye. "I meant what I said before, Theo. I can't be afraid you're going to hurt yourself every time we're together. More than that, when I see marks like this," I said, placing my hand lightly on the thigh he'd recently cut, "It breaks my heart."

"*Kardoula mou*," he said, cupping my face. "That's what it means. My heart."

Holy shit. All this time, he's been calling me his heart, and I'd thought he didn't like me enough to date me. "But you've called me that for months."

He nodded.

"Damn it, Theo," I said, swatting his chest. "I swear, if I see another mark on you, I'm wrapping you in bubble wrap, throwing you in the back of Tallulah, and driving your ass to your therapist. Then I'm ghosting you. Got it?"

He smiled and rescued my lip from my teeth again. "Would it make you feel better if I started seeing someone now?"

"Excuse me?" I said, sitting up.

He threw his head back and laughed. The fucker laughed. I crossed my arms over my bare chest and waited.

"A therapist," he said when he got himself under control.

"You don't have one?" Most artists I knew had a therapist, let alone an artist with panic attacks and self-harm tendencies. Mom put all of us in grief counseling after Dad died, and I'd used the mental health services in high school when I felt overwhelmed with my senior project and the choices I had to make after graduation.

He shook his head and my chest ached. "Because you don't think they work or because you don't think you deserve to feel better?" I asked.

He didn't answer, but his amber eyes looked a million years old. I climbed up his body and buried my face in the crook of his neck because if I looked at him any longer, I was definitely going to lose it.

"Prepare yourself for the longest snuggle of your life," I said with my face smushed against him.

He chuckled, the sound rich and warm. "I promise," he said rubbing my back, "it won't be long enough."

CHAPTER TWENTY-FOUR

Theo

SINCE MAX DIDN'T WORK Sundays, I had the shop to myself. He'd stopped trying to convince me to take the day off years ago. Sundays were for families, and I didn't have one. I'd rather leave early whenever I needed and start late the other days I worked. I reserved Sunday for custom work that required long chunks of time and focus. These tats weren't cookie-cutter hearts or Chinese symbols. Most required several rounds of sketches and lengthy discussions with the client. In other words, the most artful.

Mr. Snuggles's biker dad had come through with multiple referrals for this type of work. Today's was a challenging piece for a guy who called himself Phoenix.

"These are always tricky," I said, running my hand over his marred skin. The burn scar wrapped around his entire forearm and looked older than the ones I usually covered, more faded. "If you don't mind me asking, why did you decide to cover it now?"

"I lost my kid sister Lacey in the fire that did this," Phoenix said, pointing to his arm.

"Shit, I'm sorry."

He nodded. "It felt wrong to cover it. She was gone and I'd survived. The scar was proof of that. But the other day, I was taking my daughter to the park, and we passed a stained-glass window. She called it a 'princess window' and kept walking. I couldn't move my damn feet. Lacey's favorite Disney princess was Belle. She watched that movie over and over. There's a part at the beginning and the end where the story is told in stained glass. Have you seen it?"

I nodded. Max's girls loved the movie and had watched it in the shop more than once when they came to work with their dad.

"I realized I didn't need proof of how Lacey died; I needed to honor how she lived."

Phoenix opened the manilla envelope he'd brought with him and handed me a photo of a little girl holding an older boy's hand. The girl had lively brown eyes and waist-length hair. She looked straight at the camera while the boy looked down at her with an adoring smile.

"She's beautiful," I said. I couldn't imagine having kids of my own after losing someone so young. The fear Phoenix must carry with him every day would paralyze me.

"Can you draw us like that but like we're part of a stained-glass window?" he asked.

I saw the image clearly in my mind. Complicated work with smooth skin, but infinitely harder on a scar. I glanced at his arm again. There was enough room, barely.

"It's difficult to ink over scar tissue, but I get why you want it there. Give me an hour or two to draw it up. It'll take a couple sessions, but we should be able to nail down the design today and maybe do the outline. Mind if I snap a picture of your arm and take some measurements? I want to get this right."

"Of course. Big Tom was right about you. You know, a lot of people would have laughed at him for that cat tattoo."

"Grief is grief," I said.

He nodded and cleared his throat. "Well, take however long you need. Just text me when you're ready."

After I measured his scar and took several pictures, I lost myself in the sketch. I made a copy and played around with different shadings until the bell over the door rang.

I looked up expecting Phoenix had come back early. Instead, Aries walked in with a girl who didn't look old enough to drive, let alone hang out with a man in his early twenties.

"Theo," he said, wrapping his arm around the girl. "Heard you moving around down here and figured you could help us."

Aries and I hadn't spoken much since Poppy and I got together. Judging by the glares he sent my way Friday, I assumed she'd called him and broken their date. I didn't feel like hashing it out with him, and apart from the occasional side eye, he didn't seem inclined to talk about it either.

"My girl Sarah here wants some ink."

"I'm kind of in the middle of something," I said, pointing to the sketch on the draft table.

"It won't take long," he said.

Sarah held up her phone to an image of what had to be the most boring tattoo I'd ever seen. "I saw Aries's zodiac tat, and I want one of mine. I'm a Sagittarius, so it's just an arrow with a cross on the bottom. Nothing too thick. All black is fine."

"I'd do it myself," Aries said, "but I promised Max no more tattooing until I get a license."

"Look," I said. "I'm happy to do that or something Sagittarius-inspired tomorrow, but I'm working on a pretty complicated design right now."

"You said this guy would do it," Sarah whined.

"Come on, Theo," Aries said, glancing over at Sarah. "You owe me."

Kid wanted to get laid, and since I'd already cock blocked him once, I nodded. "But just a simple design."

"Yay," Sarah said, jumping up and down. Despite her heavy makeup and low-cut shirt, she looked dangerously young.

"I'll need your ID, Sarah," I said.

"Oh sure," she said, digging in her bag. She pulled out a loose ID and handed it to me. "I went blonde after that was taken," she said. "And, um, lost a little weight."

The ID looked real, and the picture resembled Sarah. It had her name and an October birthday that made her nineteen, but something didn't feel right. I looked up at her and frowned.

"For fuck's sake, Theo," Aries snapped. "This isn't even her first ink."

Sarah pushed up the sleeve of her oversized sweatshirt and showed me a cursive A.

"What does the A stand for?" I asked.

She rolled her eyes. "Aries of course."

"How long have you two known each other?"

"Long enough to mark her as mine," he said, eyes cold.

So, long enough he shouldn't have been trying to start something with Poppy.

I glanced at the ID again and handed it back to Sarah. "I need you to set up Max's station and sterilize it after," I told Aries. "I don't want my client to wait longer than he has to."

"Sure," Aries said, heading for the supply closet.

"Where do you want it?" I asked.

"At the base of my neck," she said, lifting her dirty blonde hair.

At least she didn't want it on her tits or ass. After she signed the consent form, I led her to Max's station. Sarah held Aries's hand and cried the entire time I worked on her. I had to wait for her to take an absurd number of selfies in front of the mirror before she'd let me bandage her up, but all in all, I only lost about a half hour.

"Go over the after-care instructions with her," I said, snapping off my black disposable gloves. "I've got to finish my sketches for my client."

"Yeah, no problem," he said, grabbing Sarah's hand. "I'll be back later to clean Max's station."

"Aries," I called after him, but he didn't stop. He snagged one of the after-care printouts from the counter and pulled Sarah through the door.

I wouldn't have charged them, but a thank you would have been nice. Not to mention there was no way in hell I wasn't sterilizing Max's station since I couldn't be sure Aries would.

After I cleaned up, I spent another fifteen minutes adding subtle white shading around Lacey's head on one of the sketches. I had several memorial tattoos of Logan. Some obvious. Some not. I'd leave it up to Phoenix to decide which he wanted his to be.

I held out the finished sketches. I always knew I'd gotten something right when it hurt to look at it. Every memorial I did felt like a punch to the chest. It's one of the reasons I'd gotten a reputation for doing them well. I could empathize with my clients, but that also meant reliving my own grief. Not a day went by that I didn't think about Logan, but some days were harder than others. I could count on a nightmare or two tonight and an extra punishing workout tomorrow morning.

I grabbed my phone to let Phoenix know I was ready and found a text from Poppy.

Mind if I stay over tonight?

Wrapping myself around Poppy was a way better option than entering a grief spiral. I felt terrible for ruining our first date, but each orgasm I gave her after had boosted my damaged ego. Holding her all night and savoring her again this morning had assured me she still wanted me, despite witnessing one of the worst panic attacks I'd ever had.

I'd love it. I'll be done here around six. I can grab takeout on the way or schedule a delivery

Either is fine since I'm already here. I'm working on something in the studio

Anything I can see?

Definitely

What are you in the mood for tonight?

I texted Phoenix and started setting up my station while I waited for her to reply. It took a minute but then my phone chimed again and again with incoming texts.

I'm really bad at sexting

Like, embarrassingly bad

If I sexted, you'd laugh at how bad I am, and I kind of want you to think I'm perfect

I laughed and called her.

"I'm not any better at phone sex," she said instead of hello.

"I've honestly never had phone sex, so I don't know if I'm any good or not. I was wondering what you wanted for dinner."

"Oh," she said. "Well, now I feel like an idiot."

"Don't. I needed a laugh, and I still think you're perfect."

She was quiet long enough that I started to worry. "Something we don't have to eat right away," she said finally. "That's what I want for dinner."

"Sushi or subs?"

"Like that's even a question."

"Two spicy tuna rolls and a California roll?" I asked even though she'd gotten the same thing every time we ordered from the single sushi restaurant in Jericho.

"That'd be great. I'll see you soon."

"Uh, and Puppy, I'm down for whatever else you're in the mood for."

"You sure about that?" she said with a heavy dose of sass.

"Absolutely."

CHAPTER TWENTY-FIVE

Poppy

I'D JUST FINISHED TAPING drop cloths to the studio windows when the doorbell rang. Hopefully it was dinner and not someone I had to get rid of before Theo arrived.

I grabbed my wallet and opened the door just as the delivery guy drove off with a friendly honk. Typical Theo. He used to cover everything when we were friends, even though I always tried to treat him. I grabbed the large bag and walked to the kitchen. There was a bottle of ketchup in the fridge and nothing else. I slid the plastic containers of sushi inside, along with the edamame he'd added to the order. He'd also gotten the green tea mochi ice cream I loved. I stashed the mochi in the freezer, which was half full of frozen entrees. If Rowan or Mom saw the contents of Theo's fridge, he'd be getting a lecture and weekly meal deliveries from our house.

Since I had everything ready in the studio, I decided to set the table before remembering Theo didn't have one. I opened the cabinets so I could at least have plates ready and took out two of the four basic white dishes he had. I slid open one drawer and then another. All were lined with '90s floral shelf paper and bare except for a box of plastic cutlery. Theo hadn't lived here long, but surely, he'd had time to hit up Target for silverware.

I opened the Notes app on my phone and jotted down a few things I could get him to make the place feel homier. I wandered down the hall to the bathroom and cracked open the closet door. The towels we'd wrapped up in last night were the only ones he owned. He did at least have a pack of toilet paper and a first aid kit.

I worked on my list in the studio while I waited and almost missed the sound of the front door opening and closing. I'd been so occupied, I hadn't had time to freak out about what I was about to suggest.

"What's all this?" Theo asked as he entered the studio. He walked around the canvas I'd laid on the floor and kissed me deeply before I had a chance to answer. Yep. Dinner was going to wait.

"Well," I said, wrapping my arms around his waist. "You made me such a thoughtful gift, I wanted to make one for you. But I'm afraid you have to help me."

He looked at the canvas spread across the floor and the drop cloths covering the windows. "Are you spray painting something?"

"Nope," I said. I pointed to the disposable pie dishes and washable tempera paint on the worktable. "You need something for your bedroom wall. Personally, I was thinking gray and an accent color. Red would work well, but it will clash with the carpet until Aiden changes it."

"I'm still not following."

I smirked at him. "I'm going to take off my clothes, and you're going to cover me in that paint. All of me, except, you know. Then you're going to take off your clothes, and I'll cover you. Then we paint."

His eyes widened and a slow smile spread across his face. Playful Theo was back, just like I'd hoped he'd be.

"Do you have green?" he asked, reaching for me.

"Just primaries, black, and white," I said as he kissed my neck and started unbuttoning my shirt dress.

He left my dress half undone and brought me over to the worktable. "We'll put the black and white on me." He grabbed an empty pie pan and started mixing blue, yellow, and white. "Look at me," he said, his tone urgent. He added more blue and held the spoon he'd used to mix the paint up to my face. "This is yours."

The man color matched my eyes. I lunged at him and started yanking at his shirt. A few moments later, we were both naked and smearing paint all over each other.

"Damn it, I want to touch you," he said as he grabbed my ass with a handful of green.

I knew exactly what he meant. I'd had to stop myself from wrapping my fingers around his erection several times. I dipped my hands in the black and white paint and ran them up and down his legs while he poured paint down my back. Glad I'd covered the floor in plastic.

"Good enough," I said, standing. I grabbed the condom I'd put on the worktable earlier, which I'd bought in Jericho because I wasn't hitting up the pharmacy in Peace Falls for protection any time soon.

My hands shook as I tried to tear open the foil.

"You OK?" Theo asked, wrapping his paint-covered hand over mine.

Yes. No. I couldn't tell him that I still didn't believe this was real. Like any moment I'd wake up and have to suffer through another day of wanting him, wondering what it was that made me so unlovable. "I just really want you, and both our hands are covered in paint, and I'm not sure what would happen if I got paint up my vag."

He chuckled and tore a paper towel from the roll I'd taken from the kitchen. After he wiped the green paint from his hands, he grabbed a new condom from the table and rolled it on before dipping both hands in the green again.

We ran for the canvas. He stretched out on his back and smiled up at me. "Probably best if you start on top to minimize internal paint splatter."

I loved seeing him like this, excited, his eyes shining with light. I wondered if this freer version of Theo was more like who he'd been before the accident.

I lowered to my knees, placing one on each side of him, spreading my legs wide. I positioned myself where I thought I needed me to be, but had to shift a little against him before I was able to take him in. He groaned as I lowered myself down.

It felt different from this angle, my clit rubbing against him every time my body met his. I started to move faster, sparks of pleasure growing to an inferno. I was moments from falling apart when Theo flipped us. My back rubbed against the canvas as he rocked into me slowly. The friction of the cloth, contrasting with the slippery paint, woke every nerve in my body.

"Sorry, baby," he said. "I wasn't going to last with you riding me like that, and I have a couple more positions in mind to cover this canvas."

He lowered his face and kissed me gently, reverently. His thrusts became languid as he broke the kiss, his warm eyes locked with mine. He laced our fingers together and took me with such tenderness, I almost cried.

My orgasm started to build again, but just before I came, he rolled us across the canvas and stopped us on our sides, facing each another.

"Are you purposefully keeping me from coming?" I asked as I arched against him.

"One more position," he said, through gritted teeth, pulling out of me.

"For Pete's sake, Theo," I yelled. "Want me to stand on my head?"

He pointed to a corner that was almost entirely blank. "Hands and knees."

"Want me to crawl there?" I asked, only half joking.

The heat in his eyes had me dragging myself across the canvas on all fours. I glanced over my shoulder and watched him lower to his hands and knees and follow my path across the canvas like a hunter stalking prey. By the time he got to me, I was so turned on I was practically hyperventilating.

He wiped his hand on the canvas and grabbed his erection. I cried out as he entered me in one swift thrust. With his hands gripping my hips, he drew himself back and then pounded into me with so much force, my hands slid forward on the canvas.

"Tell me if it's too much," he said, pulling out again.

His strokes became frantic, almost wild. My knees started to shake, and for the first time in my life, I was afraid to come. Afraid of how powerful it would be. I held back as long as I could but when Theo shouted my name, I exploded. An intense pleasure shot through me like an electric current, ripping a scream from my throat. As I started to come down, I felt Theo swell inside me as he found his release.

We collapsed to the canvas, looked at each other, and burst out laughing. His thick hair was covered in paint and sticking out in every direction. I'm sure mine looked the same. His face, which I hadn't touched, was speckled with dots of paint. No way my vag had escaped the splatter.

"Too bad Aiden hasn't put the sink in yet," he said, rubbing his hand down my arm.

"It's not my first time getting messy," I said pointing to a bucket of water under the worktable.

He raised an eyebrow at me, and I smiled. "I meant, I get messy all the time when I sculpt, and my studio didn't have a sink. If we clean our feet, we should make it to the shower with minimal fallout."

"You really are perfect," he said, pulling me close and wrapping his arms around me. "Thank you. This was just what I needed today."

He got to his feet and pulled me to mine. We stepped off the corner of the canvas onto the plastic sheeting and faced the entire work. To anyone else, it'd just be an erratic abstract with several feet and handprints. But as I studied the canvas, I could see the different ways we'd come together and apart. The area where Theo had made love to me slowly had the most paint.

He gripped my hand, and I glanced up to find him staring at the same place on the canvas. I wanted him to say something. That he'd felt the same powerful emotions I had. That maybe I wasn't the only one falling.

"This is the best gift anyone has ever given me," he said without taking his eyes from the canvas.

I squeezed his hand before I dropped it. "We should wash up before the paint dries."

He continued to study the canvas while I walked to the bucket, washed off my feet, and silently left the room.

Chapter Twenty-Six

Theo

I didn't recognize the cop who entered Marked on Tuesday. He hitched up his service belt as he walked toward the counter, hand draped casually on his weapon.

"Can I help you?" I asked.

"I'm looking for Theodoros Makris."

My blood chilled. No one called me by my full name except my parents and Aiden when he was being a prick. Up until the cop did, I assumed he was dropping in to schedule an appointment for when he was off duty.

"That's me," I said, laying my hands on the counter where he could see them. Aries stepped out from the back but did an about face when he saw the officer.

"Theodoros Makris," the cop said, pulling at the cuffs on his service belt, "you're under arrest for violating Section 18.2-371.3—"

Everything he said after that was lost. Panic roared as loud and fast as a freight train through my body. My breath came in desperate bursts and my vision narrowed, the black creeping in from all sides.

"The fuck he is," I heard Max shout as though he was on the other end of a tunnel.

I turned toward the sound of his voice and watched Max lunge at the cop. Aries rushed forward and yanked him back, but Max was strong and extremely pissed. More pissed than I'd ever seen him.

"Put your fucking cuffs away," he shouted.

"Sir, you need to stand back," the cop said.

"Hope you have two pairs of those," Max said, fighting off Aries's hold and stepping into the cop's face. "Cause the only way you're cuffing him is after you cuff me, asshole."

The officer obliged, turning Max around and shoving him to the floor before locking a pair of cuffs on his wrists. Seeing Max restrained flipped something in my brain. I could freak out later, but right now, I had to stop Max before he got himself in serious trouble.

"It's all right," I said, placing a hand on Max's shoulder as he struggled against the cuffs. I stepped between him and the cop and held my hands in front of me. Being cuffed behind my back was the last thing I wanted, so I hoped by offering the cop my hands in the front, he'd choose the easier option.

"This is bullshit," Max shouted behind me. "I don't care if he inked a fucking five-year-old, you don't need to cuff him."

"Max," I said, calmly, as the cop snapped the cuffs on my wrists. "Don't make this worse."

That seemed to deflate him. "Don't say anything until your lawyer arrives," he said as he rose to his feet.

"I don't have a lawyer," I said.

"Not a fucking word, Theo," he said.

Aries winked at me.

It was odd. Maybe he was trying to lighten the mood or send me some signal, but whatever it was, his meaning was lost on me.

The cop put his hand on my arm and Max's shoulder and guided us toward the door. His grip wasn't tight. Not like the cops who'd escorted me to and from places during my trial. It was more like the correctional officers after I'd proven to them enough times that I'd cooperate. I took it as a good sign.

We stepped onto the sidewalk, where a few people had stopped to gawk at the patrol car parked at the curb with lights flashing.

"Please, don't take him in," I said, motioning my chin toward Max. "He's calm now, right?"

"The hell I am," Max shouted.

"Watch your heads," the cop said, opening the back door.

Someone shouted my name, and I looked down Main Street. Aiden sprinted toward us with Poppy trailing behind him, pumping her arms as she tried to catch up. No telling what either of them would do, let alone the pair of them.

"Let's go," I told the cop as I slid into the back. "Max is tame compared to those two."

The cop slammed the door and hauled ass to the driver's seat, pulling away from the curb before Aiden reached us. The officer looked in the rearview mirror and gunned it down Main Street toward the police station. I turned in my seat to peer out the back. Aiden had his cell to his ear, and Poppy was running back down the block toward her hearse.

Max sat perfectly still beside me.

"Did you do that on purpose so you could ride with me?" I asked.

"I lost my head there for a minute, but since I'm here, I'm doing whatever I can to help you through this until we can call a lawyer."

"Pretty sure Aiden already has," I said as the cop turned into the station parking lot and pulled into a spot facing Main Street.

By the time the officer removed us from the cruiser, Poppy and Aiden were on the sidewalk in front of the station. No doubt they'd broken a few traffic laws to get there so fast. Poppy stepped toward me, but I shook my head. She shrank back to Aiden's side and watched as the cop led us to the entrance.

"Everly is on her way," Aiden shouted after us.

The cop put Max in a holding cell but walked me straight into an interview room and closed the door.

"Have a seat," he said motioning to one of the uncomfortable wooden chairs. I did as he asked and tried not to hurl while he read me my Miranda rights. Just as he finished, the door flew open and Everly Hendricks breezed in.

"I don't believe we've met before," she said to the cop as she extended her slender hand. "I'm Everly Hendricks. Mr. Markis's attorney."

The cop looked stunned and left her hand in the air an uncomfortable moment before he shook it. "Officer Stafford," he said, studying her carefully. "How did you get back here?"

"I told Peggy you were interviewing my client without representation. She sent me right back."

"We haven't started the interview," he said, sitting down in a chair so close to me our knees brushed.

"Great," Everly said, pulling a chair from around the table and wedging it between us. Officer Stafford and I were both tall, and Everly was a good five foot eight without her heels. "Let's get started," she said as though she wasn't practically sitting in both our laps. "Could you please tell me why you brought Mr. Markis here today?"

Office Stafford cleared his throat and had the decency to scoot back a foot. Everly adjusted her chair enough so our legs weren't pressed together.

"Your client has been accused of violating Section 18.2-371.3, which is—"

"I'm well aware of Section 18.2-371.3. I'm confused why he wasn't released on summons," Everly said.

"He's a convicted felon, Ms. Hendricks."

"With a spotless criminal record since he served his time."

"Look, ma'am, we take repeat offenders seriously in Peace Falls."

Everly's eyes hardened. "Theo is not a repeat offender. He has never once been arrested for tattooing a minor. And if you knew anything about Peace Falls, you'd know his felony conviction was based on a technicality, not criminal intent."

"Tell that to the guy he killed."

"I'm sure my brother would have agreed," Everly snapped.

Officer Stafford looked utterly perplexed.

"The guy I killed was Logan Hendricks," I said. "Ms. Hendricks's brother."

"My brother died in the accident that led to Mr. Makris's unjust conviction," Everly amended. "Now, can we please discuss the current charges?"

Officer Stafford shifted in his seat and shuffled some papers in front of him. At Marked the man had remained calm and controlled while Max attempted to rip his head off, but Everly had clearly knocked him off his axis. "He tattooed a sixteen-year-old without parental consent."

"Allegedly," she said.

Officer Stafford flipped open a folder and slid a single photograph across the table. A lower neck tattoo of a Sagittarius zodiac sign. Sarah.

"Do you recognize this?" he asked me.

"Don't answer that," Everly said.

Officer Stafford shrugged, regaining some of his composure. He pulled out another photograph and slid it across the table. "How about her?"

In the photo, Sarah looked straight ahead. With her face scrubbed clean of makeup, she looked much younger than she had on Sunday. Far too young to get a tattoo without her parents.

"Her name is Angela Lacosta. Does that ring a bell?" Officer Stafford asked.

The A was her initial, not Aries's. I leaned into Everly to tell her about the ID, but she shook her head.

"Do you have Ms. Lacosta's statement?" Everly asked.

Officer Stafford pulled out another piece of paper and started reading. "Miss Lacosta's parents discovered the tattoo this morning. When they questioned their daughter, she told them she received it on Sunday at Marked in Peace Falls from a tattoo artist named Theo."

"Have you questioned Ms. Lacosta?" Everly asked.

"No," Officer Stafford said, sliding the paper back into the folder. "Miss Lacosta's parents made the statement and filed charges. They supplied both photographs as well."

Everly nodded. "So, all your evidence is based on a second-hand statement and images brought to the station?"

"We'll be taking Miss Lacosta's statement this afternoon and official photos. She had a chemistry test today, and her parents wanted to wait until after school to bring her to the station. Miss Lacosta also informed her parents that another employee at Marked named Aries could corroborate her story. I'll be taking his statement this afternoon as well."

"So, you arrested my client at his place of employment before you obtained statements from the alleged victim or the first-hand witness?"

"As I said before, Mr. Markis is a convicted felon."

"I'm well aware," Everly said, leaning back in her chair. "I'm also aware that standard practice is to issue a summons and release for non-violent class-one misdemeanors, which maybe you didn't know since you're still in your probationary period."

"How would you—" he started but stopped.

"I suggest you release Mr. Markis before I file a complaint on his behalf."

"What about Max?" I asked.

Everly's answering smile looked a little scary. "I'm happy to represent him as well, but I wanted to give Officer Stafford the opportunity to reconsider issuing a citation before I called Chief Fitzwilliam to let him know his brother-in-law is being detained at the station. Assuming Peggy hasn't already."

Officer Stafford kept his face emotionless but paled slightly.

"Theo," Everly said, turning to me. "Isn't Chief Fitzwilliam's father a student in the art class you volunteer to teach at the community center?"

I nodded.

"Got to love a small town," Everly said with a genuine smile.

"He'll need to sign the summons," Officer Stafford said, shuffling the papers again.

"Of course." Everly uncapped a pen that probably cost more than my rent. "I suggest you uncuff him first."

I rubbed my wrists after Officer Stafford removed the cuffs. My hands shook as I signed my name on the bottom of the summons and returned Everly's pen.

"We'll appear in court at the requested time. I'd also like a copy of the statement from Ms. Lacosta's parents and any you obtain prior to the court date. My email address and fax are here," she said sliding her card across the table to Officer Stafford and tapping it with her red fingernail.

Officer Stafford nodded. "I'll get the parents' statement for you now."

After he copied the statement and collected Max from the holding cell, Officer Stafford walked us to the crowded waiting room. Aiden, Cal, who was still in his scrubs, Rowan, and Poppy rushed toward us.

"What the hell happened?" Cal asked as Poppy wrapped me in a hug.

I pulled her close and everything inside me calmed enough I could draw my first deep breath in an hour.

"Outside," Everly said in a voice that left no room for argument. We trudged into the parking lot, then followed Everly to the building two doors down that housed the firm where she worked. When we entered the lobby, a young woman popped up from behind the reception desk.

"Ms. Hendricks, I'm sorry the conference room is booked," she said.

"That's ok, Hattie. I'll be speaking with Mr. Markis in my office. Everyone else can wait here."

"The hell we will," Aiden said. "Ev, I'm not—"

"Going to be a potential witness to the conversation I need to have with Theo. Got it?" She made eye contact with each of them.

Rowan sank onto one of the leather sofas and Cal took a seat beside her. Max leaned against a wall. Aiden wrapped his arms around Poppy and pulled her onto his lap on one of the chairs. A flicker of anger shot through me before she elbowed him in the stomach. That's my girl. My heart ached. She deserved so much better than me.

"Hands off," she yelled, squirming.

"Simmer, Hell Cat, before I pop a boner. I'll let you go once Everly locks her office door."

Poppy called my name, but I turned and followed Everly. She motioned for me to enter a room at the end of the hall.

"Should I lock this?" she asked, pointing to the door as I took a seat in one of the plush chairs in front of her desk.

"Probably," I said. "But no guarantees someone won't pick it."

She snicked the lock and took a seat next to me instead of behind the desk. "Tell me what happened."

I blew out a breath. "I tattooed the girl, but she showed me an ID of a nineteen-year-old named Sarah. The picture on the ID was close except the girl had brown hair and a fuller face. I could feel something was off."

"So why'd you give her the tattoo?"

"The new guy at Marked brought her in, and she already had ink."

"Aries?" she asked, scribbling on a legal pad she'd pulled from the stack of papers on her desk.

"Yes," I said. My stomach sank. Finally, that odd wink made sense. He'd planned the whole thing. "I think he set me up."

"Why would he do that?"

"He was interested in Poppy before she and I got together."

Everly nodded.

"How bad is this?" I asked.

"It's a class one misdemeanor. Usually, these are just a fine up to $2,500, but as Officer Stafford said, you're a convicted felon." Her eyes softened and I braced myself. "There's a possibility of jail time."

"How much?"

"Up to a year."

My vision swam. I dropped my head between my knees and focused on taking deep breaths.

"I won't let that happen," Everly said, rubbing my back. "You checked her ID. I bet she has a sister or a cousin named Sarah who's nineteen."

"Sagittarius," I forced out. "What are the dates for the Sagittarius zodiac?"

"Um, I'm not sure how that relates but let me check." After a few moments she said, "November 22nd to December 21st."

I yanked my hair. "The birthdate on the ID was in October."

"Theo, not knowing the specific dates of the zodiac signs isn't a crime. Besides you said she already had a tattoo."

"Of her initial. She told me it was A for Aries, and I believed her."

"Because that's believable," Everly said, keeping her hand on my shoulder when I straightened. "We can fight this. Just so I have all the facts, did she pay with a credit card? If that had a different name, we'll need an explanation."

"She didn't pay. I did it as a favor to Aries."

"Did she sign any paperwork? A consent form?"

I nodded. "She signed with the name on the ID."

"Did anyone other than Aries see you give her the tattoo?"

"Only about five cameras."

"Marked has cameras?"

"Some clients have crossed the line before. Gotten physical over pricing or the way a piece turned out. Max has assault charges in his past, so he wanted to document any altercations."

"Smart. That could work for us. It means there's proof you did the tattoo, so there's no sense arguing that, but there's also probably proof you checked her ID."

But would it matter? I was a felon who'd tattooed a sixteen-year-old girl. Someone without a record would probably pay a small fine and be done, if they were convicted at all. But many people in Peace Falls thought I hadn't served enough time for Logan's death and would use any opportunity to put me behind bars.

"Look, Everly. I appreciate your help today. No doubt I'd be in custody right now if you hadn't shown up, but I don't want to waste your time. I'm screwed."

I stood, unlocked the door, and hurried to the reception area. Everly ran behind me, her four-inch heels clicking on the shiny wood floor. I walked straight to Poppy, who was pacing the room, and pulled her into my arms. I'd be damned if I took anyone else down with me. I breathed deep, savoring her lavender scent one last time.

"What's happening?" she asked, looking up at me with those snaring eyes.

I took a step back. "The inevitable. You can't be with me. I'll only hold you back."

"What?" Poppy said, her eyes widening. "Are you breaking up with me?"

I nodded. I was. In front of everyone. Because I knew if we were alone, I wouldn't be able to let her go.

Cal jumped to his feet. "The hell you are."

"Yeah, I'm with Cal on this one," Aiden said, standing. "You can't dump his future sister-in-law in front of him and not expect to get your ass kicked."

"I'm not dumping her," I snapped at them. "I'm not," I said taking Poppy's hands. "I'm letting you go."

She yanked her hands from mine. "What if I don't want to be let go?"

"Theo, this has been a stressful day," Max said, quietly. "I'm sure you're spinning to the worst possible scenario. Don't do anything rash."

"He's right," Everly said. "This could all be resolved with a single court date."

"Or I could spend another year in jail," I yelled.

Cal staggered back, bumping into the couch before flopping onto it. Max and Rowan looked near tears. Aiden paled, then turned green. But Poppy stared me straight in the eyes.

"Whatever it is," she said, stepping closer. "However long it takes to straighten out, it doesn't matter. I'm with you."

I shook my head.

"At least tell me why?"

"Because I love you. I love you so much I can't stand the thought of the life you'll have with me. I won't survive that guilt. If you care about me at all, you'll keep your distance."

"Care about you?" she yelled. "I fucking love you too."

"Then stay away from me," I said and walked out the front door before anyone could stop me. I headed toward Marked where my truck was parked. When Max caught up with me, I ignored him.

"What the hell were you thinking?" he asked.

"I checked her ID," I said.

"I'm sure you didn't do anything to deserve the charge. I meant breaking up with Poppy."

"It was the right thing to do, and you know it."

Max was silent a while, his hands gripping the back of his neck as we continued toward Marked. Eventually, he muttered something.

"What's that?"

"I was asking the good Lord to help me get your head out of your ass." He didn't say another word the rest of the way.

Chapter Twenty-Seven

Poppy

THE DOOR HADN'T EVEN closed behind Theo before the pain crawled into every cell and took over. I'm not sure how long I stood in that law office before Aiden picked me up fireman style and carried me to Cal's SUV. I don't remember the drive back to Sullivan Street or getting out of the car or walking into Cal's house and sitting on the sofa. Maybe Aiden carried me again.

I hadn't heard anything since Theo said he loved me and then told me to stay away. My brain was still trying to reconcile those two statements and didn't have space for anything else. I'd heard both plenty of times. Just never together. OK, so Theo was the first nonrelative male to utter those three words in my direction. But based on my limited romantic experience, aka observing Rowan and Cal, you usually want to be *with* the person you love.

Unless the person you love is me, apparently.

Eventually, I felt something warm in my hands and looked down at the mug releasing wisps of steam at my face. Rowan wrapped her fingers over mine and lifted the mug to my lips. I drank automatically. The tea had a kick I wasn't expecting. It burned my throat on the way down and made me cough.

"What the hell is this?" I asked.

"My granny swears by a cuppa with whiskey for just about anything," Aiden said.

"That's disgusting," I said, handing the mug to my sister.

"Got you talking, didn't it?" Aiden said. "I was starting to think you'd become one of those comatose people who live in psych wards."

"Catatonic," Chris said, walking out of the kitchen with a bowl of chips. "Comatose is for people in comas."

Aiden snapped his fingers. "That's right. Is there any dip?"

"What kind of messed up party are y'all throwing right now?" I asked.

The front door opened, and Cal ran in. I hadn't realized he'd left, or noticed when Chris arrived, for that matter. "Theo's not home yet," Cal said.

Aiden pulled his phone from his pocket and opened an app. "Looks like he's still at Marked."

Cal leaned over Aiden's shoulder and let out a relieved sigh. "I'm sure Max is with him."

"I wouldn't mind cooling off a bit before we head over there," Aiden said. "Enjoy this party a little," he added, winking at me.

"What if Max isn't with him?" I asked, my voice rising to a pitch I hadn't heard since elementary school. "He can't be alone." I stood before I remembered Theo wanted nothing to do with me. Maybe if I was sweet like Rowan, he'd be willing to lean on me. He probably figured I'd make things worse, yelling at the injustice of it all instead of being a source of comfort.

"Easy, Hell Cat," Aiden said, placing his meaty hand on my shoulder. He might have done me a solid earlier when I turned into a statue, but I was getting sick of him manhandling me.

"Do you know what he does to himself?" I yelled as I yanked Aiden's hand off my shoulder.

Chris and Rowan looked baffled, but Aiden and Cal nodded.

"You knew and you never made him get help? Some friends you are."

Cal ducked his head and Skye dashed over to him. Rowan shot me her mom look, the one she used whenever I crossed the line from irreverent to hurtful or potentially illegal.

"We're all fucked up," Aiden said. "Theo just has a creative way of showing it."

"All y'all need therapy," I said, crossing my arms over my chest. "But for now, which one of you is going to Marked to make sure Theo doesn't cut himself? Someone needs to, and he doesn't want me."

Rowan's eyes widened, further confirming she knew nothing about Theo's self-harm history. Then she turned her focus on me. "You know that's not true. He told you he loved you."

"Yeah, well, not enough. I get it. I'm not the most lovable person."

"I'm still catching up with what's going on," Chris said. "But from what I'm hearing, Theo's more messed up than I thought. Whatever happened has nothing to do with you being lovable, Pop. But for the record, you're one of the most loveable people I know, and I'm pretty sure Theo would agree."

I didn't want to cry in front of everyone, so I pushed past my siblings and headed for the door. I figured I had about thirty seconds.

Soon after my dad died, I'd learned how to hold my tears. My eyes would start to burn a little, and I'd imagine I was a semi-aquatic rodent, the kind who built dams in rivers and streams with sticks. Yes, I know their name. But even kid me knew better than to call myself a beaver. I'd made a point at an early age to learn curse words and inappropriate slang to nettle Rowan whenever I could. So, I'd imagine myself as a semi-aquatic rodent, holding back my tears until I could duck into the janitor's closet at school or hide in the shed behind our house. The more I wanted to cry, the less time I had to get somewhere private.

This felt like holding back Niagara Falls. If I ran, I could maybe make it out of sight of Cal's house before my face got all blotchy and snotty. Too bad Lauren and Cammie rolled up to the curb at the exact moment the floodgates opened. They rushed me like a pair of perky linebackers and tackled me in a double hug.

"He's just scared," Cammie said, squeezing me so hard my boobs ached. "Give him time to process the arrest. He'll come around."

Guess Rowan had been texting the entire time I checked out.

"He told you he loves you," Lauren added, rubbing my back. "Focus on that."

"He only said that because he felt bad for dumping me." I sobbed into Cammie's shoulder. I was probably getting snot on the fluffy pink sweater she'd tossed on over her scrubs, which for some reason made me feel a smidge better. She looked like a wannabe Muppet. I was doing her and the rest of Peace Falls a favor, though I had to admit the sweater felt really nice.

"I don't care if he's your best friend, Caleb," Rowan shouted behind me. "Let's go, Chris."

"Oh shit," Lauren said. "You've triggered the Stevens Suicide Squad."

"The what?" I asked, lifting my head from Cammie's comfy shoulder.

"It's when someone wrongs one of you and the other siblings go all Kill Bill," Lauren explained as Chris shoved past Aiden to join Rowan on the porch.

Cammie clapped her hands and did a little bounce thing that should have looked deranged but somehow felt on brand for her. "I've been dying to see it ever since Lauren told me you filled Rowan's ex's apartment with dog poop."

"Brad-hole deserved it. Theo doesn't," I sniffed. "And you can't mix movie metaphors like that, Lauren."

"It fits," Lauren said as Rowan wiggled away from Cal, possibly throwing an elbow, and started down the stairs with Chris.

"Stop," I yelled. "Stand down."

They both halted but their fury remained. Rowan's face had turned almost as red as her hair. Chris had his hands fisted at his sides. He looked ready to break someone, and I wouldn't put it past Theo to let him.

"Do not mess with Theo," I said, drawing myself up as much as I could to point my finger in my giant brother's face.

"Don't listen to her," Rowan said. "She's love blind."

"So are you," I snapped, which seemed to get their attention. Rowan's face dropped down to level pink, and Chris's nostrils stopped flaring like a raging bull. I may not be everyone's favorite flavor, but I've never questioned my family's love for me.

Of course, the damn tears decided to start up again. Chris glared at Aiden and Cal who had snuck behind him on either side. Amateurs. As far as brutality went, it was me, then Rowan, then Chris, who had the soul of a kitten despite his football physique.

I took a deep breath and got the waterworks under control before I spoke again. "He hurt me, but this isn't the same. I'm just collateral to the damage he's doing to himself. Plus, he'd probably like it if you took a swing at him. He'll want someone to hurt him if he hasn't already done it himself."

"She's right," Cal said, rubbing his forehead.

"Fine," Chris said. "I'll just plastic wrap his toilet and mess with his shampoo."

"Just remember I own the house," Aiden shouted after Chris as he cut across Twill's backyard.

"I'll make sure he doesn't do anything permanent, unless it's to that hideous carpet in the bedroom," Rowan said, following him.

"Promise me one of you will stay with Theo," I said to Aiden and Cal.

Aiden surprised me by pulling me into a hug. He kept his thick arms around me until his warmth had me full-out sobbing. The big lump had a soft side and for some reason he'd decided to share it with me. I got a good burst of tears out before he started laughing.

"What's wrong with you?" Lauren snapped.

Aiden pointed at Cal, who looked like he wanted to murder someone, and Lauren started cackling right along with Aiden.

"Hell Cat will claw her way out of this," Aiden said, stepping out of the hug, but pulling me to his side. "But if you can't contain your brotherly rage, Cal, you should stay here."

My future brother-in-law did look as pissed as Chris, which meant I wasn't just some package deal that came with Rowan. He actually liked me. I rushed Cal, burrowing my face in his scrubs. He patted my back awkwardly and cleared his throat.

"Go," I said, stepping back. "Theo needs you. I'll let Rowan and Chris in so they don't break a window."

Cal nodded, still looking miffed, and headed for his SUV. Aiden followed him, still chuckling.

"I know you're heartbroken and all, but I'm really excited to see the Squad in action," Cammie said, looping her arm in mine as we cut across Twill's yard. I caught a glimpse of him holding back a curtain in one of the upstairs windows, which was cracked despite the cold. Great. Now everyone in class would know Theo and I had imploded.

"So, Theo told you he loves you and you have a key to his place?" Lauren asked.

"That sounds serious," Cammie said, squeezing my arm.

"Don't read too much into it. I only have a key because he lets me use his studio," I said as we crossed into Theo's yard where Chris was digging a brick out of the walkway that wrapped around the house. "I have a key,"

I shouted and ran, dragging Cammie with me since she refused to let go of my arm.

Chris dropped the brick.

I glared at Rowan, who stood by the new sliding glass door, apparently waiting for Chris to smash it. "You were supposed to keep him from doing something permanent."

She shrugged. "I'm pissed at Aiden for holding you back at Everly's office. He needs to stop handling you like a rag doll whenever he wants."

"He's the worst," Lauren said.

I rolled my eyes as I dug through my jacket pocket for Theo's key. "I don't agree with this," I said as I unlocked the sliding door. "Don't touch anything in the studio. It's mostly mine." I'd go through the house after they got the bloodlust out of their systems and undo whatever they did. Our retribution pranks were usually temporary in nature, though the fact Chris had gone for a brick had me a little worried.

"Do you think we have time to drive to the store for deer pee spray?" Chris asked as he walked toward the kitchen.

Perhaps I'd underestimated their wrath.

"Wow, they don't play do they?" Cammie said.

I couldn't answer her. I'd left the canvas Theo and I painted on the floor to dry after I coated it with sealant. When I saw it right after, I thought it showed the passion between us. Now, it just looked chaotic, the image fractured and without a center.

"Interesting," Lauren said, joining Cammie and me. "Is that his or yours?"

"Ours," I said, the word burning my throat.

Cammie and Lauren both tilted their heads and looked at the canvas.

Lauren laughed. "You little freak."

"I don't get it," Cammie said.

"You want to build a bonfire in the backyard and light it up?" Lauren asked.

"No." I pulled a drop cloth from the cabinets and tossed it over the canvas. I didn't need Rowan or Chris figuring it out as fast as Lauren had.

"Does Theo even live here?" Chris asked, stepping back into the studio. "The cabinets are practically empty. I'll have to go home for plastic wrap."

"I can short his sheets," Rowan said, joining us. "But that's the best I can do with how little stuff he has unless I ruin his clothes and books. I'm not really comfortable doing that. Maybe we should grab deer pee and douse the sofa."

"I don't know, Ann," Chris said, scratching his chin where he had actual scruff. When did that happen? Clearly, I'd been Theo-focused for too long. "This place is sad enough. I don't think I have it in me to ruin his only place to sit. Sorry, Pop."

Rowan put her hands on her hips. "He needs to replace the sofa anyway. Let Lauren and Cammie decide."

Cammie and Lauren glanced at me and waited until I motioned them toward the kitchen. Knowing them, they'd have agreed with Chris without snooping around, but I figured Rowan needed convincing. I followed behind them as they opened every cabinet and drawer. They stopped in the living room to take in the floral couch and the books stacked on the floor before continuing down the hallway where they split up to look in all the rooms.

"Who only owns three towels?" Lauren asked from the bathroom.

"Three?" I asked, joining her. A fluffy white towel hung beside the worn, faded one I'd used before. I ran my fingers along the soft fabric. It felt like a fancy hotel towel, the kind you wanted to take home but would cost a fortune if they discovered it missing. I opened the closet and found the other ratty towel folded neatly inside.

"This is nice," Cammie said from Theo's bedroom.

We all joined her, and Lauren gave an appreciative nod. "This one isn't bad."

"If I hadn't been staying over," I said. "I bet he'd still be on an air mattress or maybe a cheap foam mattress on the floor."

"Sorry, Rowan," Lauren said. "I'm with Chris. You should leave him alone."

Cammie nodded.

"Whatever," Rowan said, throwing her hands in the air. "Come on, Chris. We're making monkey bread with bacon for Poppy."

They locked arms and walked down the hall together.

"Your sister comes up with some odd combos, but they always work," Cammie said. "I think they could have gotten away with putting deer pee on this carpet though. They'd be doing Theo a favor since Aiden would have to replace it."

"Guess they figured it'd be more effective to show you their love with food," Lauren said.

Just like Theo had showed his by constantly trying to make my life better. Finding art shows for us to attend. Knowing my favorite foods and surprising me with them. Making his bedroom comfortable for me to stay over. And that's when I knew what I had to do.

"Rowan and Chris had it backwards," I said. "We don't need to trash Theo's house. We need to make it nicer. The only reason he bought furniture for the bedroom was for me. The new towel in the bathroom was probably meant for me too. He doesn't think he deserves anything for himself."

"So, you want to get back at him by decorating his house?" Cammie asked.

"No, I want to show him he's loved. That he's worthy." And that I would never abandon Theo like his parents had. That I can be the kind of woman he wants when life got hard, the kind he'd never imagine pushing away.

"With decorative pillows?" Cammie said, looking at the bed, which, probably could use a throw pillow or two.

"Most guys I know hate those," Lauren said.

"Focus," I snapped, shaking her shoulders. "I don't know how long we have before Theo gets home. I need some framing wood, kitchen crap, and a fuck-ton of towels, preferably white or navy to go with the yellow. Maybe a chair or two. Pillows optional. Oh, and snacks. The sweeter the better."

"Ok," Lauren said with the authoritative tone of a boss. "I have no idea what framing wood is, but I can handle the towels and basic kitchen supplies. Cam, you go with Poppy and try to find some decent furniture at the consignment shop in Jericho. I'll call Rowan and tell her to bring over treats once she's cooled down."

This was going to work. It had to. Because the more I thought about life without Theo, the more certain I was my heart wouldn't survive.

CHAPTER TWENTY-EIGHT

Theo

ARIES WASN'T IN THE shop when we arrived at Marked, but footsteps thudded in the apartment above. It sounded like someone pacing.

I needed to watch what the cameras had caught before I told Max my suspicions. "Can you pull up the security footage from around 4 on Sunday?" I asked.

Max headed straight for the system and found the recording but didn't move from the screen. I peered over his shoulder and watched the entire interaction. The doubt on my face, the anger on Aries's when I first refused. The cameras had caught me checking the ID before giving Sarah/Angela the tattoo, so I guess that's something.

When the recording reached the point where Aries and Angela left, Max stopped the video and yanked his phone from his pocket.

"Heads up," he said to the person on the other end. "I'm firing Aries and evicting him."

"Max?" I asked.

Max turned his back to me. "Effective now. He's never paid rent," he said after a brief pause. "He's a guest, not a tenant. I'll give him an hour to get his shit and clear out, but after that he's your problem."

Max ended the call and tossed his phone on the counter.

"What's going on? Who was that?"

Max rubbed his forehead as he walked into the back. "Aries's parole officer. I'm not sure I can go up there without doing something immoral."

A phone rang upstairs and both of us glanced at the ceiling.

"Aren't you worried he could end up back inside?" I asked.

Max glared at me. "He set you up. I'm throwing that punk out on his ass. Whatever happens to him after is none of my concern."

I'd never seen this side of Max. He was always so kind and forgiving. He believed in second and third and even fourth chances. "I don't want you to do anything you'll regret."

"The only thing I regret is getting you into this shit by bringing him here. He fucked with my family. There's no coming back from that."

Hearing Max call me family filled me with warmth. My parents had abandoned me when I needed them most; my dad's disgust still haunted my thoughts. But this man had accepted me at my worst and done everything he could to help me.

"For goodness' sake, Theo, don't look so surprised." Max pulled me into a one-armed hug and thumped my back. "You know I consider you one of my kids."

"What the hell, Max," Aries shouted, throwing open the door that separated the apartment from the shop. "You're kicking me out? I thought you were decent. You pretend to be all holy and shit, but you're a dick like everyone else."

I was grateful for every burpee before breakfast I'd ever done since it took every muscle I had to hold Max back.

Aries put his hands up and stepped back toward the stairs. "Hey, no need for that. If you don't want me here, I'm out."

"What did you think would happen?" Max yelled, still struggling against me. "You bring a teenager to my shop to get back at Theo. Do you have any fucking clue what you've done? He could go back in because of you. What were you even doing with that girl in the first place? I bet you slept with her, you piece of shit. I should call that girl's parents and tell them to file statutory rape charges."

Aries jabbed his finger in the air. "That's out of line. I'd never rape anyone."

"Age of consent is eighteen in Virginia, dumbass," Max yelled.

Aries's eyes widened before his face went completely blank. "I don't know what you're talking about. I don't mess around with high schoolers."

For a moment, I believed him. Angela could have told him she was nineteen too. But that wink. It didn't sit right. Still, the thought of making someone homeless, even a shithead like Aries, made my stomach tightened. "Maybe—" I started.

Max let out a hollow laugh. "The only good thing about being a re-formed piece of shit is being able to recognize a current one. I gave you a chance, Aries. You blew it. Grab your stuff and get the hell out of my sight before Theo gets tired and can't hold me back no more."

"Whatever," Aries said, heading for the stairs. "This town sucks any-way." He slammed the door behind him, locking it from the inside, and thudded up to the apartment.

"Thanks, son," Max said patting my arm. "You can let go. I'm good, but if Aries hasn't left in an hour, I'm calling Officer Stafford back here."

I followed Max to the waiting room, relieved to put a little distance between him and the door to the apartment. We reached the counter just as the door opened and Cal and Aiden walked in.

"Could have used you a little sooner," Max said, setting the timer on his phone. "For a second there, I didn't know if Theo could keep me from Aries."

"The new guy?" Cal asked. "What'd he do?"

"The fucker—"

I elbowed Max in the stomach. "There's only one of me," I said calmly.

Max nodded and pressed his lips together. After he let out a breath he said, "I'm in a bad mood is all."

"Same, man," Aiden said, flipping through a binder of popular designs on the counter. "Wouldn't mind punching someone though, if you need me to, just not Theo."

"I'd like to take a swing at him," Cal said as he flipped through another binder beside Aiden. "But since he loves hurting himself, he'd probably like it."

Max's mouth fell open. "What the hell is he talking about?" he asked me.

"Theo cuts himself when he's upset," Aiden said in a bored tone. "He claims it makes him feel better. I guess taking a punch to the face would work too, so you better not, Cal."

I glared at my two best friends, but they kept flipping through the designs like they were about to select a spur-of-the-moment tattoo. Nothing good could come from Max knowing about my cutting. He'd worry himself sick and probably force me to strip once a week to make sure I wasn't hiding anything.

"What?" Max looked from Aiden to me, then over to Cal, who looked up from the binder and nodded. Max's hands shook slightly before he gripped the counter. "How long?"

"They're making a bigger deal out of it than it is," I said.

They all ignored me.

"He started that shit while he was waiting for his trial," Aiden said.

Max glared at Aiden, then Cal. "And you're just telling me this now?"

Aiden closed the binder and looked Max in the eyes. "No offense, but we didn't know you well enough to tell you. We've kept tabs on him. If he'd gotten worse at any point, we'd have filled you in."

"But we figured anyone who'd get themselves handcuffed to protect Theo was someone we could trust to keep an extra eye on him," Cal added.

"How did I miss it?" Max asked.

"He got good at hiding it by the time you met him," Cal said, walking away from the counter and staring at the framed photographs of some of my best work. He looked completely at ease, strolling around the shop, but I knew he wasn't. He had his hands shoved in his pockets, no doubt balled in fists. "You have to know what to look for. If he cuts his legs, his walk changes."

Max paled and gripped the counter harder.

"Go ahead and puke if you need to, Max," Aiden said. "I know I did when I found out."

"I punched a hole in my closet door," Cal said casually. "Cost me my security deposit."

"Y'all never told me that," I said. I didn't think I could feel any worse today, but I did.

Cal and Aiden looked everywhere except at me. Max took deep breaths through his nose and out his mouth. Gradually, the gray left his complexion. Throughout the conversation, Aries's footsteps had pounded overhead, but in the quiet, I could hear every drawer he opened and closed.

"Sounds like a herd of elephants up there," Aiden said after an uncomfortable stretch of silence.

"Kid better hurry the hell up," Max mumbled.

As if Aries had heard him, the sound of boots thudding down the stairs echoed through Marked. Aries walked through the front room without sparing a word for any of us and out the door carrying everything he owned in a trash bag before turning and giving the bird to the shop window. He spat on the sidewalk and headed toward the bus stop down the street.

Max gripped my shoulder. "When was the last time you hurt yourself?" he asked, staring me hard in the eyes.

"Recently," Aiden answered for me.

"They're making it sound like I'm suicidal or something," I said. "I'm not. It's just—"

"Unacceptable," Max said. His grip tightened on my shoulder, and he pointed a finger at my face with his other hand. "If I find so much as a paper cut on you, I'm taking you in for a psych hold, got it?"

I nodded.

"We're not done talking about this, but it's been a hell of a day. I'm canceling the rest of our appointments, and you're coming home with me."

I shook my head. "You have my word, Max. I won't hurt myself. Go be with your girls. Don't worry about me."

"I don't think there's any way I'll ever stop worrying about you, Theo," Max said rubbing his forehead. "It's not in a parent's nature."

"It's not in your nature," I said. Patera had no problem turning off his concern. "And it means the world to me to hear you say that. Go home. I'll make the calls and lock up. It's good for me to be busy."

Max glanced at Cal and Aiden, who both nodded. He blew out a breath and headed for the door.

"You good?" I called after him. "I'd never seen him this upset, and I worried today might have tempted his sobriety. "You're not going to do anything stupid either, right?"

He shook his head. "I'm going home and loving up on my girls. You call me anytime. Middle of the night. I don't care. Got it?"

I nodded and he opened the door. It looked like he was fighting against a current when he stepped over the threshold and pulled it shut behind him. I kept an eye on him until he got into his car and took off in the opposite direction Aries had gone.

Cal glanced at his phone and frowned. "Mind if I go too? I need to let out Skye." He glanced at Aiden who sank into a chair like he intended to stay awhile.

"You should head home. I'm fine," I told him after Cal left.

"Can't. Left my car on Sullivan Street. I need a ride to your house. I can walk from there."

"And you didn't think to get one from Cal?"

Aiden shrugged. Once I finished canceling appointments and locking up, he followed me to my truck. He pretended to mess around with his phone on the drive to my house, but he kept glancing at me and biting his fingernails like he always does when he's nervous and doesn't have a napkin to shred.

At least the windows were dark when I pulled up. I half expected Rowan, or even Poppy, to be waiting inside. An icy wind cut through me as I walked to the door. I just wanted to crawl into bed, which hopefully still smelled like Poppy, and fall apart. Unfortunately, Aiden wouldn't stop treating me like a toddler who couldn't be trusted with a metal fork. Instead of heading toward Sullivan Street, he trailed behind me like a shadow.

"Gotta take a leak," he said.

Before I could unlock the door, Cal tromped around the house with Skye. "This is ridiculous," I said as they worked their way through the yard and up the steps. "I don't need either of you to babysit me. Let alone both of you and the dog."

"Yeah, well, we need you," Cal said, staring at his feet. "And we're making sure you're safe."

"Sorry, man." Aiden gave my shoulder a friendly thump as he grabbed my keys, unlocked the door, and walked past me.

I sighed and motioned for Cal to go ahead of me into the house. There was no point telling them yet again that I wasn't suicidal and never had been. If anything, I needed more years than the average person to atone for what I'd done. But I did feel the urge to cut myself, if for no other reason than it would confirm my breakup with Poppy. Too bad Max would drag my ass to the nearest psych ward if I did.

When I entered the house, my mouth fell open. The couch was the same shape but had somehow changed from floral to dark gray. I walked closer and pulled on the fabric. It snapped back as soon as I released it. A low black coffee table sat before it with a small abstract sculpture I recognized as Poppy's.

"Good call on the slipcover," Cal said, collapsing on the couch. "Looks nice."

"What the hell's a slipcover and how'd it get on my couch?" I asked.

"Probably the same way you got a new shower curtain and a toothbrush holder," Aiden said from the bathroom doorway.

"What?" I asked, pushing past him into the bathroom. Someone had replaced the plastic shower curtain I'd bought at the dollar store with a fabric one that somehow worked with the mustard-colored tiles. The towel racks held plush navy towels in all sizes, and my toothbrush stood upright in a porcelain holder.

"Looks like they hit the kitchen too," Cal called. "No more plastic forks. You can eat your microwaved meals like a civilized person."

"The bedroom is pretty much the same," Aiden said from down the hall. "Except for the painting."

My heart sank to my stomach. I knew without looking that Poppy had framed the canvas we'd painted together and hung it over the bed like she'd planned. She wasn't giving up on us. I yanked the new shower curtain aside, collapsed on the edge of the tub, and put my head in my hands. Nails clicked softly on the tile floor before Skye shoved her big gray head onto my lap.

"I figured they'd mess the place up," Aiden said, walking down the hall. "Rowan and Chris were pissed. But I guess making it nice is the equivalent for you."

His thudding footsteps stopped right outside the bathroom. I knew he was watching me, but I couldn't lift my head from Skye's fur.

"Rowan and Chris didn't do this," Cal said, a few moments later, his voice echoing off the bathroom tiles. "They've been baking all afternoon. Chris dropped off a ton of food earlier."

"Ah," Aiden said. "No wonder Theo's a mess. Hell Cat's sending him a message."

I finally lifted my head and found them both crammed into the small space between the sink and linen closet.

"When you punish yourself, I don't think you realize how much it hurts the people who love you," Aiden said, yanking on a fingernail. "I can look past all the hurt you've caused me over the years because I understand where you're coming from. But the pain you're causing Poppy is on another level. It's hard not to intervene."

Cal nodded. "You might think you're being noble by denying yourself a decent life, but honestly, it's selfish. You drag everyone down with you."

I glared at them. "Are you trying to make me feel worse?"

"We're trying to make you understand," Cal shouted. "It's not a choice to love you. Believe me, if it was, I'd have let go of this friendship by now. But it is your choice to let your guilt rule your life. It's your choice not to get the help you need and to hurt the people who care about you."

"You're not obligated to be my friend," I said, quietly. "You can leave anytime you want."

"He didn't mean it like that," Aiden said.

"Yeah, that didn't come out right," Cal said, sliding onto the tile floor beside me and leaning his back against the tub. Skye went back and forth between us. We grew quiet, each of us taking turns giving her head a pat.

It might sound self-centered, but I'd been so focused on my own suffering since Logan died, I hadn't considered that I could be adding to my friends'. Despite having a great career and a fiancée he loved, Cal looked miserable hunched on the ugly tiles. Aiden hid his emotions well, like always, but he hadn't stopped yanking on his fingernails.

Eventually, Cal turned to me. "If you were just anyone, I wouldn't put up with your shit. I've overcome too much to let someone bring me down. But you're my best friend, Theo, my brother. I'll never stop fighting for you. For years, I assumed everyone was judging you, for what happened, for the way you look. I fought every comment, every glare. I even questioned Rowan last summer when she trusted you to stay out with her sister. She about took my head off, and I started to wonder if you needed me to defend you. Maybe it was necessary when you first got out, but I'm realizing the only person I should be fighting now is you. The way I see it, you're the only one standing in your way."

A scorching heat filled my chest. "You don't get it," I said. Cal's eyes widened at the anger in my voice. "And I hope you never will. Apart from the crushing guilt I'll never escape, I'm a murderer and a felon, marked for life. You saw what happened today with your own eyes."

"I saw a cop trying to prove himself to his new department," Cal said. "And an idiot unwilling to accept the help he's being offered."

"If Everly helps me and I end up in jail, like I know I will, she'll be devastated. I can't do that to her."

"She'll be devastated if she doesn't help you and you end up in jail," Cal said, gripping his hair. "You'd rather do time again than accept the truth that you never should have been a felon in the first place. Your BAC was .04. If you'd been twenty-one, you wouldn't have been charged at all."

"Even if you think you deserved your conviction, let Everly help you fight this ridiculous charge," Aiden said, leaning against the sink. "Because you have a life worth fighting for. You've got a job you love and more talent in your pinkie than I have in my whole body. Friends who would do anything for you. And out of all the women on the planet, you somehow found the perfect one for you, and despite your obvious faults, she loves you. Shit like that doesn't happen every day. It may never happen for some of us. You can't throw it all away."

"I never meant to hurt you," I said, standing and holding out my hand to Cal. "Either of you," I added looking at Aiden. "I'm sorry."

"Words are just words, brother," Cal said, but he allowed me to pull him to his feet and into a hug. "You want to show me you're sorry, do something about it. Talk to a professional and figure your shit out. It's long overdue."

"Mind hanging out somewhere else?" Aiden asked. "I really do need to take a leak. I held off when we started finding Hell Cat's love gifts."

Cal smirked and leaned against the linen closet.

Aiden shuffled from foot to foot. "You have five seconds or I'm pissing in the sink."

Cal chuckled and led the way out of the bathroom. Aiden didn't even bother shutting the door before he started relieving himself. We walked down the hall to the living room with Skye. She and Cal flopped onto the couch together, looking like they were settling in for a while.

"Y'all can go home," I said, taking a seat beside them. "I'm not going to hurt myself."

"You already have," Cal said quietly. "And until you start pulling yourself out of this pity hole you've dug, we're glued to your ass."

I threw my hands up in the air. "For fuck's sake, what do I have to do to get you people to leave me alone?"

"Invite Poppy over to spend the night," Aiden said, joining us. He was looking at his fingernails, which were now bleeding in a couple places.

"And call Everly and tell her you want to fight this underage crap," Cal said.

"If not for yourself, do it for us," Aiden said. "We need you here. You'll ruin Cal's wedding if you're in the slammer."

I glanced between my best friends, their faces filled with pain, and my resistance cracked. "I'll think about Everly helping me with this new charge. But that's a hard no on Poppy. I'm not dragging her into my mess. And I need some time and space to pull myself together. I can't do that with y'all hovering."

Aiden and Cal exchanged a look.

"Fine, but if I see one fresh mark on you, I'm handcuffing you to Hell Cat again," Aiden said, walking toward the front door.

"I'm leaving Skye here tonight," Cal said, standing. "I'll swing by to get her first thing tomorrow." Skye hopped off the couch and nuzzled his hand.

My palms started to sweat. As much as I loved Skye, even needed her, I hated having the responsibility of caring for her for so long. "That's not necessary."

"It is for me," Cal said. "I won't sleep knowing you're here alone. Just put a bowl of water on the floor for her and let her out to pee before you turn in."

I could tell by Cal's clenched jaw that he wasn't backing down. Either Skye stayed, or they both did.

"Thanks," I said, "I'll take good care of her."

"Go to Theo," he said told Skye.

Skye looked from me to Cal, who was clearly making his way to the front door. She hesitated a moment before placing her head on my lap and looking up at me with her soulful eyes while Aiden and Cal left. I rubbed her ears and she jumped onto the couch beside me before laying her head back in my lap.

We stayed like that until I could barely keep my eyes open. Skye pranced around my feet when I finally stood. I walked into the kitchen and opened the cabinet where I'd stashed the plastic Chinese containers I'd saved from dinner last week. The containers were gone, but a set of gray dishes were stacked neatly in their place. I grabbed a bowl and filled it from the tap. When I set it on the floor, Skye started lapping the water, her tail wagging. When she'd had her fill, I walked her through the studio, which appeared the same, apart from the missing canvas on the floor. I opened the slider and Skye dashed out to do her business, sniffing the new yard with interest until I called her inside.

I walked with her from room to room, taking in all the changes, leaving my bedroom for last. It almost looked like a home. When I couldn't put it off any longer, I motioned Skye into the bedroom and walked in behind her.

I'd assumed Poppy had put the canvas over the bed and was surprised to find the space blank. I turned and all the air rushed from my lungs. Poppy had wrapped the canvas around a frame that spanned the entire wall opposite the bed. As soon as we stood and looked at the piece, I knew we'd made something incredible. The paint marks were unrestricted. No technique or second thoughts, just the movement of our bodies in pleasure. Absolute freedom. It hurt to see it now. Unless I slept with my feet against the headboard, I'd open my eyes every morning to the proof that, for however briefly, I'd allowed myself to have her.

Skye sniffed around, her tail wagging. I wondered if she could smell Poppy here as I imagined I could, her scent lingering like a powerful dream pulled into consciousness. I flopped face first on the bed. Maybe it was my imagination, but it smelled more like her than it had this morning. Despite every reason I had to lay awake worrying, I closed my eyes and fell asleep pretending she was still beside me.

CHAPTER TWENTY-NINE

Poppy

I HADN'T SEEN THEO since he left Everly's office a week ago. I'd kept my phone glued to my hand that first night, waiting for him to text or call. Crickets. I felt like an idiot for thinking a few decorative touches and a set of dishes would convince him he couldn't live without me.

When class rolled around on Thursday, I spent the evening icing hearts and flowers for the cookie bouquets. We had so many orders, I had to teach Rowan a few basic piping techniques, so she could help me while the cookies baked. I'd started getting up early to help her mix all the dough we'd need for the day. Little by little, we were learning to limp along at each other's jobs.

Mom breezed in and out of the house at random hours to catch sleep in tiny increments. As much as it sucked to make all this Valentine's Day crap with a broken heart, at least Mom was too busy to fuss over me, a role she'd apparently delegated to my siblings, who'd hugged me more in the last week than the last year.

Construction on the new space had ramped up with Aiden stopping by the house with daily updates. Though, I suspected his reports were a handy excuse to check on me.

"I put the sink in today," he said, leaning against the prep table where I was icing a dozen flowers assembly-line style.

"How?" Rowan asked as she slid another baking sheet into the oven. "I thought we were going to Jericho next week to pick it out."

"Utility sink for the studio," he said, reaching for a cookie.

My hand stilled. His fingers hovered over the cookie while he watched me. Usually, I defended my work like a ninja, smacking hands left and right whenever Chris or Aiden or even Mom tried to sneak a sample, but I just didn't have it in me.

Aiden pulled his hand back and grabbed a paper towel instead. He twisted it for a few moments before he spoke again. "Theo asked me to install it. He thought maybe you're avoiding the studio because you had to come inside to clean up."

I gave him my best bitch face and he sighed.

"Yeah, I figured," he said. "But just so you know, there's a working sink, and he keeps the kitchen door shut. You could go in the sliding door and work without seeing him."

The problem was, I wanted to see him. I was just afraid of how I'd react when I finally did. It was fifty-fifty whether I'd scream at him or fall to a sobbing mess at his feet. Neither one felt like a dignified option, so for now, I was letting his absence fuel mine.

"That was very thoughtful of Theo," Rowan said, coming to stand beside us. "And of you, Aiden, for getting it done so quickly."

Aiden shrugged. "I'm over there every day anyway to check on him."

I pressed my lips together to keep myself from asking how Theo was holding up. The thought of him alone in that house twisted my stomach.

"Would you like a slice of caramel apple cake?" Rowan asked Aiden. "It's a new recipe, and I'd love your honest opinion." It wasn't lost on me that Rowan didn't ask how Theo was doing either. I'm sure she got regular updates from Cal, but being the excellent sister she was, she didn't force the information on me.

Aiden picked up Rowan's not-so-subtle hint to back away from the Theo talk and smiled at her. "I'll take it to go if you don't mind. I got a couple more stops to make before I head home."

"Of course," Rowan said, slicing him a huge hunk of cake and placing it in a bakery box. "Let me know what you think."

The conversation reminded me of Rowan's attempts at baklava, which of course made me think of how sexy Theo looked eating it. I pushed back from the table, intent on getting upstairs before I started bawling like a baby, but Aiden put his calloused hand on my arm. "Go to the studio, Poppy. Please."

He let go of me and I ran, shoving Chris aside on the staircase, so I could get to my room before the first tear escaped. I sat on my bed, waiting, ready to bury my face in my pillow to muffle any embarrassing sobs, but my eyes stayed dry. I still felt like crying, but for whatever reason I couldn't get it out. I stared at the door until it opened and Chris slinked in.

"I thought maybe I could walk you over to the studio, Pop," he said, shuffling his feet.

Great. Clearly, Aiden had enlisted my little brother to get his way. But why? Pretty sure Theo wouldn't be popping in to say hi if I went there to work. I raised my eyebrows at Chris.

"Don't let him take your art," he said, holding out his hand to me. "I promise you'll have your own space soon if I have to build it myself, but for now, all you have is Theo's."

That should have gotten the tears flowing. Maybe I'd finally gone dead inside, my interior as bleak as my wardrobe. Or maybe I really did need to work some shit out in the studio. Nothing made me feel more alive than sculpting, and that lump of clay I was battling in early January hadn't been touched since.

"You planning to stay with me the whole time?" I asked, trying my best to sound annoyed even though I wanted to beg him not to leave me alone at Theo's.

"Yep," he said. "I need to take another practice SAT. I'm good for a few hours."

"You know I don't like anyone watching me work."

"Which is why my nose will be buried in my laptop. It will keep me focused. Maybe I'll even give you my phone."

"Wow, your other practice scores must be awful."

He smirked, which meant his scores were stellar. I doubt he even needed another practice test, but I crossed to my dresser and yanked out one of my dad's old, oversized shirts that I liked to wear when I worked. "Let's go," I said, tossing the shirt on over my clothes.

Chris chattered about school, how much he missed football season, and the SATs as we walked to Theo's house. I'd been so busy with baked goods and self-doubt, it'd been a while since I'd checked in with my little brother. Even though I knew he was trying to distract me so I didn't bolt home, I appreciated hearing about his life. Everyone had been treating me like spun glass, so listening to someone complain about vocabulary-in-context questions and Shakespeare felt amazing.

We cut across Twill's backyard into Theo's. Several lights were on in the house, including the studio lights. Through the bare windows, I saw the room was empty and the door to the kitchen was closed. I unlocked the slider with my key and motioned for Chris to go in ahead of me.

Everything looked exactly as I'd left it, except for a deep stainless-steel sink in the corner and a wooden chair, which I'm pretty sure came from Cal's house, placed in front of the closed kitchen door. I wondered if that subtle gesture was Cal's idea or Theo's.

Chris lowered himself into the chair, which gave an ominous creak, and started pulling crap from his backpack. I yanked the long-neglected clay from the sealed bucket and began rolling it in my hands. Five minutes. Ten minutes. Nothing.

"What's this?" Chris asked behind me.

I spun to find him peering under the drop cloth that hid my failed sculpture from last fall.

"Stop that," I said, tossing the clay on the table and smacking his hand. "You know I don't like y'all to see anything until it's done. Besides, that piece didn't work."

"Why not?" Chris asked, putting his hand on my forehead to hold me off as he ripped away the cloth. It was embarrassing how easily he held me back. I used to change his diaper for crying out loud.

"It just didn't," I said, stepping out of his reach and crossing my arms over my chest.

He tilted his head. "What was it?"

I sighed. Now that he'd seen it, I might as well talk about it. I hadn't realized how much I'd missed talking about art. Theo had always been the best sounding board for ideas and the inevitable problems that came with each piece.

"It was supposed to be our family but as a tree."

Chris squinted. "I see it. But it's a little confusing with the pieces wound together. Maybe we should be the roots to your tree."

I smiled at him. If I were a tree, he, Rowan, and my parents would be the roots, but that wasn't the point of the piece. I'd sculpted a tree with separate trunks, twisting together to grow.

"Plus, you left out Dad," he said, matter-of-factly, before walking back to his chair.

"I did not," I said, walking around the piece. Much of my work examined the grief of losing my father. I'd been old enough to remember him, unlike Chris, but young enough that his death left a gaping hole in my childhood. There were no holes in this family tree and only four trunks.

"I did leave him out," I said, quietly.

"You should have left mom out too," he said, typing on his laptop. "Or put her in the roots with Dad."

I could see it. A tree with two roots and three entwined trunks.

"But honestly, it's a little creepy," he said, still pretending to study. "I mean, I love you and all, Pop, but the whole twisted together part is gross."

"Yet another reason why it failed, I guess," I said, covering the piece again. I must have felt the mistakes without being able to articulate them.

"Yeah," he said, "It's too sexual."

"Ew, Chris," I said, walking back to the worktable. "Don't ever say that word in front of me again."

He shrugged. "It could work for a wedding gift for Rowan and Cal if you trim it down to two trunks with separate roots."

"I don't want to think about Rowan and Cal's sex life either," I said, rolling the clay in my hands again.

My fingers started to work and before I knew it, I'd created a rough version of what Chris had described, except the two trees had split in half before twinning together. Two fragile pieces finding strength in each other. I could leave the broken parts bare and add leaves to the sections of the trees that supported each other.

I grabbed a sheet of drawing paper and started sketching the image in my mind. I'm not sure how long I worked before I sat back and stared at the page. At some point, the trees had morphed into actual people, their shadows images of the damage they'd left behind to be together.

"That's incredible," Chris said over my shoulder. "But that's not Cal."

"I know," I said. "It's Theo."

"You have to make that, Pop. I'll bring a sleeping bag and camp out here if you need me."

"I know you would, but I want to do this on my own. Plus, if Theo was going to come out here, he would have by now. You can head home."

"Great, because that chair is really uncomfortable."

Chris pulled me into a hug before he slipped out the sliding door. Just because I wasn't ready to see Theo, didn't mean I couldn't show him how I felt. It'd be tight, but if I skipped a ton of sleep and the handmade cards I'd planned, I might be able to finish a clay model and ice all those damn hearts-and-flowers cookies before Valentine's Day.

CHAPTER THIRTY

Poppy

MY ENTIRE BODY RELAXED as I stood back from the table. After working several long days decorating and sculpting, I'd pulled an all-nighter to finish the cookie bouquets. As the sun rose, I'd snuck into the studio to complete what I hoped would be the first model of the sculpture. I'd either be back at some point making a cast of the piece or leaving it, and Theo, behind.

I cried a ton while I sculpted the embracing figures because I knew Theo and I could have a beautiful life together. He just needed to see it as clearly as I did. When I began work on my shadow self, my thoughts focused on all my imperfections. But the longer I worked on the piece as a whole, the more I came to realize that I was enough, flaws and all. I didn't need to be sweet like Rowan, or perky like Cammie, or citizen of the year like Lauren to deserve the love I wanted. Rowan had inspired Cal to leave his fuckboy lifestyle, but only after she'd ended their casual relationship when she wanted something more. To be with her, he'd had to work through all the reasons he'd been afraid to commit to someone.

I'd pressed every ounce of pain, hope, and love into the clay, adding more and more details because I wasn't ready to leave. It'd taken hours of sculpting to finally accept Lauren's advice. If Theo couldn't heal himself enough to love me the way I wanted, I had to let him go. Because no matter how much I loved Theo or he loved me, only he could do the work he needed.

I'd sculpted without music since I didn't want to wake him, but as the hours stretched into mid-morning, I started listening for him. Eventually, I heard the thud of boots and the front door close with a finality that made my heart ache. Afterwards, I'd blasted my music and kept working long after I initially thought the piece was complete. Each detail felt like a piece of us I was letting go: Art discussions and shared sushi, my sassy mouth and his kind eyes, our friendship and our passion. The sun had already begun to sink behind the mountains when I finally put down my chisel.

"That's incredible," Mom said, making me jump a foot. The music was so loud I hadn't heard her come through the slider. I turned off my speaker while she leaned close to the sculpture, her nose almost touching the clay.

"What are you doing here?" I asked. "The shop must be slammed."

Mom waved me off like it was any other day and not the evening before the second-busiest day of the year for florists. Only Mother's Day surpassed the chaos of the next twenty-four hours at Red Blossoms. "I'm here to help. I see you're all packed up."

"Yeah," I said, glancing at the boxes of art supplies. I'd packed in fits and spurts whenever I needed a break from sculpting, leaving only a handful of tools on the table.

"This is the best work you've ever done," she said giving my shoulders a squeeze.

Whatever happened, I felt a surge of pride while I studied the piece from all angles. No question, it was my best. I'd hacked the shadow figures into pieces then replicated the lines on the entwined figures in the middle, making sure any missing parts that remained were in places where Theo's figure and mine entwined. It was a little Jerry McGuire "you complete me," but it was the truth. Plus, I'd left it up for interpretation if we filled each other's gaps or simply shielded them from the rest of the world.

"Wow," Chris said, running into the room through the open slider. "That looks great, but I have a paper to finish, so can we move this along?"

"I didn't ask either of you to help me."

"No," Chris said, stacking two boxes and lifting them. "But we figured you didn't want to move out while Theo was here, and it's getting late." He took off without another word, almost running into Lauren.

"I'm here," she said, breathing hard like she'd sprinted all the way from Karma. "I have ten minutes, so load me up."

"How did you even know to be here?" I asked as Mom shoved a bucket of clay toward Lauren.

"You told Rowan you were moving out when you used Cal's bathroom, and she's finally realized she's not helping anyone by stressing her back," Lauren said, grabbing the bucket and a stack of drop clothes.

I'd told my sister to keep me accountable, but I didn't expect her to call in reinforcements to help me move.

"Thank goodness she's being sensible," Mom said, grabbing another box, leaving only my tool chest and portable speaker. "Especially this close to the wedding."

"Thanks for the help but get back to whatever you need to do. I can get the rest," I said as I wrapped the last of my tools and placed them in the chest.

After Lauren and Mom took off, I opened the kitchen door, placed my key by the uncovered statue, and left, taking everything but my heart with me.

CHAPTER THIRTY-ONE

Theo

I DUCKED OUT OF work early to stop home before class. The past week and a half had been a torture of my own making. I'd blown up the air mattress in one of the spare bedrooms because, apart from that first night when my adrenaline crashed, I hadn't been able to sleep in mine. After one sleepless night spent staring at the painting, I switched rooms and restarted my pre-breakfast workouts. Waking up in a comfortable bed with Poppy in my arms had felt so good, I'd moved my routine to later in the day or skipped it all together to join my friends at the gym. But without her, the usual anxiety ate at me until I gave in to planks and pushups. The lonely air mattress was enough to put me in a bad mood, but then I'd gone and begged Aiden to get Poppy back in the studio.

A saner man would have left the house as soon as she arrived, but I found myself moving first from the couch to the kitchen before stretching out on the floor by the studio door. Poppy's music bled through the wall, but she kept it low enough I could hear her movements when she set up and the clank of tools in the sink as she cleaned. She was remarkably quiet while she worked. Being a night owl like me, she'd stayed in the studio long past midnight several times. I once fell asleep propped against the kitchen cabinet and woke hours later to a quiet house and a crick in my neck.

Every night after she'd left, I'd entered the studio to see the progress she'd made. The part of me that felt guilty for snooping took a back seat to the ache in my chest. I missed her. And if I couldn't see her face, the next best thing was her art.

As the days passed, the sculpture began to take the form of two people standing with either two people lying on the ground behind them or their shadows. As she added details, it became clear she and I were the two figures in the middle of the sculpture, locked in an embrace. She was still working on the two figures laying on either side. Perhaps they were meant to be our separate shadows or past selves or something else entirely. Even unfinished, I knew it would be one of her best sculptures. I wanted to scribble her a note and tell her how amazing it looked, but then I'd have to admit to snooping.

After days of listening to her work, I finally felt strong enough to see her face-to-face and invite her back to class. I was relieved she was working again, but I hated that she'd avoided the community center because of me. Not that I could teach her anything. Class just hadn't felt the same without her. Honestly, nothing had.

As soon as I opened the front door, I knew she wasn't in the studio. I walked to the back of the house anyway. My heart thudded when I saw the open kitchen door. I flicked on the studio lights and my eyes narrowed in on the statue. Unlike the other times I'd snooped, she'd left it uncovered.

The finished piece filled me with longing. Detailed and evocative, it would have moved anyone with half a heart, but the pain I felt as I walked closer pulled a sound from my throat that I hadn't heard myself make since the night Logan died. And like that night, the weight of everything I'd lost, all the hurt I'd brought on myself, crashed against me in waves that left me shaking and sick.

I took a few deep breaths, willing myself not to throw up. This pain couldn't be the same. Logan lost his life because of me. Poppy was still alive, still sculpting—better than she ever had before.

There was no mistaking the meaning of the piece. Poppy believed we were stronger together than apart, but she'd exaggerated the holes in her life and minimized mine. I had been better with her, but she was better off without me.

Once my stomach settled, I searched for a drop cloth to cover the piece like she usually did, only there wasn't one nearby. I went to the cabinet where she kept her things but found it empty. I flung open all the doors. My paints and brushes were exactly where I'd left them, but nothing of Poppy's remained.

I found her key on the table when I tossed one of my old towels over the sculpture. I should be relieved. If the past few days had taught me anything, it was that having her in my space was too painful, too tempting. Even so, I wondered what it meant for her art. Where would she work, if she didn't work here?

Hoping against all odds she'd be in class, I turned off the studio lights and left. The community center parking lot was filled with cars when I arrived, but Poppy's hearse was nowhere in sight. With a sigh, I climbed out of my truck and went inside.

"He looks even worse than last week," Millie said when I entered the classroom.

"What's tweaked?" Esther bellowed.

"She said Theo looks worse than last week," Gladys yelled.

"Oh, yes, he does," Esther said.

"Poppy doesn't look any better," Mrs. Adams added.

"Pale as a ghost," Mr. Twillings added.

"She's always pale as a ghost," Mr. Wilson said. "And we're not talking about her when she isn't here."

"And who's fault is that?" Mr. Fitzwilliam said.

Every pair of eyes in the room glared at me.

"You'll never find a woman like Poppy again," Mr. Wilson said.

"Thought we weren't talking about her," Mr. Twillings snapped.

"That's fact, not gossip," Mr. Wilson said.

Everyone grumbled their agreement except Esther who seemed to be having an off day with her hearing aid. "Is Poppy coming tonight?" she asked.

"Ok everyone," I said, clapping my hands. "Today we'll continue the watercolors we started last week."

"I'd rather work on your love life," Mrs. Adams said.

"I second that," Mr. Wilson said, raising his hand.

"All in favor," Gladys said, raising her hand too. Everyone else raised theirs, including Esther, though I doubt she knew what she was agreeing with.

I rubbed my forehead. "You won't work until we talk about this?"

They all nodded.

I blew out a breath. "Fine. I was arrested last week for tattooing a minor. I ended things with Poppy because I don't want to take her down with me. She deserves better than me."

"We know all about the arrest," Gladys said. "Every one of us submitted a character statement to that lovely Everly girl."

"I've called my son daily to give him hell," Mr. Fitzwilliam added. "What's the point of having the police chief in the family if he can't get rid of a little ticket? Between me, Brandi, and Max, he's at his wit's end. And we're not stopping until he calls that girl's parents and tries to talk some sense into them."

"I started a petition to have the charges dropped," added Mr. Wilson. "I have over two hundred signatures so far, and that's just the folks who've come into the pharmacy. We're knocking on doors this weekend. Our goal is a thousand."

"Y'all did all that for me?" I asked, my voice shaky.

"Of course, we did," Mille said. "I'm prepared to take the witness stand, if need be, and so is everyone else, except Esther," she added loudly, pointing to the woman. "For obvious reasons."

"My ears are shot but I can still write," Esther said. "The letter I gave Everly was five pages long."

"Now, back to Poppy," Mr Twillings said. "I understand you think you're doing the right thing, but from where we're sitting, you're just breaking her heart and yours."

"What's the point in that?" Mrs. Adams asked.

They all grunted like they couldn't think of any reason worth mentioning.

"Having known Logan," Mr. Twillings said in a small voice. "I'm certain he wouldn't have wanted you to hold on to the guilt the way you have either."

"You've got to let it go, Theo," Mr. Wilson said. "Move forward with Poppy."

Then, as if they'd agreed ahead of time, everyone but Mr. Wilson rose from their chairs at varying speeds, shuffled into the hall, and headed as a pack to the exit.

They didn't understand. No one did. The guilt. The shame. The fear that at any moment the life I'd built would come crashing down, taking everyone I loved with it.

Once the others had left the building, Mr. Wilson walked to the front of the room and handed me a business card. "You're right, you know," he said. "You're not good enough for Poppy. Not yet. That girl deserves a man who'd move heaven and earth, and more importantly, his own bullshit, to be with her. Believe me, I speak from experience. I did a tour in Vietnam, and I've been putting in the work ever since to be the man I want to be. I'm pulling for you, Theo. We all are. You just need to step up to the challenge."

He gave my shoulder a pat and left. I flipped the card over and found the name and number for a therapist in Jericho. I shoved it in my pocket and pulled out my phone to text Aiden. I didn't feel like spending the evening in my empty house, but when I unlocked the screen, I had a text from an unknown number.

As soon as I started reading the string of rebukes in Greek, I knew they were from Patera. Nothing had changed since the trial. I'd ruined my life and brought shame to the family. He wished I'd never been born. I was dead to him.

But within the usual rant, something stood out: The names of every member of Logan's family. Plus, Cal, Aiden, and both their parents. Even Mr. Twillings and my high school English teacher Mrs. Evers. In short, everyone in Peace Falls who my father might remember. Plus a few people he'd never met, including Max, Rose, and Mr. Fitzwilliam. They'd each reached out to my parents begging them to convince me to accept Everly's help and fight both the recent charges and my prior conviction.

I wondered what my life would be like if Patera hadn't disowned me after the trial. It definitely impacted the way I saw myself. I'd done something so terrible, my own father couldn't stand the sight of me, and my own mother hadn't loved me enough to fight him. It'd been easy to let the guilt I'd planted deep when Logan died spread like kudzu. A part of me was grateful. I'd never have met Max if my parents had welcomed me home with open arms. I never would have found my passion as a tattoo artist. But maybe, I would have been able to move forward.

Instead, I'd doubled the shame Patera felt and swallowed it as my own. My father had been the voice in my head for too long. Perhaps it was time I listened to everyone else around me. All the people who'd tracked down my father in another country, hoping he'd try to convince me to let go of my mistakes. Or, better yet, I could be more like Poppy and not give a shit what anyone else thought of me.

My fingers shook as I texted back one word: *Antio.* A cold and final goodbye.

I felt lighter the moment I sent it. I quickly typed a message to my group text with Aiden and Cal before I could change my mind.

> *Can someone give me Everly's number? I'm ready to fight*

Cal

> *About damn time*

Aiden

> *<Everly Hendrick's contact card>*

Aiden

> *Just the newest arrest or the whole conviction?*

> *Everything*

Cal

> *Better add yourself to the list*

> *Already started, brother. Think you can help me with something tomorrow?*

Cal

> *Depends. It's Valentine's Day*

Aiden

> *For fuck's sake, Cal, nothing you have planned for Rowan will top a happy sister*

Cal

He didn't say it was for Poppy!

Aiden

Still the dumbest smart person I know

Cal

Is it for Poppy?

Yes

Cal

Whatever you need, brother

Aiden

Why didn't you ask me to help?

You can. But I don't think you'll want to

Aiden

I'd do anything to stop my daily check ins with you two punks

I'm holding you to that

Aiden

Please tell me you're not buying her camping gear

Cal

Don't be an asshole, A. Rowan loved it

Aiden

Or she was too sweet to say otherwise

I shoved my phone in my pocket and let their banter ping back and forth without me. I had more important things to do.

Chapter Thirty-Two

Poppy

As I tossed and turned last night, I realized two things: First, Theo wasn't running to my arms the moment he saw the statue. Second, I was still loved. The first thought made me want to hide under my covers and cry through Valentine's Day. The second had me gathering my card-making supplies before the sun rose. I spread everything on the coffee table and grabbed a blanket to toss over my work if someone walked in when I was working on theirs. I tried not to think about how Theo and I had huddled under the same fluffy throw the night the tree fell on my studio.

I started with Mom and Rowan since they were the most likely to snoop and managed to get both cards finished before they got up. I shouldn't have worried though. They had too many flower and cookie deliveries to give a second glance at what I was doing. They'd chugged some coffee and left after I assured Rowan that I could hand over the last of the cookies scheduled for pickup without cussing anyone out.

I had to stop often to answer the doorbell, but by noon I'd made enough progress to feel confident I'd finish all the cards in time. Around two o'clock, I looked out our front window and noticed Twill and Mrs. Adams chatting on the sidewalk. Most of their conversations were screamed across the street from their respective porches, so I was already a bit suspicious when a minivan pulled to the curb and Theo's Fan Club climbed out.

"What the hell?" I said, leaving Aiden's card mid-cut to peer out the window.

I was about to open the door and ask them what they were doing when Theo walked through Twill's yard with something small and black in his arms. Everyone moved aside to make a path for him to my house.

By this point, the senior citizens had noticed me in the window and were pointing. Theo looked up at the house, his face pale. Whatever was about to go down between us, I really didn't want the entire art class watching. I half considered hiding in my room. Instead, I flung open the front door and leaned against the frame with my arms crossed over my chest. I'd have looked like a total badass in my combat boots. Instead, my furry Grinch slippers did nothing for my height or hard exterior. When Theo climbed the porch steps in his boots, he towered over me more than usual, which made me feel even smaller than I already did.

"Nice audience," I said, lifting my chin toward the sidewalk. "Afraid to see me by yourself?"

The faintest smile crossed his lips, and every nerve in my body lit up. Damn him and his pillowy pucker.

"Mr. Twillings heard I was coming to see you. I guess the news spread."

Just then, the little black ball exploded from Theo's arms, leaped through the air in a furry blaze, and shot past me into the house. For the first time since pre-K, I was in serious danger of wetting myself. Rowan had told me about the black squirrels in DC, but I'd never seen one. The creature was small enough to be a squirrel, though I couldn't think of any reason why Theo would bring one to my house.

"Son of biscuit," I said, putting my hand on my chest where my heart thudded wildly. The squirrel thing let out a bark by my feet and my breath caught.

"You're a dog," I said, kneeling to get a better look. It had a squished little face that looked like it belonged in the primate house at the zoo and a fluffy black coat that begged to be petted. I held out my hand for the dog to sniff, which it did before launching itself at me. Its silky fur brushed against my neck and cheek as it covered me in sloppy kisses.

My heart melted. It wiggled with excitement as I plopped my ass on the floor and buried my face in its fur.

"You're the cutest thing I've ever seen," I cooed. The dog gave me what I can only describe as a doggy grin before jumping off my lap and zooming back to Theo.

"This is Holly," he said quietly, kneeling to pet her.

Holly. A plant with red berries. I'd always given Mom shit for naming my sister after a berry and not a flower, but she always insisted Rowan was still a red blossom like Rose or Poppy.

"Is she yours?" I asked.

He nodded.

He'd gotten a dog. Given how Skye helped him, he should have gotten one years ago. But he'd never allowed himself that bit of happiness. Until now. A surge of hope washed through me.

Holly let out a yip and shot off toward the dining room.

"She's a curious little thing," he said, grabbing my hand and helping me to my feet.

It felt so good to touch him again, but I still didn't know if he was here to ask me back to art class or his entire life. "Is her name really Holly?" I asked, dropping his hand.

"It is now," he said with a smile that didn't undo the sadness in his eyes that appeared when I broke our connection. "She was a Christmas puppy someone dropped at the pound. Apparently, she had too much attitude."

Holly sprinted back into the living room. She sniffed every corner, her dark eyes bouncing from one thing to the next, her tail wagging in a blur.

"The little ones always do," I laughed nervously. "Will she always be small?"

He nodded. "She's an Affenpinscher."

It'd been a few years since my last high school German class, but I still remembered the word for monkey. "She's a monkey pinscher?" I said, trying not to laugh.

Theo shrugged. "She's unique."

"She's perfect," I said.

"She is," he said, looking at me instead of the dog, his dark eyes filled with a heat that made my stomach clench.

"What are they saying?" Esther yelled.

"We can't hear either," Gladys yelled back.

"Stop playing with the dog and get on with it, Theo," Esther yelled.

"I'm trying," he yelled, without pulling his molten gaze from me.

Okay, so he finally realized he could handle a pet and missed fucking me. That didn't mean he was all in. And all in was the only way Theo and I could be together without my heart breaking over and over again. I cleared my throat. "I left you something in the studio. Did you see it?"

"It's incredible," he said, softly. "I can't believe you made it in a few days."

"You knew I was working on something?"

He flashed me that rare smile of his, and my feet moved toward him on their own. My body, at least, was ready to jump back in, but my fragile heart begged my brain to take it slow. I stopped far enough away that he'd have to lean in to reach me.

"I checked your progress every night after you left," he said. "I know it was an invasion of your privacy, but I couldn't stop myself. I thought it was the only way I could be close to you. And when I realized all your things were gone—"

He stepped closer and cupped my face in his hand. "I want to wake up every morning with you in my arms. I want to buy all the towels and furniture you want to make the house feel like a home not only for me, but for us. Because I never want to spend another day without you. And I'll do whatever it takes to make that happen, as long as you want me."

My stomach danced with excitement, but I kept the joy from my face. As much as it hurt to admit, I knew loving each other wasn't enough. "It's going to take more than towels."

He nodded. "I called Everly last night and told her I wanted to fight the misdemeanor and my previous conviction. And I just came from a consult with a therapist in Jericho who specializes in PTSD and panic attacks. I'm starting weekly sessions. I love you, Poppy. I'll do whatever I can to be the man you deserve."

I stepped back but gripped his hands. "I love you too, Theo. But there's one more thing I need to know before we move forward."

Behind him the seniors shifted restlessly in their orthotic shoes. I swear Twill was biting his nails.

"Do you think you'll ever forgive yourself? You're already the man I want. But you have the power to crush me. Any pain you inflict on yourself, I feel. Anytime you hate yourself, my heart breaks."

"I'll try." He let go of one of my hands to brush a strand of hair behind my ear, his thumb lingering on my face. "I can't guarantee it will happen today or next week, but I promise I'll keep trying. Because this," he said, pointing between us, "is worth fighting for."

I let out a squeal that sounded an awful lot like Lauren or Cammie and leaped at him. Everyone on the sidewalk cheered. Holly barked and danced around Theo's boots as I grabbed his face and kissed him.

"About dang time," Mrs. Adams yelled before high-fiving Gladys, Esther, and Millie.

A Peace Falls police car sped down Sullivan Street. Theo tensed when it stopped in front of us. The passenger door flung open, and Mr. Fitzwilliam climbed out with his phone held to his face. "Did we miss it?"

"Turn the camera around," Wilson's voice yelled from the phone, which had to be at max volume. "I don't want to see up your nose. I want to see Poppy and Theo."

"You missed it," Twill said.

"I knew we should have used the sirens," Mr. Fitzwilliam said, glaring at the officer behind the wheel. He pointed a gnarled finger at the man. "My son will hear about this." He slammed the door closed, and the cruiser took off at a slower speed toward Main Street.

"Turn the camera around," Wilson yelled again.

"I don't know how to do that." Mr. Fitzwilliam fumbled with the screen a few moments before he shuffled to the bottom of the porch steps and held up the phone with the screen facing us like John Cusack with a boombox.

"Sorry I couldn't be there, sweetie," Wilson said. He was clearly at work with rows of pill bottles behind him and probably a line of customers at the counter waiting to be helped. "So, are you two back together?"

"Yes, sir," Theo said.

"And you're working on yourself? Poppy deserves the best man you can be."

Theo smiled at me. "I am."

Wilson beamed at him, and my chest filled with so much warmth, I couldn't stop the tears streaming down my face.

"Are you crying, Poppy?" Mr. Fitzwilliam asked. His mouth hung open in shock.

"As I live and breathe," Mrs. Adams said, her voice breaking.

The entire Fan Club gave a collective sniff and even Twill rubbed at his eyes. Damn tears. I'd never hear the end of this.

Theo wrapped me in a hug before kissing me with so much passion Wilson asked Mr. Fitzwilliam to turn the phone away, and Holly howled as though her new friends were trying to devour each other, which I guess, in a way, we were.

CHAPTER THIRTY-THREE

Theo

HOLLY WHIMPERED WHEN I closed the bathroom door, and I almost gave in and let her out. Thankfully, Poppy cracked first.

"Let's give her a few more hours to get comfortable before we tuck her into the bathroom for the night," she said.

I opened the door and Holly pranced out and hopped onto one of my boots as if to prevent me from moving.

"Sorry, babe," Poppy said, scooping the dog from my shoe. "You have to share him with me. And you'll have to learn to potty outside before you sleep anywhere but the bathroom."

Holly licked Poppy's face, and she laughed.

My throat tightened. Damn I wanted to hear that sound every day. The thought of being locked away from Poppy seemed unimaginable now. But I wouldn't let what could happen ruin tonight.

I had yet to be alone with Poppy since our reunion on her porch. Rowan arrived right after, and the three of us spent the next hour helping Poppy finish the cards she'd started. Then, I drove us around town delivering them to Red Blossoms, the pharmacy, Karma, Cal's office, and Aiden's house.

Poppy's mom burst into tears the moment she saw us together, but Cal didn't lose it until he read the card Poppy made him. When he showed it to me, I got a little choked up myself. She'd crafted a detailed cutout of her entire family, plus Cal and Skye, and written the sweetest note about him becoming her brother.

I wanted to be in that paper cutout of her family. For now, I was just happy to have her all to myself.

I placed a gentle kiss on her cheek. "Hold on to Holly, please. I need to unload a few things from the truck."

Poppy laughed when I pushed through the door a few minutes later with four full bags from the pet store and an orthopedic dog bed balanced on my head. I'd picked up everything before I collected Holly from the pound, but kept it in the back seat since I was determined not to wait another minute to see Poppy.

Watching Aiden skirt the walls of the SPCA while Cal and I played with the dogs will be a memory I'll never forget. Despite the audience Poppy and I ended up with, Cal and Aiden had respected my decision to visit Poppy alone. Mr. Twillings, who must have heard us talking in my yard, had not.

"Please tell me all that stuff isn't for this little dog," Poppy said. "I'm pretty sure Skye doesn't have half as much crap, and she's been with Cal for over a decade."

I dropped the bags and took the bed off my head. Poppy set down Holly, so she could explore everything. "I might have gone a little overboard," I said.

"Nah," Poppy said, wrapping her arm around my waist. "She's had her heart broken by her last family. She needs to know you care."

"Oh shit," I said, glancing down at the explosion of doggie toys. "I meant to grab flowers for you. We were even at your mom's shop."

Poppy gave my waist a squeeze. "Fun fact about me: I hate cut flowers. It's basically the only thing that stuck from my glorious teenage rebellion.

Well, that and the hair dye. There's just something so sad about flower arrangements. You're basically killing something beautiful and handing over the corpse as a gift."

"Sounds right up your alley," I said and laughed when she elbowed me in the side. "I promise no flowers."

"No *cut* flowers," she said. "I'd never turned down a potted plant. Speaking of which, you better give Holly more attention than this devil's ivy my mom gave you. It's just sad," she said, touching the brittle leaves.

"Good thing you'll be around to keep an eye on it." I leaned down and placed a kiss on the delicate curve of her neck. "I meant what I said earlier about you being here every morning."

Poppy sagged against me. "You know," she said, placing her hand on my chest. "Holly looks really happy with all her toys."

She reached down and ran her hand over my hardening cock and I groaned. After a quick glance at Holly, I decided we could leave her to enjoy her new things for a few minutes. I grabbed Poppy's hand and pulled her down the hallway to the bedroom and closed the door softly.

"It turned out well, don't you think?" she said, nodding toward the painting.

"Too well," I said, tugging at her shirt. "I haven't slept in here in days."

She put her hands on mine to stop my progress with her shirt. "Hold up. Where have you been sleeping?"

I cleared my throat. "The air mattress in the other room."

"Crap on a cracker, Theo," she said, shoving me onto the bed. "I wanted to remind you how good we were together, not torture you." She straddled me and leaned forward until our noses touched. "How should I make it up to you?" she asked rocking against me. Even with our clothes on, I could feel her heat.

"Fuck," I hissed as she moved again.

"Rowan made me get on the pill," she said, rubbing her body against mine in slow, languid waves. "And since I've never been with anyone but you—"

Before I even knew what I was doing, I'd flipped her onto her back and started to peel the leggings from her body. "I'm clean," I said, kissing the delicate skin beneath her throat. I unbuttoned her shirt and found her bare. Fuck me. Her chest rose and fell, pushing her perfect tits closer to my lips before pulling them away. I sucked a taunt nipple into my mouth, and she let her legs fall open, inviting me closer. I quickly tore off my clothes and positioned myself at her entrance.

"Are you sure?" I asked, dragging my cock through her slick folds. "I can grab a condom if you want."

"All I want is you inside me, now," she said, digging her nails into my back and pulling me close.

We both cried out when I slid into her. You'd think it'd been years, not days, since we'd been together. She was so tight and wet, I had to work my length inside her inch by inch until I buried myself completely with a hiss.

I stilled to stave off the orgasm that threatened to overtake me.

"Please, Theo," she begged. "I'm so close."

I pulled out slowly and she moaned, the sound rich and deep and far too sexy. "I'm never going to last if you keep making sounds like that, *kardoula mou*."

She tightened around me but pressed the back of her hand to her full lips to muffle the sounds she made every time I moved, her pussy squeezing me tighter and tighter until I snapped.

I started pounding into her so hard the bed smacked against the wall in time with her moans. She gave up trying to silence them, and I gave up any pretense of taking her slowly. She screamed my name as she came, and a moment later I emptied myself inside her, the pleasure rushing through me with such intensity my legs shook.

I collapsed beside her, but before I could catch my breath, Holly scratched at the door and whimpered.

"I'll get her," Poppy said. She pulled her fine ass from the bed, tossed me my boxers, and slipped on my t-shirt before opening the bedroom door.

I yanked on my boxers as Holly bounced into the room, alert for danger.

"Better get used to it, babe," she said, scooping up the little dog and planting a kiss on her furry head. "Your daddy and I will be making a lot more noise tonight." She hopped onto the bed with Holly and snuggled into my shoulder.

I couldn't remember the last time I felt so content. Perhaps I never had. When I lived with my parents, I'd always felt pressure to be the right kind of son, and I always fell short. My time in prison had been filled with raw grief and the crushing anxiety of life without any choice or control. I thought I'd found contentment in the small apartment above Marked, but really, I'd created a new cell. I was finally free, but for how long? It could all disappear with a second conviction.

"Talk to me," Poppy said, placing her hand on chest. "Your heart is racing and not in a good way."

I ran my fingers down Poppy's arm while Holly curled into a ball between us and let out a sigh. "What happens if Everly can't beat the conviction?"

"She will," Poppy said, propping herself up to look me in the eyes. "She'll fight it. And so will everyone who loves you."

"But what if that's not enough?"

Poppy shrugged. "We petition the court for house arrest. I'm basically a cave troll, so no complaints from me if we have to hunker down here for a few months."

"I'm serious, Poppy."

"So am I," she said, her green eyes blazing. "No matter what happens, we'll face it together. You're stuck with me, Theo."

I pulled her hand to my lips and kissed it. "I still feel bad I didn't get you anything for our first Valentine's Day."

"You gave me this," she said, clutching the poppy charm I'd made her. Despite everything, she hadn't taken it off.

"That was to celebrate the beginning of us. I want to give you something to mark the end of us ever being apart."

"I have an idea," she said with a devilish smirk that told me I was in for something unexpected and amazing and 100% Poppy.

CHAPTER THIRTY-FOUR

Poppy

"ARE YOU SURE ABOUT this?" Theo asked.

I nodded but refused to look at him.

"I got the trashcan right here if you need it," Max said and winked at me. He sat across from Theo, ready to hold me down if necessary. Though I'd prefer to stare at Theo for the next hour or so, I figured it was best I didn't look.

"I'm a fainter, not a puker," I said and took a deep breath.

Max shrugged. "Either one ain't a problem. I've seen it all."

"Please don't puke," Aiden said, gripping my left leg. "I have a sensitive stomach."

"I can handle both her feet if she does," Rowan said from my right leg.

"Or I can just sit on her like I offered," Chris said, where he sulked in the corner with Mom, handing her tissues, while Wilson patted her shoulder.

"I'm so proud of you, sweetheart," Mom sniffed.

"Bet you don't hear that every day," I said to Max.

Max shrugged again. "You'd be surprised. Most people aren't trying to get over a fear of needles like you, but we often do tattoos to commemorate achievements or overcoming obstacles. I've heard plenty of parents say they're proud."

"You really don't have to do this," Theo said, his voice tense.

"Stop stalling," I said, taking another deep breath.

He flipped on the machine and the room filled with a buzzing sound. I let out a little yip when he pressed the needle to my skin, and he pulled it away. "I'm not sure I can do this. Maybe Max should take over."

"Theo Markis," I snapped turning my head so I could see him. He had the tattoo needle poised right above my arm where he'd placed a stencil of the drawing he'd made of our statue. He'd simplified it to the two central figures to allow space for the intricate shading that characterized his work. "You are the only person on earth I trust to do this."

The anxiety in his eyes faded, and he flashed me a smile.

"Aren't they adorable?" Wilson said to no one in particular.

"You want to watch?" Theo asked me.

"Heck no. But you can't stop every time I make a little noise."

"You'll tell me if it's hurting too much?"

I nodded. Of course, it was going to hurt. He was burying a needle in my skin. I didn't expect it to feel pleasant.

I turned to face Max again, and he leaned down to whisper in my ear. "Just let me know if you need a break, and I'll tell him I need one." He winked at me again and lifted his head to watch Theo work.

After the first few minutes, I grew accustomed to the sting and the changing pitch of the needle when it connected with my arm. Sometimes the pain sparked through my overstimulated system, but I did the best I could to keep my winces to a minimum.

Max patted my shoulder. "You're holding up better than most."

"Yeah, I don't think we need to hold your boots down anymore," Rowan said.

"You're supporting your sister," Mom snapped.

"I can do it without holding her germy shoes."

"I'll take over, Ann," Chris said, stepping away from Mom.

"Son of biscuit," I yelled, when the needle hit a particularly tender part. "Why don't y'all go bother Lauren and bring us back some coffee."

They all seemed to like the idea, especially Aiden, and filtered out of the shop, which was thankfully closed to everyone but us. "Back in a bit," Rowan shouted before the door closed.

As soon as they were gone, I let the tears flow freely. Max kept his expression stoic, and Theo worked several more minutes before he noticed my face was wet.

"Fuck, Poppy," he said, switching off the needle and brushing a tear from under my eye. "Max why didn't you say anything?"

"If she'd wanted you to stop, she'd have told you. You picked a tough one, son. Sometimes women just need to cry. Ain't that right, Poppy?"

"Yep," I said, with a shaky voice. It hurt like a mother, but I wanted to get over my fear, and as cave woman as it sounded, I wanted Theo to mark me.

"Let's take a break," Theo said, rubbing his gloved finger across my cheek. "Do you want to see what I've done so far?"

I shook my head. "It won't be as much as I've imagined."

"I've just about got the outline down."

"Really?" I asked glancing at my arm.

Big mistake. Little drops of blood rose from the black lines Theo had etched in my skin. My vision swam, but I took a steadying breath through my nose and out my mouth and looked again. He really had finished most of the outline.

"That's incredible," I said, admiring his work. When I focused on the details instead of the blood, I could look at the tattoo without feeling dizzy. "I can't wait to see what you do with the shading."

Max gripped my shoulder. "Pretty soon you'll be begging Theo to let you tattoo him."

I laughed so hard I snorted. "The only place he has left is a small space on his chest, and I'm not putting a needle anywhere near his heart."

"Nah, that's taken now," Max said. "All you've got is his ring finger or places I'd rather not think about."

Theo turned an adorable shade of pink.

"What's he talking about?" I asked.

"Well, I was going to show you after I finished yours, but since Max can't contain his excitement, might as well show you now." Theo pulled his shirt over his head. A bandage covered his chest just above his heart. He peeled it back slowly to reveal a bright red poppy.

My eyes filled with tears again. "It's beautiful," I said, reaching forward to touch it. Max placed his hand gently on my mine. "Thank you. It's some of my better work. But let it heal a bit."

I turned to Max and gave him a watery smile. "It's perfect."

"It was Theo's design," Max said, but I could tell he was pleased with the work he'd done. "I just traced and colored."

Theo chuckled as he applied a fresh bandage to his chest and slipped his shirt back on.

"His ass would probably be easier for a tattooing debut, but I don't want to mess with perfection," I said, which made Theo laugh and Max look a little uncomfortable.

I couldn't stop myself from looking at Theo's left hand while he prepared the colored ink for the rest of our session.

"Ring finger it is then," Max whispered when the front door burst open. As everyone sipped their coffees and chatted, I found my eyes drawn again to Theo's left hand. I could see the design so clearly in my mind. Theo might have to handle the actual needle to skin part, but I knew exactly what I wanted. Thinking about wedding rings this early in a relationship should scare the crap out of me. But with Theo, it was easy to imagine. Something simple and uncomplicated because, despite how complicated we both are, the love I felt for Theo was effortless. I only hoped he felt the same.

I caught Max's eye, and he smiled at me as the needle buzzed to life.

"Ready, Poppy?" Theo asked.

"Absolutely."

EPILOGUE

Theo

TWO MONTHS LATER

Skye and Holly chased each other around the empty living room in a never-ending loop. I could already tell we were in for a long week watching Skye while Cal and Rowan were on their honeymoon.

"Can't you lock them up until we get the furniture in?" Aiden whined.

"Maybe we should lock you up," Lauren snapped and then looked at me and blushed. "Please ignore me, Theo. I haven't been myself lately." She set down the floor lamp in her hands and pulled me into a hug. "I'm so happy for you both."

"Thanks, Lauren," I said, giving her a tight squeeze. She had seemed off since the bachelor/bachelorette trip last month. It couldn't be easy watching Rowan and Poppy both move on to the next phase of life without her. We did our best to include everyone, but inevitably Cal, Rowan, Poppy, and I ended up spending extra time together. I made a note to suggest Poppy plan a girl's night out with Lauren while Rowan and Cal were on their honeymoon.

"Come on, Stud Man," Poppy said, slapping Aiden's back. "The dogs are fine where they are. Besides, we both know I'm the scariest bitch here."

The first time Poppy used Aiden's nickname in front of me, I spit out the water I was drinking. Apparently, it had something to do with an argument they had while hanging floating shelves at Red Blossoms Bakery. I'd gotten used to it. Scratch that. I secretly loved it. Poppy and I had blended our lives so easily, it felt like we'd been together years, not months. Which was why I'd already bought a black diamond and set it in a band I designed and made myself. Poppy and I left for Greece right after Cal and Rowan returned, and I planned to propose our first night there.

"Want me to pick up the couch from the furniture store?" Aiden asked, pressing himself against the wall as the dogs zoomed past.

"Take me with you," Chris said, sticking his head out of the kitchen where he was setting up a table and chair set with Rose.

"Mom hugging you too much?" Poppy asked with a laugh.

He pointed at her. "It's your fault, you know. Mom had just gotten comfortable with the idea of Ann moving down the street when you announced you were moving out."

"At least I waited until after the wedding to actually do it."

"One day, Pop. One stinking day."

"I can hear y'all," Rose said, storming out of the kitchen. "And for the record, I'm thrilled Poppy is moving in with Theo."

"I'd find that easier to believe if you hadn't been crying into a dish towel for the past ten minutes," Chris said.

My stomach sank. It was understandable Rose would have reservations about me. I was five years older than Poppy with a truckload of baggage and a panic disorder. Rose must have seen the worry on my face because she hurried over and grabbed my hands. "I couldn't be happier for Poppy," she said, giving my hands a squeeze. "And you."

My relationship with Rose was an unexpected bonus. I hadn't realized how much I missed Mana until Poppy's mom started treating me like one of her kids. It was Rose who convinced me not to let my father's rejection keep me from visiting the country I loved or from reaching out to Mana. Turns out, Rose had started texting my mother with updates of my life soon after Cal got with Rowan. Which went a long way to explain the change in frequency and tone of Mana's texts around the time I was evicted.

I wasn't sure what I expected when I told Mana about my trip to Greece, but her excited response healed something that, despite hours of therapy, I hadn't been able to work through. We agreed to meet up in a little village about an hour from where she and Patera live. Poppy and I applied for expedited passports that same day.

Since Poppy had never been abroad, I wanted her first trip to Greece to be one she'd never forget. I only hoped I could keep the ring a secret until then. As far as Poppy knew, the trip was to celebrate Everly having the charges against me dropped.

We still had a long road ahead to try to get my prior conviction reduced and expunged, but whether the law still considered me a felon, I'd started to let go of the shame that came with the label.

Working on Logan's memorial had helped. It'd been difficult at first, and more than one work session had already ended in a panic attack, but Poppy had been with me every time. She'd even joined me for a few therapy sessions to learn ways to help me ground myself. Little by little, I found my mental health improving. We were on track to install the sculpture this summer once Aiden and his crew completed work on the tree house.

"Don't forget the rug and the recliner," Poppy called after Aiden and Chris as they bolted for the door.

"I was trying to organize your clothes, but how do you separate things when they're all the same color," Lauren said, coming out of the bedroom with a pair of black pants and a black dress in her hands. "At least your underwear is colorful."

"Paws off my panties," Poppy huffed, grabbing the clothes from Lauren. "Go help my mom in the kitchen if you want to be useful."

As soon as Poppy headed down the hall toward the bedroom, Lauren gripped my arm and pulled me out the front door.

"You cannot keep an engagement ring in your sock drawer, Theo," she whispered, pulling the ring from her bra and handing it to me. "Now that you're living together, Poppy's bound to do your laundry sometime, and she's going to snoop when she's putting away your clothes. It's only natural." Her checks tinted and she broke eye contact.

I was too worried to ask Lauren why she was in my underwear drawer. "Do you think Poppy already saw it?"

Lauren shrugged, recovering quickly from her embarrassment. "Maybe. Maybe not. I give it 50/50. But she has been pretty busy with Maid of Honor duties, so maybe 60/40 in your favor. Regardless, you should keep that somewhere else."

"I know just the place," I said and shoved the ring in my pocket.

Later that night, after every box had been unpacked and every piece of furniture placed, Poppy and I flopped onto our bed. Usually, we'd be fighting for space with Holly, but she and Skye were sleeping curled together in the living room. The day had been long and tiring for everyone, yet I couldn't remember a time I'd been this happy.

"Welcome home, *kardoula mou*," I said.

She rolled toward me and grabbed my face with both her hands. "What should we do to celebrate?"

I had an intense urge to pull the ring from its new hiding place behind the canvas we'd made together. But I stopped myself. Poppy was a romantic in her soul. She deserved a breathtaking proposal she could share with our children and grandchildren. I just had to be patient a little longer.

"We could practice your Greek," I said.

"That wasn't what I had in mind. I do want to learn, but I doubt I'll get very far in a week." She wrapped her small frame around me and dug her heels into my ass to pull me closer. I groaned when she slid her hand between us and cupped me. "At least parts of you understand the word celebrate," she said as I hardened beneath her talented fingers.

I brushed the hair from her face and looked deep into her eyes. "No matter what we're doing, every moment I spend with you is worth celebrating."

Poppy's eyes got a little misty, and I smiled. Despite all the twists and turns of my life, we'd somehow ended up together. "Thank you for never giving up on me, on us," I said.

"Will you hurry up and fuck me already," she sniffed. "I'd rather have an orgasm than an ugly cry, and we're close to the point of no return."

I wasted no time chucking our clothes and sinking into her. I'd denied us both too much already. I planned to spend the rest of my life trying to bring her as much joy as she's brought me, even if I knew we'd never be even. Nowhere close. Even if it meant letting go of my guilt. I'd love her with everything I had because she'd loved me when I couldn't love myself, and a love like that was worth healing for.

MORE FROM HANNAH

Can't get enough of Poppy and Theo? Sign up for my newsletter for a bonus epilogue of their engagement.

Visit https://dl.bookfunnel.com/qq09ygm60x

If you enjoyed *For You I'd Mend*, you'll love the rest of the *Peace Falls Series*.

Book 1: For You I'd Break Available Now

Book 3: *For You I'd Bloom* Available January 7, 2025

Acknowledgements

To Jamie for discussing your mental health so openly on social media. It has made all the difference. I hope one day I can help someone else how you have helped me. To James Carpenter and Gerri Mahn for hyping me up when I need it and mercilessly tearing my writing apart the rest of the time. To Claude and Melyssa, thank you for your invaluable feedback and continued support. A special thanks to Kaytalin McCarry for your patience with a new author and your beautiful cover designs. Finally, to all my family and friends who have embraced my new career. For a time, I thought I'd never tell any of you that I'd written a romance novel, let alone three. I'm incredibly grateful I did. Your enthusiastic support has meant the world to me. But sorry, Mom and Dad, you still can't read beyond this page.

LETTER TO READERS

Dear Reader,

This book was hard to write. Not because I didn't love the characters or their story, but because it often brought up my own feelings of loss. As a nonfiction writer, I use words to work through my emotions all the time. I didn't anticipate doing the same in a romance novel. I contemplated omitting parts of this work of fiction because they cut too close and too deep. I'm still worried they might trigger grief in others. Ultimately, I decided to leave them because, like Poppy's sculptures and drawings, those sections are the most meaningful to me as a writer. And, perhaps, to some of you as readers.

Having struggled with my mental health for years before seeking treatment, I also worried about the message I'd be sending the world with a character like Theo. I hope it's this: Mental health matters. Anyone who has fought their own mind knows how overwhelming it can be. But it is a fight worth fighting. I could not have written *The Peace Falls Series* without proper treatment. My only regret is not taking the first step sooner. If you are reading this and struggling, I hope you will get the help you need.

Despite the serious moments, writing this book was a blast. In case you couldn't tell, Poppy has been my favorite character from the start, and writing the HEA she deserved was a joy. Theo really is a unicorn of a man, and building the complexities of his character (balancing his weaknesses with his appeal) was an entertaining challenge. The friendship between Aiden and Poppy also helped me fall a little bit in love with him, which was exactly what I needed to write his and Lauren's story. I can't wait to share *For You I'd Bloom* with you.

I appreciate the time you've given Poppy and Theo's story and would love if you'd leave an honest review.

Thanks for reading!

Hannah

P.S. Please keep in touch! For news and exclusive content visit https://hannahjordanauthor.com and sign up for my newsletter.

ABOUT THE AUTHOR

Hannah Jordan grew up in the Blue Ridge Mountains of Virginia but moved to South Jersey after falling in love with her complete opposite. She's got all the advanced degrees of a "serious" fiction writer but only smiles when she's writing romance. She lives with her husband and two daughters in a picturesque town outside Philadelphia where she enjoys reading in all genres, especially the spicy ones, and confusing people with her half-Southern, half-Northern accent.

Milton Keynes UK
Ingram Content Group UK Ltd.
UKHW040835141024
449705UK00006B/270